**"You're _____"**

Just what Christian wanted to hear; still, he was inexplicably annoyed. "I don't want to be involved any more than you want me to be, but it would be respectful to at least consider her last wishes."

Kezia thrust out the letter, waiting until he took it. "I can manage on my own."

It had always been her mantra—more than that, the truth. Now the words rang hollow, but she could not allow Christian back in her life. And she wouldn't cry in front of him, though she wanted to. Worse than the prospect of losing her heritage was realizing her grandmother hadn't trusted her enough to confide her troubles. She lifted her hand to her heart and pressed against the almost physical surge of pain.

"Don, more whiskey." Christian guided her to the couch with gentle hands while the older man hurried from the room in search of the bottle. "Relax." His breath was warm on the nape of her neck. "I have no intention of coming back."

Dear Reader,

In *Mr. Imperfect*, an old lady's will is the catalyst for bringing two people together. My father died suddenly when I was halfway through writing this book, and a couple of months after I'd taken a year off work to follow my writing dream. The money he left me allowed me to extend that year to two and resulted in the sale of this, my first book.

I feel very much as though his spirit imbues it, not with grief, but with the power of love—even beyond the grave. I hope that emotion shines through when you're reading it.

*Karina Bliss*

www.karinabliss.com

# MR. IMPERFECT
*Karina Bliss*

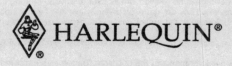

TORONTO • NEW YORK • LONDON
AMSTERDAM • PARIS • SYDNEY • HAMBURG
STOCKHOLM • ATHENS • TOKYO • MILAN • MADRID
PRAGUE • WARSAW • BUDAPEST • AUCKLAND

ISBN-13: 978-0-373-71373-8
ISBN-10:     0-373-71373-8

MR. IMPERFECT

This edition published by arrangement with Harlequin Books S.A.

® and TM are trademarks of the publisher. Trademarks indicated with ® are registered in the United States Patent and Trademark Office, the Canadian Trade Marks Office and in other countries.

www.eHarlequin.com

**Printed in U.S.A.**

## ABOUT THE AUTHOR

Karina Bliss figured she was meant to be a writer when at age twelve she began writing character sketches of her classmates. But a scary birthday milestone had to pass before she understood that achieving a childhood dream required more commitment than "when I grow up I'm going to be." It took this New Zealand journalist, a Golden Heart and Clendon Award winner, five years of "seriously writing" to get a book contract, a process she says helped put childbirth into perspective. She lives with her partner and their son north of Auckland. Visit her on the Web at www.karinabliss.com.

To my wonderful mother, Kathy Bliss, for instilling self-belief in a born skeptic. And to the memory of my father, Derek Bliss, who believed having five daughters made him immortal. It did, Dad.

# CHAPTER ONE

CHRISTIAN KELLY CRIED at funerals. For a man who never wept it had been an appalling discovery. He figured the combination of somber hymns, gentle sobbing and church rituals struck some sentimental Irish chord and caused him to blubber like a baby.

He solved the problem by never attending funerals, which solidified his reputation as a hardened sinner. So it was a testament to his affection for Muriel Medina Rose that he came back to the New Zealand hometown he loathed, wearing the darkest pair of shades he could find, and stole into the last pew midway through a stirring rendition of "When the Saints Go Marching In."

Kezia Rose appreciated the irony. Knew her grandmother would have, too. Still, it started a fit of giggles she fought to control—hysteria wasn't far away. It didn't help that she stood in full view of the congregation, shaky hands clasped, waiting to do her reading.

She dug one spiky heel into the top of her other foot until tears came to her eyes. Then looked at the coffin and had to force them back. Not yet. Not until she'd done her grandmother proud.

Why hadn't she expected him?

When she felt herself under control, Kezia looked again, coolly now, to where Christian sat, a big-city cat among country pigeons. Maturity had chiseled his features back to strong bone, his thick black hair finally tamed by an expensive cut. Beneath a pair of reflective sunglasses he held his full mouth tight, almost disdainful. In thrall to a newer, stronger grief, she looked—and was not burned. A small sigh of relief escaped her.

The music faltered to a stop in that ragtag way of amateurs and the minister gave her the signal. Three steps to the podium, deep breath. She found her place in the Bible's tissue-thin pages.

Her voice cracked on the first line; she stopped. Began again, one word at a time, found a rhythm, shut out emotion. The mantle of responsibility soothed her, reminded her who she was. A pillar of the community—teacher, chair of numerous country guilds, churchgoer. New owner of a hundred-year-old ramshackle hotel in Waterview.

The bone-dry Hauraki Plains town had sprung up around the Waterview pub, both named by Kezia's Irish forbears in a fit of whimsy and not—as Christian had once joked—to provoke a powerful thirst in the locals.

Not thinking about him right now.

The words on the page ran out; the last full stop looked like a bullet hole signaling the end of one of the happiest times of her life. Dazed, she looked up to see Christian, in classic Armani, disappear through

the arched church doors. And she was glad. Glad
he'd made the effort to come, gladder he'd left
without making contact. She had enough to cope
with today without saying goodbye to someone else
she had loved.

And lost.

CHRISTIAN STUMBLED TOWARD the car park, barely
able to see through his fogged sunglasses. Damn it!
Temples pounding, he groped through the open
window of his car for a box of tissues, yanked off the
shades and mopped up the damage. Kezia's fault.
The first break in her voice had brought a lump to
his throat, then her words—thin, brave and clear—
had sliced at his self-control like stiletto knives until
he had to get out of there.

He swung around to face the gabled church and
glared at its white clapboards and gray iron roof,
mottled with lichen. An old-fashioned church, gravestone companions rising to the left, rose beds to the
right in a riotous clash of pinks, reds and yellows.
Whoever had planted the damn things had been color
blind. Funny he'd never noticed that when he was
growing up.

But he remembered the scent. Sweet. Lush with
summer heat. He'd always been attracted to women
wearing floral scents—now he knew why.

Kezia.

In a prudish black suit at odds with her body.
Christian was annoyed at his relief that she still wore
her dark hair long. Of course he'd expected her to

still be beautiful in that remote, untouchable way that had once driven him mad—but that no longer attracted him. He preferred easy women these days, easy to win, easy to leave. He'd even expected to feel something when he saw her again. A backwash of teenage emotions agitated by shared grief. A reflex, no more. Like crying at funerals.

He hadn't expected to be irked by her lack of recognition. Christian grimaced at his egotism. Maybe Miss September had been right. He was shallow and self-centered. Beholden to no woman and proud of it.

Then why was he wiping away tears in the backwater he'd left in anger fourteen years ago? Wearily he replaced his sunglasses and turned back toward the car park.

Beholden to one woman, then. Muriel Medina Rose. A surrogate mother to a motherless boy—when he'd let her. Which hadn't been as often as she would have liked.

He'd loved that old woman.

Loved taking her out gambling on the rare occasions she visited the city. She, outrageously provocative in an ancient fox-fur stole with its glassy eyes and tidy paws draped nonchalantly over one shoulder and carrying an equally impolitic diamanté-studded cigarette holder. He, in his sharpest suit, entertaining his best girl with his wildest stories.

And not even residual bitterness toward her granddaughter—and this hick town—could keep him from paying his last respects.

"Christian Kelly."

His hand on the car door handle, Christian turned, an easy smile disguising his irritation. "Don—how are you?" He reached for the lawyer's hand, still as dry as he remembered. In fact, everything about the sandy-haired old man suggested he was slowly crumbling into dust, from the furrowed jowls and droopy eyelids to the rounded shoulders and widow's hump.

Except he'd looked like this twenty years ago when he'd first represented Christian in the local courthouse. They'd come to know each other well in a resigned "not you again" sort of way until Muriel stepped in and Christian's life as a juvenile delinquent came to an unceremonious end.

"Sad day, sad day." The lawyer shook his head. "Good to see you here, though. Muriel would have liked it and it saves me a stamp."

Christian tried to make the connection but failed.

"The will," Don explained kindly. "Or rather, the letter. She was most particular about you getting the letter."

"I thought her heart attack was unexpected?" The notion that Muriel's final illness might have been deliberately kept from him increased his sense of misuse.

Don glanced back as though to ensure he hadn't been followed, and Christian remembered the man had a flair for the dramatic. "Doc told her two months ago she could keel over anytime," he confided, "but she didn't want a fuss. Told Kezia she was retiring to get her to take over running the hotel. When the end came, my girl was playing bridge—a glass of whiskey in one hand and a grand slam in the other."

Their eyes met. The two men exchanged the "Muriel smile"—equal parts tribute and frustration. Over at the church, the organ started up with a wheeze and voices rose in song for the final hymn. Christian's hand tightened on the car keys.

Don noticed. "Nice Bentley. A Continental GT, if I'm not mistaken." He ran a finger across the silver-gray bonnet, his rheumy eyes twinkling. "A bit understated for you isn't it?"

"It's my funeral car," said Christian.

"You have another?"

"One or two." He looked at Don's shocked expression and grinned. "Actually, four altogether."

Don opened the door, inhaled the smell of expensive leather with relish. "Well, you can give me a lift to the wake in this one. Damned if I'm going to watch them bury her."

Christian's grin faded. "I wasn't planning on staying."

"An hour won't kill you," growled the old man. "Muriel put a fine whiskey aside for this. The least you can do is toast her memory. Then we'll step into my office and do the handover."

Don Muldoon, being a pragmatist, owned the building adjoining the hotel. "Be where your customers are," was his maxim. He'd even gone so far as to add an interconnecting door, fuelling gossip about the true nature of his relationship with Muriel, which both had reveled in.

*He'll miss her badly.* Christian wished he hadn't thought of that, wished he'd just handed the old codger some money for postage and left the dairy-farming flatland behind him—with a squeal of tires for old times' sake. But he still owed Don for keeping his secret. Sighing, he crossed to open the passenger door. "Thirty minutes."

Then wondered if his sympathy had been misplaced when Don winked at him. "I'm sure even you and Kezia can exchange pleasantries for that long."

KEZIA NEARLY DROPPED the cupcakes when she pushed through the saloon doors into the cool dimness of the lounge bar and saw Christian leaning against the fireplace mantel, flanked by her grandmother's elderly cronies.

The afternoon rays beamed through the stained-glass window and fell in prisms on the group. Bernice May was yellow, Don Muldoon, green, and Christian—very appropriately, she thought—glowed red. But nothing could leach the color from those extraordinary eyes—pupils like black atolls in a sea of Pacific blue. Eyes measuring her reaction as she measured his, each looking for a cue from the other.

Kezia rearranged the pink-iced sponges that had tumbled off their pyramid while she decided how she felt. So many times over the years, and in so many moods—hope, despair, righteous anger—she had imagined this meeting. Even when she no longer loved him she'd fantasized about what psychologists called closure and Kezia called having the last word.

How ironic that in this maelstrom of grief for her grandmother she felt...nothing.

Across the room he smiled at her and her heart remembered why she'd loved him, while her mind thanked God she'd got over him. One woman could never hold a man with a smile like that. There were shadows under those intensely blue eyes, she noticed, and shadows in them. Through her numbness she saw an understanding of her grief, and she frowned because she didn't want to connect with anyone ever again. Least of all Christian.

Civil, she decided, putting the plate on a sideboard already groaning under the weight of cakes and club sandwiches. She would be civil. As she headed toward the group, holding out a hand in greeting, Kezia returned Christian's smile. "How nice of you to make the trip." She heard how facile that sounded even before his eyes narrowed. "Nice" had never applied to Christian. He made no move to take her hand. "I mean, Nana would have appreciated it." Even now, trying to retrieve the situation, she'd put the stress on the wrong word. The unspoken implication—but I don't!—hung in the air. Kezia stared up at him helplessly. "Will you please just shake my hand?"

"I don't think we need to be that formal." Christian put down his glass and drew her into an embrace that was half awkward, wholly familiar and so full of reluctant sympathy that Kezia was torn between burying her face in his broad shoulder and never coming out and giving him a sharp slap for his insensitivity.

She jerked away to see his eyes leveling the same accusation at her and realized with a shock that she was being selfish. Others suffered, perhaps as much.

On an impulse she took his hands—big and broad with long, tapered fingers—and cradled them, trying to ignore the frisson of awareness that passed between them. "How are you coping?"

Christian removed his hands, reached for his glass. "Like a man," he said lightly. "Work harder, play harder."

She remembered the tabloids and couldn't resist the temptation. "How is Miss September?"

His eyes gleamed. "I'm between months at the moment."

A laugh, almost painful through disuse, escaped her.

"Toast Muriel with us," said Don approvingly. "We're celebrating her life by telling outrageous stories about her."

Oh, that sounded tempting. But Kezia eased her shoulders back. "I need to pour coffee and serve food."

"No, Kez." Christian handed her a glass. "You need a stiff drink and to talk to old—" he paused "—friends. Let someone else dole out the culinary relics."

"Keep your voice down. Everyone brought food," Kezia cautioned. They hadn't parted friends but if Christian had the manners to pretend otherwise then so did she.

"And I was one of those volunteers," said Bernice May tartly. She poked Christian in the ribs with a bony finger and pointed to the fairy bread on the mahogany bar beside them—thin triangles of white bread topped with multicolored sprinkles embedded in thick yellow butter. In the heat, the corners were as curled as Aladdin's slippers.

"Bernice May, you've been peddling that rubbish ever since I can remember." Unrepentant, Christian refilled the old lady's empty glass. "You're a terrible cook and you know it."

"Bernice May is famous for her fairy bread," Kezia insisted, biting into one. Sugar balls grated against her teeth.

"She's always saving people's feelings," explained Bernice May complacently, watching Kezia try to swill down the sprinkles with whiskey. The combination was indescribably foul but it took Kezia's mind off Christian's raised eyebrow. "Anyway, I thought you were a ladies' man these days," the old lady complained. "Where's your legendary charm?"

"Saved for ladies," said Christian.

Kezia choked midsip but Bernice May laughed until she cried and ended up wiping away most of her pencilled eyebrows. "Come home, Christian," she suggested. "With Muriel gone we need another hell-raiser to keep this town interesting. Don't we, Kezia?"

"Yes," said Kezia, emboldened by his instinctive recoil. "Come home, Christian. Swap the penthouse for a farmhouse, the Bentley for a tractor and your tourism empire for a pitchfork. I believe there are at least three single women for you to date." She realized she was enjoying herself in a perverse way, taking on someone who could match her, whose feelings she couldn't hurt, even if she wanted to. But she was also appalled at her meanness—and at a time like this.

"Do you count yourself, Kez? If so, we'll have to drop that number back to two. I never date the same woman twice."

"And I never repeat the same mistake twice." Somehow the fun had gone out of it. "What makes you think I'm single anyway?"

"You're doing this alone," said Christian, and Kezia fell back into the bleak present. She put down her glass. "I should mingle," she said, and saw quick remorse in Christian's eyes.

"Kez—"

Don interrupted. "First I need you both in my office to go over the finer details of Muriel's estate."

"Why?" Bernice May's voice echoed Kezia's.

"It'll be private in my office," Don added pointedly.

Kezia shot a suspicious look at Christian. He shrugged. "No idea. But let's get this over with. It's time I left."

She needed no further convincing. "Okay." Besides, pretty soon she'd need to cry. He had to be gone before that.

DON DIDN'T BEAT AROUND the bush. He pulverized it.

Mentally, Kezia collected all the pieces and tried to fit them together. "The hotel is verging on bankruptcy because Nana's had a bad run on the horses?"

"It appears Muriel remortgaged some years ago but most of the capital was spent on meeting running

costs, interest payments and, later, medical bills.
When her health started deteriorating she obviously
panicked and bet on the track to try to recoup that
money." Don shuffled papers on his battered desk.
"Which is exactly the sort of harebrained scheme
Muriel would adopt rather than admit she needed
help. I'm sorry, Kezia."

"There's nothing for you to be sorry about," she
said perfunctorily, still trying to take in the enormity
of his disclosure. "No wonder she retained book-
keeping when I took over two months ago." Swallowing her terror, she asked, "Can I trade out of
this?"

"Maybe. If you can come up with a good enough
business plan to satisfy the bank and follow it up with
solid results."

"I'll give you the money you need." She'd forgotten Christian was there, half hidden by the side wings
of an old green leather chair.

"No." Her response was instinctive; her brain
caught up and approved it seconds later.

Christian looked at Don. "How much is it? I'll
write a check now."

"I said no, Christian. I don't want your money."

"I'm not doing this for you, Kezia. I'm doing it
for Muriel."

"Muriel won't take your money, either," said Don.
"It's specified in the will." He put on his glasses and
read, "'Christian Kelly is prohibited from paying off
the hotel's debts.' This, I think, is where I give you
her letter."

Christian looked at Muriel's familiar flourish and swallowed a lump in his throat. She'd written to him weekly for fourteen years. This would be the last letter he ever received from her.

My darling, you're wondering why I won't let you pay off my debt. Too bad, I'm not going to tell you! I ask instead that you stay in town—yes, I know you hate it but it's just a few weeks—and help Kezia come up with a plan to reverse the hotel's fortunes. The place needs an entrepreneur's skill if it's to survive another hundred years. Tell Kezia I'm sorry I've left things in such a mess but it seemed necessary. God bless you both, my darlings, Muriel.

Christian handed it to Kezia without a word. *It seemed necessary?* What was Muriel playing at? Had she forgotten he had a multimillion-dollar business to run? Okay, his two partners could carry him for a couple of weeks, but to come back here— a place haunted by memories, most of them bad… He shuddered. Immediately he began thinking of ways to circumvent the will. Hell, if a hotel and tourism magnate couldn't outwit an old lady, he deserved this penance.

With grim amusement he watched Kezia's face as she read the letter, before she became aware of his scrutiny and turned away. When she turned back, her expression reflected his resolve. Implacable resistance. "You're off the hook. I refuse your help."

Just what Christian wanted to hear. Still, he was inexplicably annoyed. "I don't want to be involved any more than you want me to be, but it would be respectful to at least consider her last wishes." He ignored the fact that he had been doing no such thing.

Kezia thrust out the letter, waited until he took it. "I can manage on my own." It had always been her mantra—more than that, the truth. Now the words rang hollow, but she couldn't allow Christian back into her life. And she wouldn't cry in front of him, though she wanted to, very badly. Worse than the prospect of losing her heritage was realizing her grandmother hadn't trusted her enough to confide her troubles. She lifted her hand to her heart and pressed against the almost physical surge of pain.

"Don, more whiskey." Christian guided her to a couch with gentle hands, while the older man hurried from the room in search of the bottle. "Relax." His breath was warm on the nape of her neck. "I have no intention of coming back."

"Thank God!" He looked startled at her vehemence and Kezia added impatiently, "Surely you realize she's trying to force us together to salvage a happy-ever-after out of this mess. Why else would she have that curious clause refusing your money?"

He stared at her and she saw with relief they were in perfect accord on this one.

"It must be nice to die with some illusions intact," he commented.

She frowned. "What's that supposed to mean?"

He shook his head as though to clear it. "Nothing.

Look, let me find a way to give you the money, Kez, then I can leave with a clear conscience."

She resisted the urge to ask when a clear conscience had become necessary to him; the scars had been picked at enough. "Okay, but it's a bridging loan. Once the hotel is back on its feet, I'll arrange a repayment schedule that will include backdated interest pegged at today's rate."

He looked amused. "Whatever."

"I'm serious, Christian."

"Look—" he raked a hand through his hair "—don't tie yourself into unnecessary debt, take the money as a gift. You must know I won't miss it."

She did know, but it made no difference. Favors were something she did for other people. Accepting hundreds of thousands of dollars from Christian, the man who'd deserted her, was unthinkable. Simple as that.

Less simple was when she'd be able to pay it back. But that was tomorrow's problem. At least she'd have her home, her heritage, intact.

"I want a business arrangement but...thanks for the offer." She wished he'd move. The scent of him—crisp linen overlaying healthy male heat, a hint of cedarwood—was making her dizzy.

Don came back with a silver tray bearing their drinks. Reluctantly, Kezia took a sip for medicinal purposes, trying to remember when she'd last eaten. She had no taste for whiskey, but the association with her grandmother was comforting. She took another, inhaling the smoky sharpness like smelling salts.

Christian declined his drink. "I'm driving," he said. "Don, you should know I intend to find a way to lend Kezia the money."

"Muriel thought you would," said Don calmly, and reached for another envelope on his desk. "Here."

Irritated, Christian pulled out a scrap of paper. "What is this, Give Us A Clue?" He glanced down at it and the color drained from his face. "Damn."

Foreboding hit Kezia like a rolling winter fog. "What?"

Still he gazed down at the note, his expression remote yet curiously softened. "Damn," he said again, and shoved it into his pocket.

She knew what he was going to say, could see it in his eyes, could feel the prickle of tears in her own. It seemed she would cry in front of Christian Kelly, after all.

"Hi, honey," he said grimly. "I'm home."

Kezia began to laugh. She laughed until she cried.

# CHAPTER TWO

ONE SHUDDERING SOB led to another and then another until her body convulsed under the force of them and she curled up on the couch like a lost child, her arms wrapped around her knees. Christian reached for her, but with shaking hands she pushed him away, did the same to Don.

"Let me get someone—a friend," Christian offered.

Terror strafed through her grief. "No! I don't want to be seen like this." A fresh paroxysm racked her body. "Please, both of you go away," she sobbed, then laid her head on her knees and gave herself over to the anguish.

Dimly she heard a murmur of voices, the door open and close again, the scrape of a chair. And Christian was sitting next to her. "I...don't...want... anyone...here!" she said between sobs, but took the handkerchief he offered.

"I know," he said soothingly. "I'm temporary."

"Don't touch me."

"I won't," he promised. "I'll just sit here."

And he did, watching the shadows lengthen in the room, listening to her sobs until they abated and, emotionally exhausted, she slept. And all the while he suffered, resisting grief, resisting Kezia. He sat stiff and unyielding in his chair. He would not be moved by her beyond common pity.

When he stirred at last, his muscles ached like a prizefighter's. But he'd won. He stretched as he turned on a lamp against the encroaching dusk, found a throw and covered Kezia.

His opponent looked worse, her face blotchy, her closed lids swollen. In the circle of light her disheveled hair gleamed with velvet browns and sparks of amber. Just as her eyes did, he remembered, and because she looked so vulnerable, so un-Kezia, he smoothed her knotted brow.

An unexpected blow to the heart made him step back, shove his hands into his pockets. His fingers brushed the crumpled ball of paper and, swearing softly, he pulled it out of his pocket, smoothed the creases and glared at it.

Nothing complicated about it, just a scrap of a page torn from an exercise book. The IOU had been dated and signed, the letters sprawling loose and untidy across the page. His signature hadn't changed much in sixteen years.

*You conniving, brilliant old woman. You got me good.*

With a sigh he opened the door, saw Don and Bernice May and a host of other anxious people—many familiar—staring at him. He fought back a sense of claustrophobia and nodded acknowledgments.

"She's sleeping, but I doubt she'll want a welcoming party when she wakes. Perhaps just you, Don?"

He drew the older man away, ostensibly to talk privately, but moving closer to the pub's exit. He was in no mood to renew old acquaintances. Plenty of time for that in the following weeks, he thought bleakly. "I'll be back when I've reorganized my affairs. I'm sure Muriel's bank will allow us a few weeks' grace."

"A phone call from you will get it," Don said dryly.

"Tell Kez I'll need a bed at the hotel. Ask her to courier me the books so I can start formulating strategies."

Don looked doubtful. "I can't promise anything. She hasn't exactly warmed to the idea of you coming back."

"Then here's the carrot. Tell her I've set myself a deadline. I'll turn the hotel around in a month."

"You don't know how bad things are…."

"A month," said Christian grimly. "If it kills me."

KEZIA RACKED HER BRAIN FOR another way to tell Christian no. Spats of rain against the pane heralded a summer squall. But the storm building indoors was of more concern than racing to bring in the white tablecloths snapping on the line in the easterly below.

"Probably not," she ventured.

They sat on spindle-legged antique chairs in the private sitting room on the hotel's first floor. Much of the threadbare blue carpet was covered by piles of paper, as neat and precisely spaced as soldiers at attention, testament to Kezia's methodical sifting over the previous week.

Christian had roared back into town thirty minutes earlier in old jeans and a new Enzo Ferrari he called Consolation. If asked, Kezia would recall it as red and showy. And—like its charismatic, self-indulgent owner—not to her mature taste.

"You mean no." Christian began pacing while Kezia watched her tidy piles of paper anxiously. "I thought we agreed to cooperate—get me out of here as quickly as possible."

"It's not that I think your ideas lack merit." Kezia had spent the intervening days practicing her responses to this intrusion and had resolved on diplomacy, civility and detachment. She frowned as his foot knocked a pile askew. "I just think we need to quantify the problem to qualify the solution."

Christian grabbed an invoice from the top of one stack and her eyes followed the tug of taut muscle under tightened denim. "'Nineteen twenty-six. Two bags of chicken mash and five pounds of head cheese.'"

"That's not indicative of what I'm sorting," Kezia said stiffly. Okay, maybe she had become a little distracted by cutesy historical data, mainly because she could sleep after reading it, unlike some of the more recent accounts she'd uncovered.

"I know you want to do this properly." Christian forced a smile and Kezia's mood lightened. She, at least, had relaxed her jaw. "But we don't have the luxury of time."

For once she couldn't disagree with him. The

bank had abruptly withdrawn its forbearance when the manager discovered wealthy Christian Kelly couldn't act as a guarantor. Kezia had won a further ten days' grace based solely on her own banking history. "But cutting staff…" she protested.

"Short term. Ultimately the plan will generate jobs."

"But my people depend on those jobs now. In a rural community, employment is hard to come by."

"Even harder if the hotel closes down," Christian said bluntly. "And what's this complicated system with a dozen part-timers?"

"I work the roster to suit mothers' hours."

"Get full-time staff. The taxes and health insurances for all these people adds ten percent to your costs."

"The benefits offset that," argued Kezia. "My workforce is highly motivated because they're so delighted to be out of the house for a few hours. By definition mothers are skilled multitaskers, and adept at handling troublemakers."

"They have to go, Kez."

"No, Christian, they don't. We'll save money elsewhere." One thing Kezia *had* resolved after a week of receiving his brusque e-mails—Send this. Find that. What the hell does this mean?—was to clarify who was boss.

"Listen." She squared her shoulders. "I'm happy to consider any ideas you have with an open mind, but—"

"Starting when? You've knocked down every suggestion I've made."

"You've been here half an hour!" Kezia paused to

drag her tone back to civility. "You haven't seen your room yet, let alone toured the property and met staff. Do you really think I'll take your recommendations seriously until you do?"

"No, which is the underlying problem. This hotel is in such dire straits because Muriel let emotion overrule good business practice."

Kezia saw red. "Don't you dare attack Nana's judgment. *Never* criticize her, do you hear me?"

"I'm sorry," he said simply.

She realized she was standing and sat again, too shaken to censor her words. "I think I would cope with my grief better if I wasn't so angry with her."

He nodded, neither in pity nor judgment, and Kezia felt strangely absolved. All week she'd vacillated between tears and guilt-stricken fury. For the first time it seemed forgivable. "You've had time to assess the mess. How do you rate our chances of success?"

"If we keep emotion out of it?" Their shared past flickered like a ghost between them. "Fifty/fifty."

"Better than the odds I came up with." She hesitated. "As long as you understand that I'm John Wayne in this picture."

"You're going to need his balls," he replied dryly.

The door swung open before Kezia could think of a suitable retort. A trolley appeared first, lurched left across the doorway, then right, then surged into the room and rode roughshod over one of Kezia's neat piles.

"Your horse needs breaking in," remarked Christian.

The small woman pushing it raised her head. Marion Morgan looked like a benign witch, mainly because of her wild blond hair—closer to mist than curls—but also because of the perpetual myopic bewilderment in her big blue eyes.

A bewilderment that had intensified since her alcoholic husband had abandoned his family three months earlier. Kezia saw with relief that Marion's preschooler was nowhere in sight.

Christian was the one who needed breaking in.

He hated being here already, she could tell by his inability to sit still. It reassured Kezia that the ties that meant everything to her were binds on him; he wouldn't outstay his welcome. There was also a curious relief in having the decision she'd made all those years ago reinforced as the right one. Restless and mercurial, he would never have stuck by her.

"Well, this is a surprise." Christian crossed the room to give Marion a hand. The trolley rattled to a rest, slopped coffee shivering to stillness in the saucers.

Marion flung her arms around him and kissed him. "You're a lifesaver for rescuing us like this."

Over her head Christian stared unnerved at Kezia who shrugged, half exasperated, half amused. The man was only here because of some IOU he refused to explain, but bless Marion, she always suspected the best in people. Especially bad boys.

Christian changed the subject. "You work here?"

Marion released him to search through her jeans for a handkerchief. "Most evenings. The job's a godsend as well as my little bit of sanity." She dabbed at her eyes. "I guess Kezia has told you of my troubles."

"All we've done so far is argue," said Kezia, hoping to deflect her. One litany of woes at a time.

"About the past, I expect." Marion recovered enough to hand out cups of coffee, and Kezia wished she'd kept her mouth shut. The things her youthful self had once done and said to Christian's boy-man had haunted her all week.

"No. About the hotel."

"It must be *so* awkward," said Marion sympathetically, "deciding what to talk about, what not to talk about." Kezia frowned at her; they'd already had this chat.

"We're opting for the not," replied Christian. "Is that shortbread?"

Marion offered him a slice. "Very wise," she approved. "First loves are so embarrassing years later. All that overwrought intensity, the passion and the promises. You haven't learned it's safer to hold something back."

"Marion!" Kezia caught her friend's eye, sent a desperate message. "We're not talking about any of it."

"And I'll make sure everyone knows that," Marion soothed.

"Still scared of spiders, Muffet?" Christian used Marion's old nickname with relish.

She paused. "We're not talking about it."

A smile, unguarded and complicit, flickered between Christian and Kezia. Maybe we can forgive each other, after all, she thought.

"So—" Marion reached for her coffee "—did you ever settle down, Christian?"

His grin hardened with cynicism and Kezia looked away, feeling foolish.

"Marry, beget 2.5 kids and get talked into a pet hamster?" His mouth quirked. "No, I didn't."

"That's my life you're describing, so you'd better stop there. Except my son chose a rat." Marion looked sad again. "Come to think of it, so did I."

"I'm sorry to hear that—" Christian stopped, puzzlement on his face. The ancient linen tablecloth that enveloped the trolley billowed like a poltergeist.

"John Jason, you come out of there," yelled his mother, pulling up the cloth. "No wonder I couldn't steer this thing."

A miniature Batman clutching a white rat rolled onto the carpet, scattering papers. With a yelp, Kezia lurched forward to save them and succeeded only in splattering coffee down her best white linen suit. Served her right for trying to look coolly austere for Christian's arrival.

"You should have left that rat at home, Batman." Christian grabbed the child's cape and swung him away from the few remaining stacks. "Hotel inspectors don't like them. I have to say, I'm not too fond of them myself."

"Roland lives here." John Jason's tone suggested Christian should know that. Kezia found herself crossing her arms defensively.

"The rat lives…here?"

Christian's shortbread was at just the right height. John Jason leaned forward to take a bite. "With me."

"You live here, too?"

"Me an' Mum an'—" in a singsong "—Roland an' Kezia."

"Normally he's in a cage." Kezia made a futile attempt to sound responsible.

Christian asked nicely, "What about the rat?"

"I COULDN'T SAY NO," argued Kezia.

"You have no problem saying no to me," Christian pointed out.

"They needed a home after the farm sold. I asked Muriel to take them in. It's temporary."

An unwelcome suspicion distracted Christian from the beguiling sway of Kezia's hips under the soft swish of silk-lined linen as he followed her down the narrow corridor. "Temporary." He picked a rational figure and doubled it. "So they've been here six weeks?"

"Here's your room." She stood aside to let him pass. "It's the honeymoon suite," she encouraged, urging him forward.

"God, we're talking months, aren't we?" Through the doorway Christian found just what he'd expected—more shabby gentility perfumed with beeswax and mothballs. He dropped his bag and hauled the lace curtains back to throw light on the room's bones. "Quit hedging," he demanded. "Just how long have the Munsters been in residence?"

"Three months. The rat—four weeks."

Christian's attention, hijacked by the sight of an ancient iron-framed bed, snapped back to Kezia. "You approved the rat?"

"I bought him." Her brown eyes, lit with rueful humor, met his and he resisted an impulse to smile back. There would be no repeat of his weakness at the funeral.

"Why?" Making a mental note to buy rat poison at the first opportunity, Christian tested the bedsprings. The white linen coverlet was so thin it had the translucence of skimmed milk.

"John Jason was missing his dad, wetting the bed every night. I thought a pet might help. Except any pet for that boy needs a powerful survival instinct." Her rueful grin intensified. "Hence Roland."

Damn, he smiled before he could stop himself. Amazing that the intervening years hadn't wearied Kezia's philanthropy, more so that he still found it a turn-on. "Rats only leave sinking ships so I guess his presence is a good sign under the circumstances," he conceded, reluctantly discounting the rat poison. "But the rodent stays in the kid's room." An experimental bounce on the mattress evoked shrieks from the springs. "How the hell does anyone have sex in this bed?"

"It's been a while..." Kezia faltered and he watched the color heighten in her cheeks. So this unwelcome awareness was mutual "...a while since we had honeymooners staying. And the springs have only got worse because...only recently," she finished vaguely.

"Just how much rent are your strays paying?"

From the financial accounts, Christian already knew the answer but he wanted her to acknowledge some culpability for this mess. It would give him the moral high ground, a position he found useful in business and avoided like the plague in his private life.

"If you think I'm going to fall on my sword because I helped out a friend, you're not smart enough to be useful," she said coolly. "And I can stop fighting the impulse to tell you to go to hell."

So the intervening years had put steel in that fragile backbone. Shame she hadn't had it when they were eighteen.

"Keep fighting it, I just got smarter." This time his smile was deliberate, the wattage turned high enough to melt all female resistance. "I won't underestimate you again, I promise."

Kezia snorted. "Christian, please remember that I knew you when you were a sixteen-year-old bagging up chicken shit at Old Man Norton's poultry farm."

"Kelly's Compost Activator. You know I've never bettered that profit margin. Four hundred percent return."

"Mostly spent on soap," Kezia reminded him, and for the first time their unspoken past lay lightly between them.

He decided to trust her with honesty. "We have to get these rooms back into inventory as quickly as possible. The bank must believe we can generate more income."

"So you expect me to evict Marion."

"Yes," he said dryly. "I like nothing better than to toss women and children out onto the street. If only it were snowing."

She sat beside him, hands clenched together in her coffee-splattered lap. "Sorry, I don't usually shoot at the cavalry."

"More like the Lone Ranger." Under her makeup he saw the blank weariness of grief. "We'll work around Marion until she finds a place. I can subsidize it." Impatiently he overrode her protest. "At least let my money solve someone's problem."

His frustration that it couldn't solve this one grew as he toured the upper floor. With his buyer's eye he could see the red-oak floors stripped of their threadbare carpet, fretwork restored by a craftsman's careful hand and the rooms dressed in lush fabrics and colors by one of his interior designers.

Instead, he and Kez would have to give the place yet another cosmetic overhaul with cheap fabrics, cheaper paint and their own inexpert labor. He'd funded himself through college as a builder's laborer and hated it. *Thanks, Muriel.*

"This is Nan—my room." Kezia opened the door adjacent to Christian's room. "It might work as a second honeymoon suite."

Christian blinked. Ruby-velvet drapes coiled around the mahogany frame of a massive four-poster, the bed made plump with white faux fur cushions. A crystal chandelier winked at its reflection in an ornate gilt mirror and a candy-striped couch with the curves of a languishing woman merged into matching wallpaper. "It's like a bordello in a spaghetti Western."

"Muriel's tastes were expensive but the results were generally cheap. I don't think she ever made the connection—" Kezia smiled "—and no one had the nerve to make it for her."

"Maybe it's a good thing she never had the money to redecorate."

"Actually she did." Kezia straightened a cushion that had fallen out of formation. "The bank told me yesterday that upgrading the hotel was the reason she gave them for re-mortgaging five years ago. As far as I can tell, only the foundations were reinforced— and this room decorated." She hugged herself in an unconscious gesture of comfort. "Needless to say, they're less than thrilled the place is still in disrepair."

Christian kept his face blank while he mastered his emotions. "Why didn't you call me with this last night?"

"You might not have come."

Her accuracy didn't bother him; the hope implied by her words did. "I'm not a miracle worker, Kez."

Her mouth softened into a wry smile. "There's your first miracle."

He raised a brow in enquiry.

"I just admitted I want your advice."

"No, the miracle would be if you took it." His gaze swept the outrageous room. "We could always add turning tricks to our business plan." She grew thoughtful enough to startle him. "It was a joke, Kez. You're not on the streets yet."

"Themed rooms would give us a point of difference with the romance market, perhaps tied in with local culture."

Now that was funny. "How about one called the Milking Parlor? Cowpat-brown carpet, hay in the mattress, Bovine Breath room freshener and milking cup light fixtures."

She gave him a look that reminded him forcibly of her grandmother. "I won't even dignify that with a reply. Shall we continue the tour?"

## CHAPTER THREE

THE KITCHEN WAS an enormous, high-ceilinged room, gloomy even in midsummer. Long, scratched stainless-steel benches and a large table in the center of the room added to the barracks feel.

There were three women in the kitchen, aprons protecting their clothes, one buttering slices of white bread, one mixing cake dough and the third plating chicken pies, oven-bronzed and fragrant, doing their desperate best to cheer the dank room. Déjà vu slammed Christian against the wall and held him there.

"Are you all right?"

He couldn't answer, closing his eyes against the faintness stealing over his senses. The scrape of a chair, then Kezia's hands forcing him to sit, pushing his head down between his legs, the sharp exclamations of anxious women.

By sheer force of will he sat up. "I'm fine now."

"Are you ill, son?" One of the woman asked, her white apron encasing her generous girth like an overstuffed pillowcase.

Son. Christian closed his eyes again, racked by an

old guilt. "Didn't eat breakfast," he managed to say. It got the desired result.

He sensed movement as they hastened to gather food, releasing him from scrutiny. He opened his eyes, his emotions unguarded and raw, and his gaze collided with Kezia's. She still crouched anxiously in front of him.

"Oh, my God, Christian." She reached for him as one would a child, to comfort and console.

He stopped her with a glance. "I need to get out of here."

"Fresh air will do you good," she agreed.

He pushed to his feet. "I mean, leave, Kez."

"Okay." But her dismayed expression made him understand that he couldn't do this to Muriel—or to her. He sat again.

"My mother worked here," he said in a low voice. She'd died of cancer when he was twelve, well before Kezia's arrival at sixteen, and he'd never talked about it. "I used to come here after school, eat the leftovers and study at that table. I'd forgotten...until I walked in." He dredged up a weak smile. "This place is caught in a time warp."

"We'll change the kitchen first," she said seriously.

"No, the public areas have precedence. Anyway, I'm over it now. Stupid to get a hit for someone twenty years dead."

Kezia frowned, but before she could say anything the coffee arrived—steaming hot and so full of sugar he could smell it. With it came a slice of bread, door-stop-thick and slathered with creamy butter. "We're cooking you a decent meal, son," said the large woman. "You and Kezia take yourself to the dining room and I'll bring it out."

"This will do fine," Christian answered. "Please don't put yourself to further trouble—" he looked at her name tag "—Peach?" It suited her round-cheeked abundance.

"We can't have you fading away or we'll have nothing to look at," said Peach.

"Just as long as I know what I'm here for."

Peach glanced at Kezia. "Oh, we can think of a few uses for you. I hear you two were sweethearts once."

"We're not talking about it," they said together.

SITTING IN THE DINING ROOM, watching Christian scan her summary report while they waited for his meal, Kezia wondered how he did it. Ten minutes ago he'd revealed a grief so deep she still ached to give him sympathy. Now his self-possession was intimidating.

Peach arrived, carrying two plates piled high with bacon and eggs, hash browns and toast. She forestalled Kezia. "No arguments. Coffee does not count as breakfast."

"Just so we know who's in charge here," Kezia grumbled as she picked up her knife and fork.

"You are," said Peach. "Except when I am." She turned to Christian, her face softening, and Kezia was torn between amusement and irritation. The damn man exuded a potency that dazzled anyone with estrogen. Thank God she'd been immunized.

"She got skinny living away," Peach confided, "but I'll fix that." On that ominous promise, she departed.

Christian put the report aside. "You moved out?"

Kezia stabbed at her bacon. "No, time stopped the day you left."

His blue eyes glinted across the table. "That sound patronizing?"

"Very." He waited and she added shortly, "Up until two months ago I shared a town house in Everton with another teacher." In the district hub, a township barely ten kilometers south of Waterview. "I hadn't officially lived here for a couple of years although I came back to help out most weekends."

"Tell me about your life, Kez." Christian picked up his cutlery and attacked his heaped plate. "When I'd ask Muriel, she'd turn frosty and say, 'Call and ask her yourself.'"

"Did she?" Kezia paused in her breakfast. "She told me the same thing." She reached for the last piece of toast. "Of course, I have the advantage, the tabloids had no such reticence."

He laughed at her, unrepentantly male. "So much for my hobbies. What about yours?"

She took her time applying butter. He lived his life on a big canvas and could never appreciate the incidental pleasures of country life. But not telling him meant his opinion mattered. "I taught primary school for most of it, though it was always understood I'd eventually run the family business. I'm also on the Waterview town council, I help out with Age Assist once a week—"

"Those are duties, not hobbies. What do you do for fun?"

"Meetings can be very social." Kezia didn't like the defensiveness in her voice. She had to lighten up. "Did I mention I'm a campanologist?"

That intrigued him. "You study camping?"

Kezia tsked. "And you with a college degree."

"I'm mortified." He looked no such thing. "Now explain."

"Some call me a swinger." She enjoyed the play of expressions on Christian's face.

"Baseball," he concluded.

Kezia made a moue of disappointment. "A man of the world not knowing what a swinger is? Pass the honey, please."

"You're pulling my leg."

"There is a lot of pulling involved," she allowed, "but not of legs. The honey?"

Christian handed it over, his gaze assessing, but Kezia kept a straight face. "Come along to our next meeting, we're always looking for new members." She put just the tiniest emphasis on the last word but the gleam in his eye told her she'd overdone it. Fortunately, Peach arrived and started clearing plates.

"Kez tells me she's a swinger," he said while his subject, unconcerned, applied honey to her toast.

"One of our best," said Peach proudly. "There's some that think giving it a tug and setting up a racket is the go, but you need a light touch to be any good at it."

For the first time Kezia saw Christian nonplussed. "You swing, too?" he asked carefully.

"No, but my husband does when his back isn't playing up." She turned away with a stack of plates. "It's great to hear you laugh again, Kezia," she called over her shoulder.

"Okay, put my imagination out of its misery," Christian demanded. "What the hell is campanology?"

"Church bell-ringing," she gasped. "Very difficult to do."

He evinced skepticism with one eyebrow. "Pulling a rope?"

"Knowing when to let it go takes more skill," she answered, regaining her composure. Campanologists were used to teasing.

"Sounds like it ranks with bungy-jumping for excitement."

"And danger," she added serenely.

"Rope burn?"

Kezia bit her lip, determined not to smile. "People have—"

"Gone deaf?"

"Died! The bells can weigh up to two tons a piece." Okay, those five fatalities were probably spread over several hundred years, but no point in spoiling a good story.

"I'm sure the insurance premiums are huge," he remarked, and she laughed despite herself. Christian grinned back with a boyish charm that made Kezia catch her breath. "You know," he said, "the biggest surprise for me was finding you single. Somehow I expected you to be married with lots of kids. You always wanted them."

Abruptly she changed the subject. "We should get back to work. Now that I've bought you up to date, what's your verdict?"

Shrugging, he reached for the report. "Please tell me you own that town house in Everton, because we haven't a snowball's chance in hell with the bank without some security or cash."

Kezia had known it would come to this. Still a miracle would have been nice. "I don't own the town house but I do have something to sell—six acres about two kilometers from here."

She stuck to the facts, her tone brisk. But in her heart, dread grew like a tumor. "It has a huge mortgage so it's no use as security, but I've had an offer to buy. It's low—Bob Harvey knows I'm desperate for money—but I'd net twenty thousand dollars."

"You don't want to sell."

She told him about the house she'd wanted to build there. "Wide decks overhung with grape leaves in summer. A big pond to encourage water fowl, a vegetable garden and chickens—"

"Don't forget the white picket fence."

"Too much work to paint," she said wistfully, then registered the irony. "Sounds like your worst nightmare?"

"Actually, it makes an attractive picture. One I'd like to hang in my inner-city penthouse." His tone softened. "Choose your dream, Kez. I'm sorry, but right now you can only afford one."

For a split second she was eighteen again and panicky until she remembered that her hardest choice had been made then. And she'd survived. She gestured toward Christian's phone. "May I?"

He made no move to hand it over. "You still let duty drive you." There was a critical note in his voice that stung.

"Better than still evading responsibility."

His eyes narrowed. "I'm here, aren't I?"

*Under duress, you bastard!* The words trembled on the tip of Kezia's tongue. "Yes," she said at last. "You're here now." Coward, she said to herself, wanting to say it to him. "My point is," she continued, "I have to consider other people's interests as well as my own."

"But none of them are taking your risk." Christian's tone was equally rational. "And you could be throwing good money after bad. If your heart's not in it, let the bank have it."

"If the hotel closes, it may never reopen. I can't— won't—let that happen to Waterview."

Without another word he handed her the phone and she punched in the number of the estate agent. "George? Kezia. You can tell Bob the land's his if he'll agree to an immediate settlement—".

Christian repossessed the phone. "And is prepared to pay a fair price. You're supposed to be representing the interests of the vendor, George, so why the hell are you letting Bob Harvey dance on an old lady's grave? Yes, I'm back…well I look forward to seeing you again, too. In fact you don't have long to wait because in thirty minutes Kezia and I will be in your office. Make sure Bob's there." He rang off and saw the irritation on Kezia's face. "I know, I know. You're perfectly capable of handling this. But you're grieving and you shouldn't have to deal with assholes like Bob Harvey."

Once again, he'd disarmed her.

"ONE HUNDRED AND TWENTY thousand dollars and not a cent more, damn you—not you, Kezia. You, you robber's dog!" Bob Harvey ripped off his tie, worn in deference to the occasion, hitched up his trousers, pushed south by his belly, and glared at Christian, who inclined his head graciously at the compliment.

Dissatisfied with this response, the grizzled farmer turned on the estate agent. "Oh, yes, you can smirk with the commission *you're* getting. Well, use it to buy a vote when you stand for racecourse chairman next week because you won't be getting mine!"

Having wiped the grin off somebody's face, Bob signed the contract, then patted Kezia's knee. "Don't worry, love, I won't let this affect our relationship."

Judging by the broken veins fanning out from the old farmer's bulbous red nose, Christian suspected that relationship to be one of publican and best customer.

Kezia's words confirmed it. "Next one's on the house, Bob."

"One!" Bob heaved to his feet. "The pub will be buying beer until I'm bloody carried out, after today's chicanery." His disgusted gaze swept over Christian's casual attire. "Someone needs to tell you how to dress for business, boy." He crossed his arms, causing the buttons of his white shirt to strain across his expansive belly.

"Bob!" Kezia's rebuke had a wobble of amusement in it.

Christian kept a straight face only by not looking at Kezia. He could tell Bob what the jeans had cost him and be called a bloody fool. He could mention that *Sartorial* magazine had voted him Australasia's best-dressed man for the past five years and be called a bloody pansy. Or he could enjoy the moment. He chose the last course, figuring his pleasures would be few and far between in the coming days.

Emboldened by Christian's silence, Bob grunted and picked up the contract. "Let's get over to the pub before bloody Kelly remembers to swipe the change out of my pockets. Once a thief, always a thief, eh, Kelly?"

Christian remembered a desperate boy who would rather steal money for food than admit to paternal neglect, and his jaw hardened. He'd amputated sentiment from his life when he'd left Waterview, yet all day he'd been plagued by phantom pains. "As I recall, I labored four weekends paying back that two dollars. But then, you always did know how to exploit a situation, didn't you, Bob? Nothing's changed there, either."

"I offered a fair price." The old man blustered. "And Kezia was happy with it—" as she tried to interrupt Bob simply raised his voice "—until you showed up playing the hotshot with your fancy car and fancy attitude. Well, you're home now, boy, and we know you for what you really are."

"Now, guys," said George nervously. The man still ducked and dived his way through trouble, Christian noted, just as he had when they'd played rugby together in high school.

Ignoring him, Christian gave Bob a contemptuous once-over. "And that is?"

"The same loser your father was."

"Give me that contract!" Kezia stormed toward Bob with a look in her eye that made Christian wonder whether he should step in and save the old blowhard's life.

Bob obviously read the same message because he took a couple of steps back and held out the document. Christian neatly intercepted it. "You're forgetting which cause you're martyring yourself for," he reminded her, amused and touched. It had been a long time since anyone considered him in need of a champion.

"Damn it, Kelly, if you imply I'm a martyr once more I'll—"

"Let the bully have me?" He resisted her efforts to seize the contract by holding it aloft. "It's okay, Kez, he didn't hurt my feelings. I don't have many so they're a hard target."

"I don't care, he crossed the line." She was on tiptoe now, straining breast-to-chest with him, one arm upstretched, and Christian had a sudden urge to kiss her and put all that passion to better use. It scared the hell out of him.

"Forget your principles for once," he said more sharply than he intended to. "We need his money and we need it now." Out of the corner of his eye he saw George wince.

Kezia drew herself up to her full height. "*Now,* Christian!"

"What the hell's going on?" demanded Bob, mystified. "Why does she want the contract?"

"To rip it up, you fool!" Anxiously, George gestured to Christian to hand it to him.

Christian obliged, passing it over Kezia's head. She spun around, her dark hair flying, but it was too late. George had wrenched open the door and sped down the road with it.

"So," said Bob after a moment's stunned silence, "how about that drink?"

KEZIA DIDN'T SPEAK TO CHRISTIAN for several hours, which suited him perfectly. He'd mainlined into her concerns when he'd only meant to dabble, and that annoyed him. What he needed was space, to reestablish his autonomy.

So he shut himself in his room with his laptop and mobile and connected to the real world, taking dinner on a tray and ignoring the whispers of children outside his door.

It was approaching twilight when he sought a change of scene and discovered the upstairs deck overlooking a quarter-acre yard with a large vegetable garden and a couple of flower beds. Beyond that was pasture, traversed by the highway heading to the city. The sight taunted Christian, but not enough to seek the bar and run the gauntlet of old acquaintances.

Instead he found a pack of cards and took them outside where he sat at a wicker table and played Patience. He figured he needed the practice. He'd only played one game—and lost—when he heard Kezia at the open French doors behind him. "I won't bite if you don't," he said, shuffling the deck and dealing two hands.

"I haven't come to play with you," she began and he raised his head to enjoy the discomposure that always followed her unintentional double entendres. Since he knew from experience that she was a passionate lover, he could only assume it had been a while. Ungenerous of him to be glad.

"I've come to apologize." Kezia pulled up a chair.

"Forget it." He went back to playing Patience.

As usual, she did the opposite. "It was enough that you had to listen to Bob's insults without me getting mad and trying to scupper the deal we need so badly."

He shrugged. "If you apologize to me for stepping in, then I'll have to apologize to you for not appreciating your defense. Like I said, forget it."

"You got a great price."

He heard the smile in her voice and looked up. Her silky hair was brushed to a schoolgirl's neatness, wholesome and fresh. He smiled back. "Cleared you another ten thousand."

"Thank you," she said formally.

Christian's smile broadened. She took her obligations so seriously, always had. Once, she'd taken him seriously. As a wild boy with wilder dreams he'd loved her for that. On impulse, he leaned forward and brushed his lips against hers; found them warm and firm and full like her curves. A burst of need jolted through him and he jerked back at the precise moment Kezia shoved him away. Hard.

"What the hell do you think you're doing!"

"Nothing…it was a friendly gesture, that's all." Christian affected nonchalance. "Why are you making so much of it?"

As he'd intended, she shrank back in her chair and crossed her arms. "I'm not. You took me by surprise, that's all."

Attack was a great deflector; he stuck with it. "If that's all…"

"Of course that's all." Angry color rushed back into her face. "You think I'd still be carrying a torch for you after what you did?"

"Oh, that's rich." Christian forgot his strategy. "After what *I* did?"

Kezia held up her hands in supplication. "Truce. We're not talking about the past, remember? We grew up, we got over it." She shrugged. "At least, I did."

"Of course I did," he snapped, then realized she'd turned the tables on him.

"I'll play cards now," Kezia said serenely.

He pushed the cards aside, suddenly restless. "How the hell do you stand all this peace and quiet?"

Faint and far away in the country silence came the thin hum of a car, the sound growing louder as it approached down the lonely highway. Finally it streaked past, windows lit, a female passenger poring over a map. "Don't you ever feel life is happening somewhere else?" he said, longing to be in that car.

"Listen."

Crickets' song swelled and filled the dusk. Above, the darkening sky seethed with stars. Swallows darted across its canopy, and Christian could hear the soft snort of cattle in the adjacent field, a strangely comforting sound.

He'd forgotten that he'd never had a quarrel with the land. Slowly the tension went out of him. "Maybe," he conceded finally, "some peace and quiet will do me good."

Christian's magnanimity lasted until he got into bed and the springs screeched. Damn! How could they have gotten so rusty? He lay on his back, naked, feeling the sag in the mattress suck on his spine like quicksand.

Cursing, he rolled onto his side—a squeal from the springs—and the knobbled embroidery on the pillowcase dug into his cheek. After five minutes of maneuvering around fleurs-de-lis he sat up and ripped off the pillowcase to a cacophony of protesting metal and flung himself down again. "Shit!"

"Sorry about the bed," called Kezia, her muffled voice sounding close.

Christian snapped on the bedside lamp, saw the adjoining door barricaded behind a mahogany dresser and grinned. He switched off the lamp and lay back with his hands cupped behind his head. "How sorry?" he drawled suggestively, just for the hell of it.

"Not that sorry."

He could tell by her tone she was frowning, no doubt lying demurely clothed and neatly tucked into that lush double bed, only her dark hair spilling untidily across the pillowcase. He remembered winding it around his fingers as he worshipped her ardent young body. His grin faded.

He'd never given himself as recklessly to any woman since. The bedsprings gave voice to Christian's growing disquiet as he tossed and turned on rationalizations.

Okay, he still found Kezia attractive, so what? It was only because he'd been celibate for three months, taking a break from the game.

And despite the occasional flashes of her wicked humor, Kezia wasn't the playmate type, having fossilized into an earnest, thirty-two-going-on-fifty-two pillar of the community.

*Fourteen years later, Kelly, and you're still looking for the last word. Forget your male ego.*

He turned carefully and was rewarded with only a small squeak of the bedsprings, which brought to mind the rat. In the dark he shook his head. Only Kezia would come up with such a novel solution for a bed-wetting Batman. His brain ran idly over the day's conversations, braked and rewound. "The springs got worse because...only recently."

Christian jerked bolt upright. "Who was the last person to sleep in this bed?" There was silence, followed by a smothered laugh.

Right, he thought grimly, all bets are off.

AT SIX-THIRTY WHEN KEZIA went to creep past Christian's door, running shoes clutched in her hand, she found it open.

The sleeping man lay sprawled on his belly, one arm flung over the side of the bed, his face half buried in the pillow. Bare, broad shoulders tapered down to a narrow waist, both deeply tanned against the white sheets, unlike the taut creamy buttocks the top sheet barely covered.

But what made Kezia gasp was the sight of two small boys standing patiently by the bed. One wore a Batman cape and was sucking his thumb. "Come away," she whispered, gesturing frantically.

Batman removed his thumb. "We want him to wake up." Christian stirred, opened one bleary eye and John Jason obviously thought him ripe for conversation. "You're in my bed."

"I gathered." Christian closed his eye again, opened it. "Where's the rat?"

"In my new room. I liked this one better."

Christian rolled over with a groan repeated by the bedsprings. "What time is it?"

Time to flee. Kezia tiptoed away.

"What's the o'clock, Auntie Kezia?" Batman bellowed.

Squaring her shoulders, Kezia turned around.

"Six-thirty, now shush or you'll wake your mother!" Christian, she saw, had propped himself up on one elbow and was looking at her with a predatory gleam. "Good morning," she said briskly, refusing to feel bad. Really, she'd had no idea the bedsprings were that rusty. "Did you sleep well?"

"Don't get funny with me," Christian warned her, looking downright dangerous with his disheveled hair and blue-black stubble. An effect negated by his two pajama-clad sidekicks. Kezia found it impossible to hide her smile. "You'll keep." He made it sound like a promise.

"Can you please take us for a ride in your Ferrari?" John Jason's sleepover buddy finally found his courage.

"David is my friend," Batman informed Christian in the manner of one providing a personal reference.

Christian's lips twitched. "Later I'll take you. Scram for now."

Reluctantly they trooped toward the door where Batman paused. "Why don't you wear pajamas? We all saw your—"

"Boys!" Her cheeks hot, Kezia shepherded them out. "It's too early. Go get breakfast."

When she turned back, Christian was leaning against the pillows with his hands clasped behind his head and giving her a killer smile. She asked primly, "Would you like a cup of coffee?"

"What I'd like—" his gaze ran lazily over her bare legs and high-cut running shorts and Kezia got hotter, resisting the urge to yank down her T-shirt

"—is a new bed and a lock on my door to keep out Peeping Thomasinas."

"I didn't…it wasn't…" she stuttered, then met his eyes. "Okay, you embarrassed me back, we're quits."

"Who said I was embarrassed? Let me get dressed and I'll come running with you." When she hesitated, searching for a polite way to tell him she always ran alone, he raised a quizzical eyebrow. "Are you hanging around for another glimpse of my ass?"

"Downstairs," she snapped, "five minutes." And fled.

# CHAPTER FOUR

HANDS RESTING LOOSELY on his knees, Joe Bryant sat in the clinic's Spartan foyer, feigning nonchalance and hoping Rueben would get off the damn pay phone before his courage failed. Again. He cleared his dry throat. "Other people need to make calls."

The wiry teenager, all Adam's apple and attitude, waved a dismissive hand. "C'mon, man," he wheedled into the receiver, "I'm dying in here." He glanced over to where Joe and Big Tim sat, and his voice dropped to a whisper. "It'll be easy to smuggle it in, security sucks." His voice hit normal levels and kept rising. "Whaddaya mean, you don't trust me? Screw you, then. You're no friend of mine." He slammed down the phone and stormed off.

"Dumb ass." Shaking his head, Tim hauled himself to his feet. "Well, wish me luck."

"Good luck." *To both of us.* Joe watched as his roommate lumbered over to the pay phone, laboriously fed in the right number of coins and stabbed in the number. And his heart began thumping against his ribs. *Your turn next. Your turn next.* A cold sweat beaded his brow and he couldn't keep his hands still. "Not too long now, hey?"

Tim grunted in a noncommittal way. Giving up all pretence of indifference, Joe began pacing. It gave the adrenaline somewhere to go, stopped it pooling in the pit of his stomach. Mentally he began practicing what he was going to say.

*Hi, it's me. I know you haven't heard from me in months, but there's a good reason for that.*

"Don't do this to me, baby." The anguish in Tim's deep bass broke Joe's concentration. Wanting to respect the other man's privacy, skittish enough already without someone else's emotional baggage, he moved farther away, but Tim's voice followed him. "Give me another chance, Ellie, I'm begging you."

Joe swallowed hard. His back still to Tim, he wiped his palms on his T-shirt, then began walking again. Fast. He got to the end of the corridor, changed his mind, spun around and headed back. He wasn't going to chicken out this time. This time he'd make that call. If Tim could beg, so could he.

Tim had already hung up. Shoulders hunched, one hand pressed to his forehead, he was staring down at his shoes. He straightened as Joe approached. "The kids." He shrugged helplessly. "How can I fight her when she's doing what's best for the kids?"

Joe's resolve evaporated, replaced by self-loathing. *What the hell do I think I'm doing?* He put a hand on Tim's shoulder. "You can't."

The two men fell into step. "Hey!" Tim stopped,

confusion on his broad face. "Weren't you waiting to use the phone?"

"The urge passed."

Tim wouldn't have it. "C'mon, what've you got left to lose?"

"Hope," said Joe, and kept on walking. "Another day of hope."

DAWN WAS KEZIA'S FAVORITE TIME to run, especially on a cool summer morning when the dew released the scent of pasture and pine. She also discovered, on their first run together, she could relax her guard when Christian's gaze was on the road ahead and all that Kelly charisma has space to dissipate.

In the four days since his arrival, he'd taken to flirting with her in a lazy teasing way that was clearly second nature to him, but which alerted Kezia to the differences in their worlds. She'd spent her adulthood dating governable men, she realized. Managing a wolfish ex-lover—even one she'd gotten over— was a hell of a lot more challenging.

The pace quickened; Christian was waking up.

"Had another thought," she said, panting. "Community hall...too big for smaller groups. Could... hire out club lounge."

Their running shoes pounded in unison on the blacktop road while he thought about it. "I like it. You come up with some great ideas."

They brainstormed the conversion details, Christian fluently, Kezia truncating sentences between gasps. "Damn your...fitness...I haven't got...breath to…argue," she huffed when he challenged her on a key point.

"No kidding." At the smugness in his voice, she reached out and shoved him. He laughed. Around the bend, meandering cows blocked the road. Kezia shambled to a grateful halt.

She'd just managed to lower her heart rate when Christian stripped off his T-shirt and used it to towel down. Kezia's mouth went even drier and she averted her gaze, but as he mopped his face, her curiosity won. She wouldn't call it temptation.

Once she'd known Christian's body intimately, but it wasn't the body he had now. He was taller, broader, with muscle hardened over a powerful frame. If the boy had been liquid grace, the man was hewn rock.

Her appraisal picked up other differences—a smattering of silky hair on his chest and belly where none had been before and the sort of muscle definition that called to a woman's hands. Made a woman want to start at the smooth, taut pectorals and slide her palms slowly down over the masculine planes and angles, down the flat stomach, all the way down.

"Your body's changed, too."

Kezia started as though she'd been shot.

Casually, Christian made his own inspection, scanning her curves in a male appraisal that set Kezia's teeth on edge. "It's more…womanly." His gaze lifted and she saw it was nowhere near as dispassionate as his tone. "Your breasts—" he began huskily before she found her voice.

"Don't."

"Don't what? Look? Wonder?"

"Anything!" The last of the cattle passed, flanked by two border collies. A man on a farm bike tooted his thanks and Kezia waved, glad the tension was broken. "Don't flirt with me," she said, and started running.

Christian caught up effortlessly. "Why? Do you have a jealous lover?"

The loaded question shocked her into mistiming her stride. Christian put out a hand to steady her but she shook it off. "That's my business!"

"I thought not," was his cryptic reply.

She stopped short and stared after his retreating back. "What's that supposed to mean?"

Christian turned and started running backward. "You act like a woman who isn't getting any."

She put her hands on her hips. "And how is that?"

He halted to think about it. "Uptight. Orderly in an obsessive way. Eating too much chocolate. Practical clothes and plain underwear."

Kezia didn't know where to start, she was so furious. "For your information, all my underwear is scarlet lace," she retorted, then remembered the clothesline was under his window.

"But mainly…" He turned for home.

"Oh, yes?" She powered up behind him.

"Mainly…" He turned suddenly and she fell back. "You're jumpy as hell around me. Either we still have chemistry or you're out of practice. Which is it?"

She forced herself to bridge the distance and run alongside him. "Definitely not the chemistry thing.

Definitely," she repeated. "I'm out of practice." She really didn't want to be telling him this but he had to believe she wasn't attracted to him. "Like you, I'm between lovers. Unlike you, discrimination governs my sex life, which means I get a dry spell occasionally." *You mean a drought.* "I happen to be in one."

They jogged around the hotel to the fire escape leading to the top floor.

"Well, I guess I'm wrong then."

"You are," she said emphatically, and headed up the fire escape before her nose started to grow.

She was halfway up when he called, "Let me know if you want to practice."

CHRISTIAN GOT THE PHONE CALL late that afternoon when he and Kezia were on their hands and knees pulling out the last of the carpet tacks. He picked up his mobile and talked into it, sitting dirty and disheveled on a roll of discarded and moth-eaten carpet.

Kezia hid a smile, wondering if London, Toronto or Japan—or whoever it was this time—realized they were doing business with someone covered in carpet fluff. She removed a piece from her mouth and tried not to listen, but when Christian swore loud and long, she sat back on her heels and frowned.

He cut the call short and with deadly accuracy hurled the phone across the room and through the open window. Kezia had grown so accustomed to his unshakeable sangfroid that she could only stare at him.

"Sorry." He didn't sound it. "I'm being played for a fool and there's not a damn thing I can do about it."

"What's the problem?"

"I've got a spoilt heiress who's refusing to sign an eight-million-dollar deal her father and I negotiated because I'm not at a meeting in Auckland. In three hours, she's flying to Europe for four months."

Christian began pacing. "Meanwhile, thanks to one crazy old lady, I'm stuck in Hicksville pulling out carpet tacks to save a few hundred lousy dollars! Her lawyers will have no trouble sinking the deal." He looked around for something else to throw and Kezia hid the hammer.

"I think I can fix it," she said calmly as she went downstairs to retrieve his phone from the flower bed. It still worked.

Upstairs, Christian leaned out the window. "You're kidding."

She lifted a hand. "Hi, Bruce, this is Kezia. I hoped it would be too windy for crop-dusting today. Listen, I've got a guy who needs to get to Auckland within the hour. Can you do it? Oh yeah, I think you can charge him plenty. He'll be there in thirty minutes. 'Bye."

"Come up here," Christian demanded. "I have to kiss you."

"I prefer to be worshipped from afar."

"You're an angel, a goddess, words can't describe your beauty…."

"That's odd," Kezia mused. "Someone told me I was an uptight, orderly, obsessive chocoholic who wasn't getting any."

"Only because mortal men aren't worthy of you."

"You're good," she said admiringly. "Now go shower."

Fifteen minutes later she was in her ancient station wagon driving Christian, cool and composed in a summer-weight Italian suit and Ray•Ban sunglasses, to the airfield. He released a faint scent of expensive cologne every time he moved to accommodate the rough ride.

"This car," he said less-than-politely, "how old is it?"

"Too old to ask," she replied shortly, hot and bothered by his proximity. "Unlike you, I'd rather put my money into something that appreciates in value."

"Like land," he said, adding astutely, "I'm sure one day you'll be able to buy it back."

Not with prices rising the way they were. Kezia graunched the gears. "Let's talk about something else."

"Our meeting at the bank in Everton tomorrow?"

Apprehension tightened Kezia's throat. "Something *else* else."

The car forded a pothole, Christian moving easily with the swaying vehicle. "Okay. You know why you're being so helpful to me, don't you? You figure you owe me a favor for all this and want to cross me off your list."

"I'm not that bad," she protested.

"I've seen you noting every volunteer's name in your little black book."

"It's blue. And you're starting to get on my nerves."

"So how does the debt stand between us? Does this make us even?"

"It puts me way ahead. I doubt you could ever catch up."

He laughed and she kept her eyes on the road because he got too damn handsome when he did that. It was his laugh that had made her like him all those years ago. The freedom from care it promised. And at the time she'd had a lot of cares, convalescing from a serious illness and living with a grandmother—and in a country—she barely remembered.

As if reading her thoughts, Christian asked casually, "How are your parents? I expected to see them at the funeral."

She tried to keep the defensiveness out of her voice. "They're stationed in a remote part of Indonesia and couldn't get back in time."

"Your father didn't inherit."

"No. Nana was afraid Dad would sell up and give away the money."

"And charity begins at home," Christian said, quoting Muriel's favorite adage. "When did you last see them?"

The road forked and Kezia took the left. "Two years ago when they came home between assignments. I'd visit but they always seem to be working in countries with dengue fever and I can't risk another hemorrhagic attack."

"So they left you to deal with this alone?"

"They're aid workers, Christian. They have more important priorities."

"You always did make excuses for them."

"And you've always criticized them. Well, don't.

They're all I have left." When he said nothing to that, she insisted, "I had a very happy childhood."

"Sure you did," he said affably. "Almost as good as mine."

Ahead, a hawk feasted on roadkill. Kezia tooted her horn, and it lifted into the air with two slow, insolent flaps. "Why did you never tell me how bad your home situation was?"

There was a brief silence. "What could you have done, Kez?"

"Given you sympathy at least."

"I was happy with the other things you were giving me, babe," he drawled.

But she was on to him now; knew he was deflecting her. "We went to your father's funeral," she said as though he hadn't spoken. "Muriel and I and Bernice May."

Her tone told Christian that she knew about what he'd once gone to such pains to hide from her—his father's drunkenness and neglect. "Did he…did he ever hit you?"

He opted to lie. "No." Yet someone had been telling tales if both Kezia and Bob Harvey knew details of his childhood. "Who told you? I know it wasn't Muriel." *Surely Don hasn't broken faith after all these years?*

"Bernice May, until Nana hushed her up. I'd asked why you weren't there."

"I paid for the funeral," he said, "for my mother's sake. That was all I could bring myself to do."

"You used to talk even less about your mother than your father." Kezia kept her eyes on the road.

"And you've been wondering since that episode in the kitchen."

"Yes," she said simply. "So some of your childhood was happy?"

"Yes. Your turn to change the subject."

Kezia retreated into farmer's talk—bemoaning the lack of decent rainfall and, when that subject was exhausted, moving on to the merits of Rhode Island Reds versus bantams.

By the time she pulled into the paddock that passed as an airfield, she was sick of the sound of her own voice. The Cessna's engines were already whining through their warm-up.

Christian could exchange one drone for another, she thought wryly. She turned to see his mouth twisted in a half smile.

"What?"

"I didn't think you and I could ever be friends." His voice was deep and husky and sexy as hell. "But damn, if you don't make me like you sometimes, Kezia Rose."

*Oh, no... Don't do this to me. Not again.*

"I see that scares you."

"It horrifies me. Let's get this straight, Christian, once and for all." She made her tone deliberately brutal. "You and I could never be friends."

"Hell, you're right." He leaned forward and lightly nipped her lower lip with the intimacy of someone who'd done it many times before. "You and I weren't made to be friends." Then he got out and strode toward the plane.

Only when the Cessna taxied down the runway and lifted into the blue haze did Kezia realize she should have slapped his face.

"HELLO?"

Telephone to his ear, Joe hesitated. He hadn't expected his son to answer. It wasn't in the script.

"Hello?" There was silence as the kid waited for a response. "You need to talk back, you know," the boy suggested helpfully.

Joe's throat seized up. His baby sounded so grown-up...so confident. They'd only been apart three months and already Joe had missed a transition. It hurt, hurt like hell.

"Who is it, honey?" Her voice.

"There's someone there. But they're not talking, just breathing sort of fast."

"Give me the phone. Hello? Who is this?"

Joe opened his mouth. But, trapped in some kind of guilt-stricken limbo, he couldn't say a word.

"Joe?" Her voice was hesitant now. "Is that you?"

Panicked, he hung up.

He turned and banged his head against the wall beside the pay phone. Damn, cowardly, stupid *dickhead!* But the waver in her voice had killed him. A waver that might have been fear.

Last time he'd seen her, she'd been sprawled on the floor, staring up at him in shock and disbelief. She screamed at him to get out and never come back.

Because last time he'd seen her, he'd hit her.

# CHAPTER FIVE

CHRISTIAN HATED William J. Rankin the Third after ten minutes.

The bank manager was well mannered in that inoffensive style adopted by funeral directors. His robust frame carried a little extra weight, which Christian soon attributed to William J.'s inflated idea of his own importance. He seemed to be in his late thirties and, by his manner, had been most of his life.

The first real indication of trouble had been the vicelike handshake that told him William J. had competition issues, which Christian didn't help by grinning when he saw William J. Rankin III in gold-embossed letters on the door.

"A gift from my mother," William J. said shortly.

To which Christian replied politely, "Very thoughtful of her."

When the banker swung back in his chair and clasped his hands behind his head as he listened to Kezia outline her proposal, Christian wished to God he'd let Kezia come alone. His presence here was doing her no good.

Certain men reacted to his wealth this way, adopting a studied nonchalance while their body language screamed alpha male marking territory. He generally cut the negotiations short—he was too old for pissing contests. Unfortunately this man held the loan on the hotel.

So he adopted a deferential pose, his shoulders slightly slumped and his expression respectful. *How's that, you bastard?*

"So what I'm asking for, Bill," said Kezia, looking damn fine in that white linen suit that accentuated her curves, "is for the bank to transfer the outstanding loan to me. This new business plan—" she forced William J. to drop his gorilla pose and take it "—will kick-start the business and enable regular repayments."

"Your grandmother took out the original loan on a similar basis five years ago." William J. opened another file on his desk. "Her business plan included substantial refurbishment—reroofing, repainting and modernizing the accommodation to attract out-of-towners. Five years down the track the property is still in desperate need of an upgrade and—forgive me for being blunt—you're broke."

"If you look at the plan, you'll see I'll clear thirty thousand dollars when I've repaid the mortgage on the land I've sold to Bob Harvey," replied Kezia quietly. "When the money comes through next week, I'll use it for the most urgent repairs. And I'm sure my grandmother had every intention of putting the money she borrowed into the hotel but she had a soft heart. When a friend needed a hip replacement, she picked up the bill."

"Yet Bernice May could have got it free under the public health system."

Kezia made an impatient gesture. "If she'd waited five years. Look, Bill, I'm not here to hide anything. We both know Nana had a gambling habit and that she also gave extravagant gifts." She smiled mischievously. "I imagine you still have the cashmere sweater. But Muriel's spending habits have nothing to do with my application."

"Unless you inherited them." William J. plainly didn't like being shown up and Christian didn't blame him. What the hell was Kez playing at? She wasn't just airing dirty linen, she was beating it with a stick.

She compounded her error by laughing. "Thirty thousand dollars says otherwise. It's okay," she explained to Christian, "we dated for a few years."

Christian's caveman instincts stirred. "Really?"

"Were engaged, actually," added Kezia cheerfully.

"Which is why I need to be scrupulous in assessing your loan application," interrupted William J. smoothly. "And I doubt Mr. Kelly wants to hear details of our personal relationship."

Mr. Kelly did, very much. But he kept his mouth shut and struggled fruitlessly to control his imagination.

"I know we can put that aside," Kezia said in all seriousness. Christian had never heard a more deluded concept in his life—and said so.

The other two bristled. "Our relationship ended amicably two years ago," said William J. coldly, "and

I resent the implication that I would allow it to affect my professional judgment."

"Who ended it?" Christian asked bluntly.

"I did," they both chorused, then stared at each other.

"Don't you remember I gave you back your ring because…" Kezia recalled Christian's presence and faltered.

"Because I asked for it," the banker finished.

Christian hid a smile as he watched Kezia open her mouth to argue, notice William J.'s folded arms, and shut it again.

"It doesn't matter anyway," she said in a tight voice. "The point is, our relationship remained civil. That's how mature adults behave." She threw the verbal barb in Christian's direction.

Mature? In bed, William J. Rankin the Third would have to be on top. Christian's smile broadened until he remembered just *who* this jerk had been on top of. Dismayed, he jammed a lid on his jealousy, an emotion so new, so unwelcome, he refused to acknowledge it. But his fingers itched for a club.

William J. must have scented the surge of testosterone in the air. "Perhaps I'm missing something, but just what's the purpose of your being present this morning?"

"Moral support," said Christian easily.

"I didn't think moral support was your area." William J. had clearly done his homework. "And Kezia has never needed protection from me."

Christian imagined himself grabbing William J. by his maroon-and-gray-striped tie and choking the self-satisfied pomposity out of him. "You're right, of course. She did try to tell me that." He smiled as he stood up. "I'll wait outside."

"Thank you." Kezia's grateful expression made it easier for Christian to allow William J. to crush his hand without breaking every one of the jerk's fingers in return.

"Great handshake you've got there, tiger," he said, and exited to the outer office. Lightweight. Encouraging his opponent to underestimate him was a tactic that had made Christian Kelly wealthy and respected. The metaphorical uppercut, delivered when his adversary least expected it, made him feared.

"Can I get you a coffee while you're waiting?"

His mind still on William J., Christian looked up and the woman who'd spoken took an involuntary step back.

He gave her his most charming smile—the one, God help him, that always got him what he wanted. "Thank you—" he looked at her name badge "—Suzie. Worked here long?"

"Do you mind telling me what that was about?" Kezia demanded as the door closed behind Christian. "You're acting like a jerk."

"Do you mind telling me why you've got Mr. Big City Hotshot in tow? I thought he was your grandmother's protégé, not yours."

"What are you jealous of, Bill? That Christian's wildly successful, was Nana's favorite or might be sleeping with me?" If he could catch her. After yesterday's kiss, she'd run like a rabbit to Marion's new rental just outside town. Christian had been forced to celebrate his corporate victory alone when he'd got back from Auckland. Winning this loan was vital—she had to get Christian out of her life.

Bill sighed. "I'm trying to remember you're vulnerable right now."

"And I'm trying to remember you're a decent man. Why did you say you ended our engagement?"

"Because I didn't want to look like a cuckold. The man's patronizing enough as it is."

Kezia stared at him in amazement. "Honestly, Bill, he's really not like that." Except of course Christian could be like that—arrogant, dominant, opinionated. Her attitude softened. "Bear with him, please. He's helped me a lot."

Bill snorted. "So why not make a donation of his small change instead of poking his supercilious nose into business that doesn't concern him."

With a sigh Kezia told him the terms of her grandmother's will. It helped. Honesty compelled her to tell him of Christian's input into the business plan. That didn't go down as well.

"You know, I would have been happy to advise you." Still, he picked up the plan, unable to resist examining it.

"Conflict of interest," she reminded him. Despite Christian's qualms, Bill's professional ethics were unimpeachable though his tendency to seize control had been one of the reasons she'd broken their engagement. He hadn't been like that when they'd started dating, mainly, she realized later, because he'd still been subdued over his father's death. Her sympathy had initially brought them together, but the pensive, gentle man she thought she'd fallen in love with had healed into a control freak.

Much like herself, Kezia thought in her bleaker moments, though at least she recognized when she was being bossy and resolved to stop. Bill never had. He was now engaged to a coworker who worshipped him in a way most people saved for God. He was very pleased with her.

"You know, Bill, I still think Suzie would prefer I didn't come to your wedding on Saturday."

With her tousled blond-streaked fringe, Suzie reminded Kezia of a Pekinese. One that was afraid the other dog might want its bone back. None of Kezia's oblique reassurances had helped and the truth—that Kezia thanked Providence daily for a lucky escape—was unspeakable.

Bill kept his attention on the business plan. "Nonsense. We both want you there."

For the first time Kezia wondered if Bill had embroidered the facts about their breakup. Gods needed to be infallible, after all. Which meant she had to go to the wedding to prove to Suzie she wasn't still pining.

"I can't fault this." Bill made the concession reluctantly. "There are a few flashy touches—the illustrious Mr. Kelly's, no doubt—but the numbers are sound. Subject to the usual credit checks, a formality in your case, I'll approve the transfer."

At that moment Kezia loved Bill Rankin with all her

heart. "Thank you," she managed to say over the lump in her throat. She hadn't allowed herself to despair, hadn't allowed herself to hope, but now she acknowledged how badly she needed the hotel to anchor her life and give her future certainty. She had her heritage back.

"Kezia, you need a glass of water." Bill guided her solicitously across the room. *So good with enfeebled women.* "And now you can get rid of Kelly," he added as he ushered her through the door. She stumbled. "A man like that wouldn't scruple to take advantage of a vulnerable woman."

Christian looked up. "Must be some bastard you're talking about," he said dryly. "Let's round up a posse and run him out of town."

But Bill was frowning at Suzie, thigh-to-thigh with Christian on the two-seater.

"Christian's been telling me all the celebrity gossip." Suzie's face was more animated than Kezia had ever seen it. "And guess what, Bill, Baz Monteith's left his wife. For a man!" She turned back to Christian. "He's Bill's favorite country singer."

"I believe you mentioned it," said Christian, and Kezia smothered a smile. His keen eyes searched her face for clues.

"We got it."

Christian glanced at Bill. "Just as well," he said quietly, then stood up and opened his arms to her, mouth curving in a slow grin that ignited her own.

With a jubilant whoop, she launched herself at him.

Not expecting it, he stumbled and they toppled

back into the couch. Suzie shrieked. Kezia found herself splayed across two laps, her skirt rucked up to her thighs.

Face blazing, she struggled to her feet and Christian gave her backside an obliging push. "I love it when you're spontaneous. Reminds me of old times."

None too gently, Bill pulled her away from Christian's lingering hands. "For God's sake, Kezia, what's got into you?"

"What old times?" Suzie asked. Obviously her love of gossip wasn't confined to celebrities.

"We went to high school together." Kezia smoothed her skirt.

"She used to help me with my homework," added Christian, his tone speculative.

Damn, now he was wondering what she'd told Bill about them. Almost imperceptibly she shook her head and his eyes narrowed with intense enjoyment.

"Kez made me the man I am today," he said, and no one missed his meaning.

"I doubt that," said Bill. "She's led a blameless life."

Even to Kezia that sounded dull, and Christian, bless him, laughed. "She may have led one with you," he conceded.

Only Suzie looked satisfied at that one; Bill inflated like an angry bullfrog and Kezia decided exit was the best strategy. She grabbed Christian's arm to steer him toward the door, felt his biceps tighten in resistance. "I get the feeling there's something you'd like to say to me, Bill," he prompted.

"You may have taken advantage of Kezia's innocent trust once, but her friends won't allow you to do so again."

Kezia tried to leaven the threat with humor, "I think I've had enough chivalry for one day thanks, Bill. First I'm dull, now I'm simple-minded. Trust me, if the need arises I can fend Christian off by myself." She pushed but Christian didn't budge. Was the man made of granite?

"Like you did last time?" Bill said sarcastically.

"When you were teenage lovers?" Suzie had no intention of relinquishing this juicy bone. It seemed Kezia had misjudged her breed. Fox terrier suited her better.

"Once and for all, Christian didn't take advantage of me. Strictly speaking it was the other way around." Bill and Suzie looked at her blankly. Obviously she was more boring than she realized. "Nothing, forget it." Kezia renewed her attempts to manhandle Christian to the exit.

"She means to rescue my reputation," he said helpfully, "by confessing to stealing my virginity."

There was a stunned silence while Bill and Suzie struggled to adjust their perception of her. Kezia turned on Christian. "Why the hell did you have to say that?"

"I gave in too easily," he confided to Suzie. "You can tell she no longer respects me."

"Christian!"

"Wow," said Suzie. "The women's magazines would pay thousands for that. 'My First Time' by Christian Kelly."

Kezia felt sick. "Suzie, promise me that information will stay in this room."

"Of course." Suzie gave her the sweetest smile.

Kezia racked her brains to cover all bases. "That means not bringing anyone in here to tell them, either." The other woman's face fell and Kezia grew desperate. "Promise me!"

"Give in, Suzie," suggested Christian. "From personal experience, Kezia doesn't take no for an answer."

Kezia turned on him in a fury. "Will you *shut up!* And, Bill, stop looking at me as if I've grown horns. Christian *was* taking my virginity at the same time."

"But, Kezia…" Bill looked like a man who needed to cough up a fur ball "…you've always been so good."

"I couldn't agree more," said Christian.

"Rational, restrained, sensible…"

"Oh, that sort of good." Christian smiled and Kezia looked around the room for something to bludgeon him with. "I was remembering the old model, not the new improved version."

Bill stiffened. "It seems I owe you an apology for maligning you."

"You can buy me a beer at your wedding," Christian said generously. "Your bride has invited me as Kez's date."

"I THINK THAT WENT WELL, don't you?"

Kezia resisted an impulse to swing for him. Her

reputation had been tarnished enough without being arrested for assault.

They had paused on the wide concrete steps outside the bank's faux Roman edifice, impressive but for the fact that it had been built to Everton's toy-town scale.

"You always have to have the last word, don't you, Kelly?"

"Pretty much."

"I've got a good mind to make you go to the wedding."

"No, you won't," he said easily. "You're too damn grateful I helped you save your inheritance."

"I guess I am." Kezia leaned against a concrete pillar, her emotions a tangled mess.

"Come here." Christian pulled her into an embrace, and she found herself holding him tight.

"We did it, Kelly, we actually did it."

"Of course."

Laughing, Kezia pushed him away. "I forgive you for embarrassing me. Hey, I'll even buy you a coffee to celebrate your imminent departure."

There was a brief silence, then he said lightly, "My God, you're right. Forget the coffee, this calls for champagne."

"At ten in the morning? In Everton?"

"Live dangerously for once. You might enjoy it."

"Okay, let's be bad." Her inheritance was safe and, with Christian leaving, so was she.

Christian looked intrigued. "How bad?"

"We'll have cake, too."

He raised his eyes at that, and at the sight of the coffee shop, too—a tiny enterprise with only two types of coffee, black or white.

But he was engaging and funny, complimenting the owner on her chocolate cake. Kezia ordered a second piece and thought, *I am not compensating for no sex life.*

"I can't imagine what you saw in William J. Rankin the Third," Christian told Kezia. "He's way too straight for you."

"Bill has got more earnest with age," she conceded, "but he's loyal, dependable, reliable…"

"My opposite in fact."

"That was an attraction."

"Still, you broke off your engagement."

"Mmm."

"Why?" He wasn't averse to bluntness.

"Do I ask you questions about your love life?"

"Go ahead."

"I prefer to respect people's privacy."

"The first question's free."

She was torn, he could see that. "Okay, a scientific one. Are breast implants cold to the touch?"

"You wouldn't believe how many women ask me that."

"We want them to be cold," she admitted.

"Then they are," he said diplomatically. "My turn. Why did you break off your engagement?"

"Uh-uh. I only agreed to a free question for me, remember?" He grimaced and she relented. "We didn't have enough in common."

Christian sat back. "I knew he'd be lousy in bed."

She got pious, he knew she would. "Sex is not the true barometer of a relationship. Intimacy is far more important."

"Aren't they the same thing?"

"No, they are not."

"Who cares? That the sex was lousy is enough for me."

"Actually the sex was great."

He stared at her. "You're kidding me!"

"For God's sake, how would you feel if I asked you what sex was like with Miss October?"

"Miss September. She got an A for effort, we had very effort-ful sex." She tried not to laugh at that. "Go on, Kez, you know you want to, let loose."

"You're not going to make me snicker at someone else's expense."

"She had more of a whicker, actually," he commented and she exploded into mirth.

"Damn you," she said.

"Did you love him?" He couldn't stop himself asking.

"I only sleep with men I love."

"How ironic," he muttered. "After you, I made a point of sleeping only with women I didn't."

"You started this game," she reminded him softly.

He stood, annoyed with himself. "I'll go pay."

Kezia watched him at the counter, so sharp in his city suit, the old lady was clearly flustered. It had taken years to get over him and yet—he was going, so she could admit it—she was still tempted.

"Okay, Madame Publican, let's go."

With a sense of reprieve Kezia led the way out, nodding to two acquaintances coming in. From the way the women glanced from her to Christian she knew they'd been withdrawing gossip from the bank. She never had secured that promise from Suzie.

"You want me to apologize for spilling the beans?" Christian offered behind her. So, he'd noticed the stares.

"Only if you're sorry."

"I'm not."

Exasperated, Kezia started walking.

"Want to know why?" Glancing back, she caught her breath at his expression, playful and tender, masculine and intense. "I waited a long time for you because I wanted you to be my first. And I don't care who knows it."

She forced her feelings back, couldn't let him move her. "I'm sure you've learned a lot since then."

He laughed. "Has my technique improved?" His gaze lowered, laser heat all the way down her body. "Only one way to find out."

"I've learned a lot since then, too."

"I look forward to a full and frank exchange of ideas."

She frowned to stop the smile. "I mean, about men like you."

"C'mon, how about a tumble for old times' sake?"

"That's your best line? No wonder Miss November dumped you."

"Miss September. And for the record, our parting

was mutual—smoothed with the help of a diamond navel ring. You're the only woman who has ever dumped me."

"It was your choice to leave," she reminded him coldly.

Christian's tone was equally frigid. "And yours to stay."

They had reached the impasse that had parted them and it looked as wide a gulf as ever.

# CHAPTER SIX

"You still don't trust yourself, do you?"

Staring out the window, Joe was glad the psych couldn't see him roll his eyes. If one more kindly professional probed his feelings… After ninety days' rehab he was supposed to have learned how to control destructive impulses.

"That's why you haven't called your wife," prompted Dr. Samuel when it became clear Joe wasn't going to answer. "Because you're worried you might fail her again."

For all his bedside manner, Dr. Samuel had a gaze that could strip paint. Joe concentrated on Redvale House's gardens. The soldierly rows of conifers down the driveway flanked symmetrical beds of purple and red poppies. Everything had self-restraint in this place, he noted wryly, even the plants.

"Talk to me, Joe," commanded Dr. Samuel.

Joe turned to face the man who could have been his twin. Same age—mid-thirties—same lanky stature, same unexceptional brown eyes and hair. But they lived in different worlds. "I can't make promises while I'm in here." *I won't hurt my family again.* "My ninety days is up this week. If I can stay sober outside for three months, we'll talk."

"And what's your son supposed to do in the meantime?"

That struck a nerve. "What's your point?"

"Six months is too long for a four-year-old to lose all contact with his father."

Joe glared. "I'm trying to do the right thing by my family."

"You want to make yourself perfect before you take the first step." Dr. Samuel steepled his long, manicured fingers. Joe hated it when he did that. "Even if you never take another drink, that's not going to happen, Joe. Humans aren't made that way. Besides, maybe your wife doesn't want you perfect. You won't know until you ask her."

"I'll write her a letter."

Dr. Samuel shook his head. "You know that part of the twelve steps is to make direct amends to the people we've harmed."

"Except when it would hurt them more—or others." Joe met Dr. Samuel's paint-stripping gaze with one of his own.

The other man didn't flinch. "At your lowest ebb, you got drunk and struck out at your wife. Let's be very clear. I make no more excuse for that than you do." His tone was acerbic. "But it affected you so profoundly that you acknowledged your alcoholism and committed yourself to residential rehab. At the very least, don't you think she needs to hear that in person?"

Joe stared blindly out the window. He'd survived his

childhood by not giving a damn. Alcohol had put a protective visor around the scary business of living with a woman he knew he didn't deserve and a son who peeled his emotions back to tender. "I'll think about it."

"Turn around," said Dr. Samuel, and reluctantly Joe complied. "Would you risk your life for your wife and child?"

At last, an easy question. "Of course."

"Yet you won't take an emotional risk for them." The pain was so unexpected it took Joe seconds to realize he'd been cut. Having made his neat incision into Joe's heart, Dr. Samuel probed gently. "What are you really afraid of? All she can do is say no."

"Oh," said Joe, "is that all she can do? *That* thought never occurred to me."

Dr Samuel smiled. The first smile Joe had ever seen from the man. He was so surprised he returned it.

"Tell me, Doc—" he spoke gruffly to cover his momentary lapse "—are you this brutal with all your patients?"

Dr. Samuel turned serious again. "Only the strong ones." Joe refused to feel gratified. "And the stubborn ones," he added, and smiled at Joe again.

DON WAS WAITING FOR KEZIA and Christian back at the hotel, sitting straight-backed in a cane chair on the front veranda, his sparse ginger hair lifting in the warm breeze.

The sight of him distracted Kezia from her brooding and she hung out the open window with her thumbs up and called, "Success!" She was puzzled when she received no answering salute. "I'm going to have to buy that man a hearing aid."

Christian didn't reply, and she scrambled out of the passenger seat then slammed the Ferrari's door, listening for the curse and smiling when it came.

What was she doing? Provoking Christian into a fight when she was within hours of being rid of him?

With a supreme effort of will she opened the driver's door. "Sorry about that." *You were the one to issue an ultimatum and refuse to compromise.* "And thanks for all your help." *You were the one who disappeared without a goodbye.* The memory of discovering him gone without a word could still upset her. "Bastard!"

She slammed the door again. Wrenched it open. "Damn it, I want to talk about it." Her voice vibrated with passion.

Christian got out of the car and closed both doors with exaggerated care. "Tough. I don't."

"I didn't dump you. You dumped me because I wouldn't run away with you on one day's notice. 'If you love me you'll come with me.' Well, if you'd loved me you would have stayed!" Fourteen years of bitterness uncorked. "But that's not your style, is it, Christian? Better to run away than to stick it out and work on a compromise."

Christian began strolling across the car park toward the hotel. Kezia yelled after his retreating back. "That's right, you coward! Walk away!"

"You're confused," he called back. "The coward stayed."

Anger propelled her after him. "I had responsibilities."

"You had excuses."

"What's your excuse for disappearing without a goodbye?"

"You ripped my heart out. What the hell did you expect?"

Her own began to bleed, the wound as fresh as the day he inflicted it. "Did it ever occur to you," she cried with a searing anguish that cauterized the flow, "that I could have changed my mind?"

Christian swung around, his face a study in shock. "Did you?"

She was silent while she watched him suffer, wondered whether he could ever suffer enough. "I guess you'll never know now, will you?" She held her chin high to stop it from trembling.

*"Tell me!"*

Without another word, she walked past him, forcing a smile for Don as she rounded the corner of the hotel. "We got it," she enthused. Inside, her stomach was churning. "Isn't that great?"

Don's lined face remained grave and Kezia pulled up another cane chair. "You have bad news."

"My dear girl." He reached for her hand, waiting for Christian, who arrived grim-faced a few seconds later.

Like Kezia, he assessed Don's mood at a glance. "Tell me something else I don't need to hear today."

Don cleared his throat. "It's customary for the executor to notify the tax department to inquire after money outstanding but I had no idea..."

Wearily, Kezia leaned back. "A tax bill. Oh, great. I guess I could sell my station wagon."

"I'm afraid that won't be enough." Don hesitated. "Muriel has been stalling Inland Revenue for two years over provisional tax. I believe she used the tax money she should have been setting aside to pay off other creditors."

*Oh, Nana, why didn't you tell me?*

"How much?" Christian asked quietly.

Don tightened his hold on Kezia's hand.

"There's quite a high penalty regime for provisional tax. Incremental penalties as well as use-of-money interest—"

"How much, Don?" Her voice came out harsh and Kezia dropped it to a whisper. "Please. Just tell me how much."

His grip on her hand grew painful. "One hundred and fifty thousand dollars. That's core debt with penalty and interest included."

"Oh, my God." Kezia stared at Christian, becoming conscious of how much she was revealing, then leaned back in her chair. Across the street the fruit and flower shop was a splash of vibrant color.

Plump Mrs. McKlosky came out of the shop with a bucket of purple irises and pink peonies. Seeing Kezia, she gave a cheery wave. For twenty-five years she'd supplied the hotel with fresh produce and flowers. Kezia's throat tightened. "Poor Mrs. McKlosky," she said, and knew it as an admission of defeat.

Christian laid a hand on her arm. "No one could have worked harder to save this place."

She couldn't look at him and maintain her composure so she stared blindly at Mrs. McKlosky. "We're beat, though, aren't we?"

"I'm sorry, babe."

Kezia hoisted herself up, feeling like an old woman. "I'm going to lie down for an hour. Then I'll tell the staff."

"Would you like me to do it?"

"No, it should come from me." Don's old face was drawn and anxious, and she bent to kiss his forehead. "I'm one tough broad. Don't worry about me." At the doorway self-preservation kicked in. She turned back. "Christian?"

He was watching her, all arrogance gone, and she steeled herself. "That other matter. I hadn't changed my mind so a goodbye wouldn't have made any difference."

For a moment an indefinable emotion flickered in his eyes. "Thanks for telling me."

Kezia nodded and turned away. She had told the truth—just not all of it. That would have been vindictive.

A ROW OF EMPTY GLASSES between them, Christian and Kezia sat at the dimly lit bar, oblivious to the curious stares of late-night patrons. They were mostly grizzled farmers who insisted on buying Kezia another drink she clearly didn't need "for your loss." Their nods to Christian mixed sociability with "watch your step with our girl." He'd got used to it.

One of the biggest shocks in coming back had been discovering most of his peers gone. Left were the old, the young, eternal optimists like Kezia, and the hopeless, tied to their land by debt. At the center, socially and economically, was the Waterview Hotel.

Depressed, Christian took another swig of his beer and wondered if he should try to stop Kez from drinking any more. She plainly wasn't used to alcohol, but he was in complete sympathy with her desire to soften the edges of a day from hell. Not one to shirk unpleasantness, she had spent the afternoon with the tax department signing over ownership of the hotel. It was already up for sale.

Kezia picked up her glass and took a ladylike sip. Christian removed the beer mat still clinging to the base. "At least I have my teaching to fall back on," she said, "though I'll probably have to leave the area." There were no vacancies at her old school.

Christian tried to play along with her determined cheerfulness. "Meanwhile you've got your town council position."

"And my community projects."

"And your campanology."

She looked up sharply, saw he intended no irony and relaxed.

"All I've lost is a roof over my head. I'll just stay in a motel until I know where I'll end up working."

Christian nodded, unable to hide his pity.

"I'm not pretending this isn't devastating, but I refuse to fall apart," Kezia told him firmly, waving her forgotten drink. "From now on, my cup is half full, not half empty." Then she noticed her glass was in fact nearly empty and signaled for the bartender.

"Coffee," Christian told Davie before she could open her mouth.

Kezia had been about to order coffee, longed for coffee, but allowing Christian to take charge now would be fatal. "A Bloody Mary, please, and if you look to Christian for confirmation, Davie, I'll fire you."

The twenty-one-year-old kept his eyes on hers. "Okay, Kezia."

She bit her tongue, resolving to make it up to Davie with some baking when she'd resettled. If she remembered right, peanut brownies were his favorite.

"Will the motel have an oven?" she asked Christian, then laughed, both at his perplexity and at the absurdity of expecting a millionaire to know such a thing. He'd probably never been in a motel in his life.... Oh, boy. The drink arrived and Kezia took a gulp, trying to quench the fire burning her face, the fire within. Instead the alcohol inflamed her memories, all of them slick, hot and wantonly abandoned.

"Small oven," he said, and she looked at him blankly. "Big bed."

He spoke the last softly, dragging it out like every sigh of pleasure he'd won from her. Kezia put down her Bloody Mary, reached for a jug of ice water and poured a glass. Drained it. He was tormenting her deliberately. Well, two could play this game.

"Is it hard?" she asked throatily, and waited until his eyes widened. "I do so hate a soft mattress."

That surprised a laugh out of him. "Is there still a wayward streak in that pillar of the community?"

"I may have led a sheltered life compared to you—actually I can't think of a single person who hasn't—but I'm not unworldly. You think of rural life as entombment."

"And you never have." His tone was neutral but she sensed an accusation.

Alcohol made her brave. "I didn't go with you fourteen years ago because I was scared."

His expression changed to the one she hated—that of the world-weary cynic. "You were right not to trust me. Look how I turned out."

"That's not what I meant," she persisted. "You were so intense, so fearless." She struggled to find the right words. "So sure about what you wanted." *And didn't want.*

"I don't do intensity anymore. A man lasts so much longer without it." His intonation gave the words a sexual connotation but Kezia knew he was trying to steer the conversation into safer channels.

She let him. "You couldn't burn me now, Christian, even if you tried." She refilled her glass with ice water, looked up and fell into his eyes, shimmering with male heat.

Casually he took the glass, already forgotten. "No?"

Ignoring the thumping of her heart, Kezia held his gaze. She was thirty-two and in charge of this conversation even if her emotional responses were still eighteen.

"These days," she said carelessly, "I might just burn you."

"You could try."

It was on the tip of her tongue to tell him to get naked. "I got over you, Christian," she said instead. And almost meant it.

"Me, too. So there's no reason to rehash the past, is there?" To Kezia's surprise he reached out a hand. After a brief hesitation, she took it. "We have enough to deal with."

"I have enough to deal with," she corrected, and withdrew her hand to reinforce an independence she didn't feel. "Your work here is done."

"Are you counting that as one of your blessings?"

"That would be ungrateful," she said, and he laughed.

"I'll take that as a yes, then."

Yes. Go before I care. "I figure I'll leave most things for the new owner. A clean break is probably best."

In his mind's eye Christian saw her walking past the hotel every day, swinging her arms a little more briskly, giving it a cursory glance, catching people's eye so she could say brightly, "Hi, how are you? I'm fine!" Being brave.

He drained his glass, signaled Davie for another, hating this feeling of helplessness. *If you weren't dead, Muriel, I'd wring your neck.*

The old woman had put too much faith in his ability. Kezia's theory—that Muriel wanted to throw them together—he'd already dismissed.

Only a sentimental fool would chance everything

on love, and Muriel had never been that. Stubbornly independent maybe, but no fool. Her granddaughter had inherited her independence in spades so why was he reluctant to leave her like this?

Maybe because he'd suffered few failures in his adult life, and every damn one of them involved Kezia Rose.

But he could do something for her. He slid an envelope along the bar. "This is for you."

She opened it. Inside were hundred dollar bills—lots of them. "What's this?"

"Your commission for helping me close that multimillion-dollar deal yesterday."

Snorting, she pushed it away. "I'm not a pity case yet."

He pushed it back. "Pity has nothing to do with it. Like you said yesterday, I owe you."

"Okay, let's be realistic. Give me a hundred bucks toward a new church bell." She removed one bill and tried to pass him the envelope.

Christian hid his hands behind his back. "My reality has a lot more zeros in it."

"Well, mine doesn't." She reached around him to make him take the money and his arms came about her like muscle-sheathed iron.

"People around here tell me you peg your worth too low." His arms tightened. "And on the subject of unfinished business, I still haven't kissed you properly—improperly—yet."

His arms were warm against her back, his mouth inches from hers. Kezia began to struggle. Christian released her and raised his brows in mock surprise. "I thought you said I couldn't burn you now, even if I tried?"

Needing to have the last word made her reckless. "I also said I might just burn you, so don't play chicken with me. Unless you mean it." She threw the envelope down between them like a gauntlet. Then swallowed.

Christian pocketed the money, his eyes never leaving her face. "Oh, I mean it," he said slowly. "If you won't take my money—" his smile brought the butterflies back "—how about I put myself at your service for three hours?"

"That's some hourly rate," she said dryly, "but I like the idea of having you in my power."

"For three hours I'll do anything you want."

"Anything?" Kezia managed an ironic expression but her heart wasn't as good at overlooking innuendo. Unwittingly, she put a hand on her heart and Christian's smile reached his eyes. "You mean, dig potatoes or put out the trash or…"

"Get dirty," he agreed softly, and she stopped pretending she didn't understand his meaning and started pretending she could manage this.

# CHAPTER SEVEN

"OKAY, I'LL ADMIT to a little sexual curiosity." Kezia regrouped, that wasn't what she'd meant to say. *"But."* That was better. "Why would I—Miss Uptight Whatever—abandon my principles and sleep with you on your last night in town?"

"Because you want to as much as I do. Because if you don't get some serious fun, you'll implode. Because I don't need you like everyone else around here seems to."

She could say nothing to that.

"What would it be like—" his casual tone was intensely seductive when combined with the lazy eroticism of his gaze "—to give yourself permission to be selfish? To take what you want from someone who doesn't need you to care about his feelings? To have a man devote himself entirely to your pleasure?"

It was a fantasy she hadn't known she harbored. With an effort Kezia remembered he'd broken her heart and she still had painful scars. "So you're offering to be my sex slave for three hours?" she countered, deliberately reducing his offer to carnal.

"No." He sounded surprised and her cheeks

burned with mortification. Christian tucked an errant strand of hair behind her ear, trailed his fingers, feather-light, across her heated cheek. "But your idea sounds a hell of a lot more fun than mine."

"What idea is that?" Don appeared at Kezia's elbow and put his empty glass on the bar.

"She wants a sex slave," said Christian frankly, "and I'm applying for the job, so go away."

"So like her grandmother." Don patted Kezia's hand then asked Christian, "Is there really no way around that letter? We couldn't give one of your cars to the tax department, for example?"

"None of my money, in any shape or form, can come near the place," quoted Christian, and just like that a solution came to him, so simple he could have kicked himself for not thinking of it before.

Excited, he jumped off the bar stool. "I forgot to make a call." He hesitated, looking at Kezia, knowing he was losing the chance to exorcise the soul-searing memory of first love with the grown-up realism of down-and-dirty sex. "You know where I sleep."

"Sleep well," she retorted, but she looked like a woman reprieved, which bugged him all the way up to his room.

The day Kezia had arrived at high school and accepted his smile at face value, he'd liked her. All the other girls either vied for his attention or, sufficiently frightened by their parents, crossed the street to avoid him. But after school that first day, Kezia had crossed it to walk with him. "You're heading in the same direction," she'd explained. "Would you mind showing me the quickest way home?"

He'd quipped, "Baby, I'm the guy who can take you all the way," and she'd said, "Thank you very much." He'd spent most of that first walk home trying to explain that being sixteen and ignorant was all very well in some mission. But in a country town like Waterview where sex was all teenagers had to think about, she needed to wise up or she'd find herself in a barn with her panties around her ankles.

Which was precisely what he'd intended for Marion's older sister, Sally, that night, after she'd intimated that she'd go all the way with him. Instead he'd endured two years of blue balls waiting for Kezia.

As he waited for his partner to pick up, it occurred to him that leaving as the good guy had somehow become more important than sexual conquest.

This afternoon Kezia had suggested she'd changed her mind all those years ago, throwing everything he believed about her into doubt. Except it turned out she hadn't changed her mind and he could continue to think of her as an emotional coward. But that didn't square with the woman who had coolly mortgaged her future to save others.

Christian was frowning over her inconsistencies when his partner picked up. "Luke? It's me. How would you and Jordan like to own a bankrupt hotel in a rural backwater? It has dwindling business and needs thousands of dollars spent on renovations." Luke was obviously stunned into silence on the other end. Christian laughed. "And I haven't even mentioned the rat."

"Either that woman is standing there with a gun to your head or you're in love with her. Which is it?" Luke's dry comment wiped the grin off Christian's face.

"Neither," he said shortly. Quickly he outlined his plan and asked his partner to pick it over for holes.

"Jordan's here for dinner," said Luke. "I'll run it by him."

As he waited, Christian relaxed. Between the three of them, they'd make this work. Years ago, Jordan and Luke had talked Christian into getting his feet wet as a white-water rafting guide on the Whanganui River. Christian had then talked them into sinking their earnings—earmarked for masters degrees—into a downpayment on the ailing company they guided for. Now they owned a multimillion-dollar tourism concern.

Luke came back and suggested a few modifications. "Incidentally, Jordan thinks you're deluding yourself."

Christian frowned. "I'm sure we've covered all the bases."

"He thinks it's love, too."

"I hate to throw cold water on your fevered imaginations," Christian said with exaggerated patience, "but I've already been there, done that and got the T-shirt that says Sucker."

"You two have history?" Luke's tone lost its lazy drawl. "How interesting that you never told us."

"Gotta go now, thanks for the help." Christian

rang off. For a moment he stood pensive, then knuckled down to the business of extricating every-body from this mess—including himself.

AT 1:00 A.M. KEZIA GAVE UP on sleep and crept like a ghostly wraith in her satin nightdress into the sitting room. She switched on a lamp, hauled a card-board box close, and began to sift through papers. Her thoughts were in chaos. She had to bring order to something or she'd go mad.

Her tears fell on her grandmother's spidery hand-writing but she angrily wiped them away. She may have lost her inheritance but she had her health, her job skills...many of her staff were far worse off. And she'd come through Christian's visit unscathed. With a pithy curse, she reached for the tissues and blew her nose hard.

She was an astute, sensible woman with respon-sibilities she should be thinking about right now, but what was she doing? Aching for a man who offered her a respite from virtue.

No other lover had aroused the passionate side of her nature, and with Christian would go her last op-portunity to play without boundaries.

*You know where I sleep.*

Before she could talk herself out of it, Kezia stood and walked along the passageway to Christian's bedroom door. Took a deep breath and knocked.

He opened it, tie and jacket discarded, a cell phone pressed to his ear. The sight threw Kezia com-pletely. She'd expected a moonlit shape that would segue into hers. Instead she was faced with a fully dressed man in a prosaic conversation about transferring funds. It occurred to her that alcohol might still be affecting her judgment.

"N-nothing, wrong room," she stammered, and spun around.

Continuing his conversation, Christian grabbed her about the waist and kicked the door shut. "I know it's the middle of the night, but I need the deal done and you're my lawyer. Find a time zone that will make the transaction possible."

Kezia started to wiggle free but the heat generated by her satin curves sliding against Christian's resistant muscle did nothing but shiver her nipples into relief. She stopped.

"No chance," he whispered in her ear. In a normal voice he said into the phone, "Cathy, consider. Getting laid by your husband now or a dirty weekend later at my expense…and yes, that includes child care. Call me the minute you have news."

He dropped the phone into his pocket, wrapped his other arm around Kezia and growled, "Welcome to the pleasure dome."

That did it. Blushing with humiliation, she freed herself and reached for the door handle. "This was such a bad idea."

To her surprise he opened it for her. "You're wrong, it's a great idea, one of the best you've ever had." With his hands on her shoulders he propelled her down the corridor to her own room and turned on the light. "We just need the right setting."

The sight of Muriel's sinfully decorated boudoir was the last straw. "Okay, joke's over, you can stop making fun of me."

"I'm making fun *with* you. Now, sit." She didn't move, so Christian swept her up into his arms.

Kezia yelped and clutched at him and he laughed as he dumped her on the candy-striped sofa. She met his eyes at last, saw no mockery there, just desire. And her heart hammered… *Get out, get out, get out.*

Christian pressed on her shoulders as she tried to stand. "Tonight you're going to lighten up and I'm going to help you do it. Now dredge up some fantasies and tell me what you want me to do."

"That's the most unromantic proposition I've ever heard!"

"Ah, so milady wants romance?" He left her side to hit the switch for the chandelier and the room fell into darkness. Another click and the bedside lamp—a cherub holding a flaming torch—spilled its glow across the four-poster, making the glitter in the white faux fur cushions sparkle like snow. The room and the man seemed much more dangerous. "I really think—"

"Personally," Christian said, ignoring her interruption, "I don't think you want romance. I think you're more turned on by control over a dominant male." He stood by the bed with his arms folded, looking arrogant and potently masculine. "Want to give it a try?"

*Cocky bastard.* On impulse, Kezia nodded. *I'm not going to sleep with him but I am going to play with him a little because he needs taking down a peg or two.*

Christian reached into his pocket and threw her the envelope. "I know you, Kez, you're going to get cold feet. Every time you have a pang of conscience I want you to hand me a bill."

"You don't know me anymore, Christian, you only think you do. And my first order, sex slave, is to keep your opinions to yourself." It was easier now that she wasn't taking it seriously.

His mouth quirked as he inclined his head. "Certainly, mistress. Your next request?"

Kezia searched for something…anything. "Take it off," she demanded, throwing down a hundred dollar bill. Stripping him naked should deflate his insufferable ego.

One black eyebrow lifted. "You'll have to be more specific."

"Your…" her courage failed her "…shoes."

"Live dangerously."

"Okay, take off your socks, as well."

Christian sat on the bed and did as he was bid. "Babe, you need some practice at this."

"Fine," she said, stung. "Take off all your clothes. Slowly."

He came closer and she clutched the envelope nervously. He was so much bigger, closer. In silence, he held out his hand for the money, his eyes insolent and hot. With a surge of exhilaration, she gave it to him. He could look how he liked, but he still had to do as she said. The balance of power hung in the air between them like an aphrodisiac.

His eyes never leaving hers, Christian undid the

buttons on his shirt. Slowly. Kezia watched as button by button the shirt fell open, revealing first a strong brown collarbone, then the bulge of pectorals, their nipples half hidden by the crisp white shirt, finally the corrugated muscle of an iron-flat stomach.

He shrugged his shoulders and the shirt fell to the floor. His muscled arms and chest were the color of old gold in the lamplight, nipples like copper. Kezia realized she was staring and blushed as she defiantly raised her eyes to his.

He was smiling at her; his pupils dilated, his irises bleached to night-washed gray. The dim light cast shadows under his strong cheekbones, the light behind him an aureole around his body. And Kezia began to ache, a woman's ache at breast and groin.

His large hands moved to the front of his pants, one snap to unfasten, then down went the zipper. Slowly. Underneath, the briefs were sleek and black against his arousal. Easing off the trousers, Christian slid them down his long, solidly muscled thighs and kicked them aside. Then he stood there under her scrutiny.

And Kezia forgot she was toying with him, forgot she wasn't going to sleep with him, forgot she didn't love him anymore.

He held out his hand for more money and, like Sleeping Beauty, she woke to reality. Kezia stumbled to her feet and the envelope fell from her lap, spilling onto the floor. "I'm sorry," she blurted, "but I have too many hang-ups to do this." *And you're one of them.*

She almost ran for the door, but Christian caught her and pulled her back against his near-naked body.

"Please. Don't leave," he said huskily, and she thought with sudden clarity, *I'm damned.* But she had to know, had to, so she turned in his hold and lifted her mouth, blindly as a woman dying of thirst seeks water. Their lips met.

Then Christian's hands came up to cup Kezia's face and they opened their mouths to each other and drank.

The kiss became more savage, more passionate. Her arms came up around his neck and he crushed her to him as they punished each other for the intervening years, the loss and the longing. At last they broke apart, breathing hard.

"So," said Christian, "the gloves are off at last." He looked aroused and fierce and vengeful, and Kezia reached for him again because she felt exactly the same way.

He laughed, his gaze dark on hers, and this time their kiss was about tasting and teasing, about showing the other what they'd been missing. Kezia realized Christian had picked up far more tricks in the intervening years than she had. The knowledge made her self-conscious and strangely sad.

"What?" He lifted his mouth from hers.

"You've learned a lot." She wanted to be honest. "I'm not sure how I feel about that."

"Meanwhile I'm trying to pretend you haven't," he told her. "Because I know damn well how I feel about it."

Kezia laughed. She'd forgotten that intimacy with Christian Kelly was like this, frank with humor as well as lust. Reassured, she kissed him again.

And somewhere in the slow, languorous heat of that third kiss, the past lost its power and nothing mattered except that they were here. Now.

Christian entwined his fingers in her hair and pushed it back to kiss her throat, her collarbone. He pulled down the thin straps of her nightdress so that it fell to her waist, and at the look in his eyes, she ached for his mouth on her breasts.

He made her wait, stroking her shoulders, her arms, the skin above her breasts, marveling with his touch at every silken swell and curve of her upper body until Kezia felt like the most desirable woman in the world. She felt his tongue's caress on a nipple and groaned, wanting more, so much more.

Christian stepped back, his eyes languorous with passion, the message in them unmistakable. He gathered the scattered money, sat Kezia unceremoniously on the end of the bed and handed the notes to her. Nothing needed to be said.

"Come closer," she said in a low voice. "Kneel down so I can touch you." She put some money to one side and with a hand that shook slightly, rediscovered the strong curves of his face, the glossy texture of his hair and brows. Her fingers tracked the line of his throat.

She flattened her palm against his warm, broad chest and let it rest, sharing the rhythm of his breathing, before sliding it around his back and down to the swell of his buttocks. And her hand didn't shake anymore. Another bill on the pile.

Slowly, Kezia removed his briefs, freeing him to her sight, to her touch, freeing herself from her last inhibitions. She would suffer, but she didn't care. Christian closed his eyes under her caresses and she didn't have to hide her love as she moved to rub her bare breasts against his chest. If she had to suffer, then so would he. The pile of notes grew higher.

"Let me touch you," he ground out through clenched teeth.

Kezia leaned back on her elbows. Dark hair tumbling over her bare breasts, she considered with a half-smile on her face. Torture was such fun. Christian growled his frustration.

"What did you have in mind?" she asked. But she lost her smugness as he told her, graphically, exactly what he wanted to do to her—and how much it would cost.

"Sold," she said weakly, and he reached for her with a glint in his eyes that thrilled her.

And then he played her.

Played her until there wasn't an inch of her body that didn't know his touch, his mouth, until she was mad for him. With his naked body, finely covered in perspiration, poised above hers, Christian waited as Kezia scrabbled around the bed for more cash. Waited as she came to a sickening realization. "I've run out of money."

His smile suggested he'd planned it that way. "This," he whispered, entering her with slow, exquisite control that stripped her of rational thought, "is the gift part."

She let him thrust, once, twice before croaking, "Stop!"

## CHAPTER EIGHT

BREATHING DEEPLY, CHRISTIAN held himself away from her on arms sculpted out of corded muscle. She closed her eyes to block out the sight of his gorgeous male body, but that concentrated all her senses on the one place they still joined, a place hot, slick, yearning for movement. Involuntarily she lifted her hips and he groaned.

"What do you want me to do?" His voice was hoarse.

*Get off, get out, go away and never come back because I can't stand to feel like this again, alive and crazy in love.* But, oh, he felt so good. Her hips lifted again.

"Kez, please."

He pushed back and she panted. "Lend me some money."

"Take it all," said Christian, desperate now. He watched her open her mouth, form the word yes, and his phone rang, a zippy little tune programmed by a friend's ten-year-old. No, No, *No!* For an interminable moment he hung over Kezia while every instinct screamed at him to ignore it.

"Don't you dare take that call," she cried fiercely, tempting as Delilah, her body promising to bring him home.

*Home.* With a force of will he didn't know he possessed, Christian rolled off her with a groan. This call might save hers. "I'm sorry, I have to. Just... don't...move!"

He retrieved the phone from the pocket of his discarded pants and snapped into the receiver, "Make it good news." It was. He only half listened as Cathy gave him all the details that made him the new owner—once removed—of the hotel.

His gaze stayed on Kezia who was pulling the bedclothes around her luscious curves. She was angry with him for taking the call but his news would change that. He could admit it now; he wanted to leave her happy.

And he wanted to leave her. When he'd delivered his ultimatum at eighteen, she hadn't known how desperate his home situation was because he hadn't wanted pity to affect her choice. In a world that had been reduced to black and white he had given her a test of loyalty. And she had failed.

He might have matured into seeing shades of gray but emotionally he couldn't forgive her. Even if he could feel the siren's song in her touch, he could resist it. If he left soon.

"Thanks, Cathy, I'll be home tomorrow so we can finalize last details then." He rang off to see Kezia, tight-lipped and furious, pulling on her nightdress under the blanket. "You think you—this—means so little to me that I'd interrupt it for any old business call?" He tried to look wounded but he was feeling too damn elated to carry it off.

She noticed. Snap went the sheet and she was out of bed and gathering his clothes with short jerky movements. "Get dressed and get out." Kezia thrust his clothes at him and he caught her against him with a jubilant laugh.

"Get naked and get grateful. Hell, you can even do this place up properly now." Picking her up, he whirled her around, forcing her to drop his clothes and grab his shoulders.

"What are you talking about?"

"You're looking at the new owner of the Water-view Hotel."

Kezia stared at him, all the color leaving her face, and Christian steered her toward the couch. He grabbed a bedsheet, wrapped himself in it and sat beside her, taking her hands in his. "Muriel's will specified that none of my money could come near the hotel. So I got my partners to buy the place, then I bought it off them."

"It's the middle of the night!"

"I know a tax department head who saw a few hours' overtime as a small price to pay for offloading this white elephant. My lawyer prepared the paperwork and Internet banking did the rest."

"But you hate it here. You can't be thinking of staying?"

There was hope there, he heard it. Faint, barely articulated, perhaps Kezia wasn't even aware of it, but like an early warning system, it told him it was time to go.

"I'm still leaving tomorrow." She didn't flinch... maybe he'd imagined it. "And I didn't buy the hotel for me. It's for you."

She pulled her hands away from his. "For...me?"

"Tomorrow we'll sign a deed of transfer. Your troubles are over." He waited for the realization to sink in, for Kezia to throw her arms around him and hopefully drag him back to bed to express her gratitude. And he waited.

"And I'm to accept a four-hundred-thousand-dollar gift from you just like that? For what, services rendered?"

He didn't like that. "Sex has nothing to do with it. If you recall, I initiated the deal before you came to my room." At a loss, he resorted to humor. "But, hey, render away."

Her slap hit him square on the left cheek.

With stinging heat radiating from one side of his face Christian sat back. "So much for basking in your gratitude." His tone belied the anger building steam inside.

"It must be great to be Christian Kelly," she raged. "Patron of the poor!"

Now he couldn't keep the exasperation out of his voice. "In case you haven't noticed, I'm giving you your inheritance back."

"You're trying to strip me of the last remnant of pride I have left, that's what you're trying to do, mister!"

He threw up his hands in disgust. "Stop being so paranoid. I have no agenda."

Kezia regarded him with contempt. "Christian, your agenda would take up two pages. First, you're a man who pays off ex-girlfriends so he doesn't have to dirty his conscience, only in this case your recipient is an old lady. Well, live with the guilt like the rest of us. Second, you're paying back—and I quote— 'the only woman who ever dumped you,' by putting me in a situation where I'm hopelessly beholden to you. Damn it." Her hands balled into fists. "You're trying to have the last word!"

The echo of his thoughts, only days earlier, infuriated him. "That's bullshit. I got over you years ago."

"I don't doubt that." Her voice was bitter. "But have you forgiven me?" He remained silent and she rose to her feet, her eyes flashing sparks. "I haven't forgiven you, either. You wouldn't compromise then and I'm not compromising now. I will not start over again owing you for everything I have. I want to be free of you, do you hear me?"

"Let me get this straight," said Christian very quietly. "I've just spent the past week working my guts out to redecorate this dump, groveling to your ex-boyfriend banker, sleeping in that godawful bed and now—" he sucked a deep breath and stood up "—now, when we can finally do this the easy way, you're saying no?"

"Damn right I'm saying no!"

His temper exploded. "And what the hell am I supposed to do with a hotel I don't want? I'm going home tomorrow."

Kezia tipped her head to one side, considering.

"Oops," she said sweetly, "I nearly forgot. That's your problem."

Christian hadn't yelled in years but he yelled now. "Either you accept this place or I'll burn the damn thing down!"

Under his glare, Kezia stalked over to the dresser beside the bed and took something out of the top drawer. "Here!" She tossed it over and Christian dropped the bedsheet to catch it. It was a box of matches.

WHEN NIGHT LIGHTENED TO dawn Kezia gave up on sleep. Her fury had long since abated and the regret was so much harder to bear. In her mind's eye she saw herself, seminaked, tossing Christian money and asking him to…oh, God.

She scrambled out of bed and turned on the shower, determined to scrub all trace of the previous night away. If only it were that easy. Behind the walls, ancient pipes creaked and groaned, and she experienced a rush of bitter satisfaction—Christian's problem now.

The hot water stung a little. Her skin was still tender from the stubble on Christian's jaw. Even if guilt and revenge hadn't motivated his offer, accepting it was out of the question. It would strike a killing blow to her self-reliance—a thing she clung to when she lost the people she loved through death. Or abandonment.

Reaching for the soap, Kezia tried to ground herself. She was tired and overemotional. Her parents' aid work saved many lives; they'd no choice but to send their sick child home to her unknown grandmother.

A wonderful, crazy grandmother who, even in death, made people jump through hoops. Dropping the soap, Kezia covered her face with shaky hands. *I can't take his money, Nana, please understand and forgive me. I just can't.*

Christian seemed to exist to give her impossible choices.

She turned off the shower and dried herself briskly with a threadbare towel. She fully intended to make his remaining time here a misery and she would smile as she made him suffer. She got dressed in the bedroom, then, catching sight of herself in the gilt mirror—a wreck with tangled hair and dark shadows under her eyes—fumbled for a hairbrush and makeup.

As she applied the unconcerned face she would present to Christian, Kezia stopped fighting the truth. God help her, she still loved him.

Her course of action was clear. She had to get him out of her life quickly and for good before he realized how well he'd exacted his revenge. He might take her heart with him when he left, but her soul was not for sale.

KEZIA'S CHEERFUL WHISTLE PRECEDED her to breakfast. Hunched over his second coffee, Christian put his hands over his ears before his brain exploded. After storming out of her room last night, he'd raided the bar of Johnnie Walker and drank until 4:00 a.m.

"Cut the act. You can't have slept any better than I did."

She poured herself a cup of coffee from the dregs in the pot and turned to smile pleasantly at him. "Why wouldn't I? That phone call saved me from an embarrassing lapse in judgment, and all my responsibilities are now on your shoulders."

"Your lapse of judgment was sleeping with me, I take it," said Christian dryly, "and not the more serious one of rejecting my offer?"

Her smile vanished. "As it turned, out I rejected both."

"I smoked, your honor, but I didn't inhale." With grim satisfaction Christian watched her color rise. *Don't pretend with me, Kez, I remember every touch.*

He changed tactics, only because he was too hungover to do what he really wanted to do, which was shake some sense into her, kiss her into submission or both. Okay, and he was desperate to offload the hotel. "Please. Sit down. Let's talk."

Clearly reluctant, she pulled out a chair. She smelled good, some sort of apple-blossom soapy fragrance. Christian forced himself to concentrate, to look past her mouth still swollen from his kisses to the shadows under her eyes that makeup couldn't hide. So she was conflicted. The sight should have relieved him. Instead he felt protective—and more desperate to leave.

"This hotel has been in your family for over a hundred years. Don't let our history override that." He added astutely, "Don't make me that important."

Kezia said nothing but her hands tightened on the cup.

Encouraged, Christian went on. "You're right, there's some squaring of accounts in my offer. But not with you. Muriel trusted me and I failed. But it's more than that. I owed her everything and all I gave her was a weekend of my time once a year and the occasional phone call. I wish I'd taken her to Paris or New York.... I wish I'd told her how much she meant to me. I wish I'd known how much I'd miss her." He stopped. The words had poured out of a reservoir of feeling he kept dammed. "Let this be my way of making it up to her."

Tears shimmered in Kezia's eyes. "I'm sorry," she said, "but you'll have to make your peace with her another way."

His sympathy evaporated along with his patience. "And you accused me of petty revenge," he said softly, and she paled. "All that talk about keeping this place open at all costs, protecting jobs was just expedient bullshit. It's not me who wants the last word, Kez. It's you. Hell, it must really burn you up that the loser you thought you were rejecting ended up wealthy and successful."

She opened her mouth as if to argue, closed it and took a deep breath. "I will not be in your debt," she said quietly, and pushed up from the table to leave. "I can be packed up and out of here in a week, although if you need someone to oversee things until it's sold or you find another manager, I'm prepared to stay on." She raised her chin. "As a gesture of goodwill."

Christian lounged back in the chair. In business circles he was referred to as the Juggler for his ability to manage multiple deals. Those bested by him scathingly referred to him as the Jugular. Kezia hadn't seen that side of his nature. Yet.

"Very magnanimous, but if you haven't agreed to take this place by tomorrow, I'm going to board it up and abandon it." He watched her steps falter and stop.

Kezia grabbed a chair back. "You wouldn't."

"What's stopping me? Money?" Christian leaned forward. "This is just loose change. Affection for my hometown? What's it ever done for me? The sooner it cocks up its toes, the better."

"You wouldn't do that to the people who work here."

"You're right," he acknowledged. "I wouldn't." He waited for her expression of relief. "But it won't be me doing it, Kez. Turn it down and it will be you."

"You're bluffing."

"You have until after Suzie's wedding tomorrow to decide."

"Bluffing," she repeated emphatically.

Christian shrugged. "Today I thought I'd go into Everton, pick out a present for the happy couple. As my date you might like to advise me. How about a nice pair of salad servers?"

"Bluffing." Her tone was desperate.

He smiled. "Salad servers it is, then."

"HE'S BLUFFING," KEZIA TOLD Marion later that morning as they drank coffee on the deck of Marion's two-bedroom farmhouse rental and watched

John Jason try to make his rat jump through a hoop. The rat wasn't having a bar of it. Good for you, Roland, thought Kezia. A rat must keep his dignity.

"Of course he's bluffing." Marion had spoken in a soothing tone, probably the same one she used when telling John Jason there really was an Easter bunny.

"He's bluffing," Kezia told Don as she'd dropped another box of papers in his cavernous office for storage. She'd figured she might as well start moving at once and show Christian she didn't take this ultimatum seriously. *Like you didn't the last one. And look what happened then.*

Don had considered her out of hangdog eyes. "Maybe."

"A typical lawyer's remark," she'd snarled, then insisted on buying him lunch.

"He's bluffing," she told Bernice May as they stood in the cemetery, the hot afternoon breeze lifting the skirt on the old lady's mauve housedress like a playful ghost.

"You told me that ten times," complained Bernice May. She bent her rheumatic knees to place flowers beside Muriel's headstone. "And doing as bad a job convincing me as you are yourself."

Kezia started weeding the grave without another word.

"Be careful of your grandma, honey," said Bernice May in a mild tone. "She's here to rest, remember?"

Kezia dropped the trowel. "I have to believe he's bluffing because I can't bear either of the alternatives."

Bernice May shook her head. "Compromise isn't in Christian's nature. He didn't grow up in a compromising world."

"Then he was lucky," said Kezia bitterly. "Compromise was all I knew. There was always someone who needed my parents more so I compromised by being good and useful." Her laugh was half sob. "So why am I so set on being selfish now, when Nana was the only person who ever really loved me? I should just take the damn hotel for her sake. But it will kill something in me to do it."

For a while there was silence but it was a silence of acceptance. "You two need to stop fighting and start talking."

Kezia laughed at that. "Show him weakness? You're kidding!"

"Come with me," said Bernice May. She started picking her way through the graves. Puzzled, Kezia followed. The old lady moved slowly and paused often to pat the headstone of various old acquaintances. At last she stopped. "This is his mother's grave."

"Neglected," observed Kezia. "Why am I not surprised?" But she looked at the gravestone. Deborah Kelly. Beloved. Rest in Peace.

"I like to tend it for him," said Bernice May, pulling on a tall paspalum. "Least, I used to before my knees gave out."

Taking the hint, Kezia went to work on the low weeds. "Your son should be doing this," she told the dead woman.

"Except for the funeral I don't believe he's ever

visited Deborah." Bernice May picked paspalum stickies off her dress. "I think he feels too ashamed."

"That would be a first," Kezia replied tartly. She had no intention of allowing Christian further into her heart but her hands were gentle in the earth.

"I saw how he was," said Bernice May, more to herself than Kezia. "Poor little boy, all torn up and closed in on himself. 'Honey,' I said, 'I hope you're going to cry for your mother at her funeral and show her how much you love her.' Really, I wanted him to let it out, it was unnatural the composure of that child. He just looked at me and said, 'Not in front of my friends.'

"I told him straight—'Honey, if you can't cry in front of your friends, who can you cry in front of?' But it didn't happen. Even then he had an aversion to pity and that was before his father started whaling him." The weeds fell out of Kezia's nerveless fingers and she swiveled around to stare at Bernice May.

"Course I didn't know that till Don let it slip at Muriel's funeral. I tried to get more out of him but he closed up like a clam. Don might tell you more if you ask him."

Uneasy, Kezia answered, "I will."

"It was good to see Christian able to cry for Muriel…ah, you didn't know that…but then I figure a person can only bottle grief for so long."

"He hates me." Tears brimmed in Kezia's eyes and streamed down her face. "God help me, I still love him and he hates me. He's forcing me to accept the hotel for revenge."

"I doubt that, honey."

"I know he's your blue-eyed boy, but it's true."

"Then don't take it," said Bernice May. "Simple as that."

"Simple!" Wearily, Kezia stood. The tears stopped as suddenly as they'd come. "Do you know how many people depend on the hotel? Forty. I counted them last night. Forty people who will have to find work in a rural area already short on jobs." She wiped away the last tears. "Who am I kidding? If it's a choice between taking the hotel or seeing it closed down, I'll take it." She sent Bernice May a watery smile. "I'm sorry for unloading on you, I don't know what came over me."

"If all Christian Kelly does is make you realize you have friends to turn to, Miss Independence, then some good has come out of it," said Bernice May stoutly, holding out a handkerchief. "You want to go back and tell him now?"

Kezia blew her nose, gallows humor restoring the last of her composure. "And spare him another couple of nights in Waterview? I wouldn't dream of it."

*Get rid of him,* insisted her brain. *Soon,* promised her heart.

# CHAPTER NINE

THE HOTEL WAS quiet. Eerily quiet. She pushed through the swinging doors into the bar. Empty and dark, the yeasty smell of beer lingered in the room.

There should be staff shining glasses and preparing for a busy Friday night. A couple of farmers sitting over a beer before early evening milking and a clutch of lady golfers reviewing their performance over a shandy.

Her apprehension grew as she started up the stairs. The banister wobbled under her hand, and she saw it was only tacked in place. But a noise distracted her from closer inspection. Glancing up, she saw Christian sitting at the top of the stairs tying his running shoes.

"The carpenter was supposed to have this fixed today, it's dangerous." She shook the banister. "And where are the staff?"

"I've closed the place."

Her eyes widened in shock. "You told me I had until tomorrow."

"You do." His voice was reasonable as he laced up the second shoe. "Until then there's no point continuing renovations."

"The bar wasn't under renovation."

"The closure is temporary." Christian looked at her with eyes the guileless blue of heaven. "Or permanent. Entirely up to you."

Kezia reached for the banister again; it offered no support. "I assume you're paying people in the meantime."

"Assume away."

He started jauntily down the stairs and her anxiety increased with every step he took. Of course he would have paid staff. Wouldn't he?

She put a hand to her forehead and tried to massage some wits into her tired brain, but after last night she didn't trust herself to make a dispassionate judgment.

Then it occurred to her it didn't matter. In another twenty-four hours she would concede defeat and her staff would be back at work.

"Do what you like," she told him with a shrug. "It's your hotel." She carried on up the stairs without a backward glance. Yes, it was pathetic to cling to the last vestiges of her pride. Still she couldn't give it up. Not until she had to.

KEZIA'S UNEXPECTED COMPOSURE frustrated Christian so much he forgot to pace himself and ended up five kilometers past his usual circuit down some godforsaken road he'd never been before. Damn it! He stopped, bent forward from the waist and sucked in great gulps of air. Even his hangover was making a comeback.

He started to run again, slowly now, ripping off his T-shirt and wiping away sweat. Heat shimmered off the black tar road, which unfurled like a strap of sticky liquorice through the golden acres of newly cut hay.

Christian barely noticed, caught up in the darkness of his emotions. Closing the hotel was supposed to be the masterstroke that panicked Kezia into an acceptance. Instead her staff were enjoying paid leave with no benefit to himself whatsoever. It was infuriating!

And disturbing. What if she called his bluff? What did he do then?

"Aaaaaah!" As he raised his fists and yelled his exasperation, and several cows stopped chewing to stare at him.

Grimly, he cut a loop and ran back the way he'd come.

Well, to hell with it. He'd put in a manager and leave Kezia to play the martyr. *I did my best, Muriel, I really did.*

Ahead to his left, a new Power Wagon jolted down a rutted track and stopped just before the road, providing a welcome distraction. Then Christian recognized the driver and groaned. Bob bloody Harvey.

Bob leaned one meaty sunburned forearm out the window and grinned as Christian jogged toward him. "I got some hay bales need moving if you want some real exercise."

"Tempting." Christian ran past.

Behind him the vehicle rumbled into gear and Bob drove alongside, keeping pace. "I've just been driving over my new land and you know what? I figure I got the best out of that deal." With a hearty laugh, the farmer jammed his foot down and sped off, leaving a cloud of exhaust fumes in his wake.

Christian kept jogging until the 4WD was out of sight, then circled back. He followed the rough track up the hill that was once Kezia's land.

An anomaly on the plains, the fields hadn't been grazed, and from the top of the hill Christian watched the warm wind ripple across the gold. He saw at once where Kezia had intended to put the pond and how the farmstead she'd described would nestle into the side of the hill.

He sat and rested, just looking. The breeze was sweet with grass and wildflower and ripe summer heat. And he understood the real sacrifice Kezia had made when she'd sold her land to a man who would probably use it to grow turnips.

Cursing, he stretched out the tightening muscles in his legs and began the run back. Bob Harvey was right. He'd bought a piece of paradise for a song.

To hell with Kezia's principles. One way or another Christian was making her take the damn hotel even if he had to tell the truth to do it. If only he could figure out what that was.

In the shimmering distance he saw some sort of small animal on the road, with black face and pointy ears, pale chin. A goat?

As Christian drew closer, a tired John Jason came into focus, padding wearily down the road toward him, Batman cape trailing in his wake.

He had a backpack on one shoulder and his cheeks were sunburned and sweaty under the satin hood. A plastic bag of sandwiches hung limply from his utility belt.

Anxiety quickened Christian's pace. He was at the kid's side in five strides, untying the knotty bow under his chin and stripping off the cape.

"Now you'll know who I am," complained John Jason, but his struggle lacked conviction. Heat radiated from his body, and the baby-blond hair clung damply to his scalp.

"John Jason, is that you?" Christian feigned surprise and, mollified, the little boy allowed himself to be led to the shade of an ancient macrocarpa.

Christian spread the cape out over the sharp, burned grass and sat the boy on it, gave him the water bottle and watched him take gulping swallows. In that black cape the kid would have been all but invisible to a car from behind. The thought sickened him.

With an effort he kept his voice gentle. "You must never, ever, walk on the road. Where's your mother?" First, the backpack registered, then the guilty defiance on the child's face. "You're running away?"

"Me and Roland."

"Hell, you've got the rat with you—where is it?" Out came the listless white rat from a half-zipped pocket to be watered and revived, while Christian panicked about the best way to handle this. Parenthood was for idealists. His own childhood had made a benevolent worldview impossible.

John Jason's eyes filled with tears. "I'm finding my daddy. I'm gonna make him come home."

Shit. Where was Kezia when you needed her? She'd know exactly what to say. "You miss him."

John Jason started howling. *Great, Kelly.* Christian handed the kid his T-shirt, watched him wipe his nose on it, smearing snot across one plump cheek. Christian reclaimed the T-shirt and awkwardly wiped the kid's face clean. "C'mon, let's get you home." John Jason howled louder.

Christian unzipped the backpack, threw out a couple of apple cores and fashioned a bed in a pair of pajamas. "Put the rat in here." Reluctantly, Christian then swung the partially closed backpack to his shoulder, telling the rat through gritted teeth, "Stay put, vermin."

John Jason stopped crying. "He's Roland, not Vermin."

"Give me your hand."

"Carry me!"

"You can walk for a bit."

John Jason's lower lip trembled again and, feeling trapped, Christian picked him up. One small hand latched on to his bare shoulder, the other kept hold of Christian's T-shirt, trailing it down his chest. Christian felt something distinctly cold and slimy on his bare skin and tried to ignore it. He set off.

John Jason started crying again. "Mummy's gonna be mad."

"I'll tell her not to be."

The child leaned back against Christian's arm and assessed him doubtfully. The untanned portion of his face made him look like a reversed raccoon.

Christian grinned at the sight and John Jason sighed and rested his wet cheek against Christian's chest.

"Will you get my daddy, too?"

Christian patted the child lightly on the back. From what he'd heard—despite his best efforts not to—John Jason was better off without the man. "I think your daddy is too far away for anyone to find." In a hell of his own choosing.

The child said sadly, "But I need a daddy." Christian suffered a surge of helpless rage against all men who shouldn't be fathers. "I need him to do something," added John Jason.

"What?"

"Build me a tree house. Mummy says she can't do it an' she got mad when I said Daddy would have if she hadn't made him run away. She sent me to my room an' I hadn't done anything. So I ran away, too."

Christian shifted the child over to his other arm. He was surprisingly heavy. "Is that rat still lying still?"

John Jason checked. "Yep."

Around the next bend Marion's farmhouse came into view. With any luck the kid hadn't been missed. "Y'know, the real Batman wouldn't have run away. He would have known it would make his mummy sad." *Jeez, I can't believe I'm saying this.*

"Batman doesn't have a mummy!"

"Sure he does. Her name is Batmum and she fights tooth decay and snotty noses."

John Jason pushed back to gaze solemnly at him and Christian couldn't keep a straight face.

"Noooooo!" The kid burst out laughing.

"You're right I'm tricking, but running away makes things worse." *Unless you're a grown-up, then it works just fine.*

"You ran away from Auntie Kezia," said John Jason blithely. At Christian's frown he hastened to add, "Mummy said that."

"Mummy was wrong." Christian put the child down and opened the gate.

"No—" John Jason led the way down the path "—she never is."

Christian was tempted to cast a seed of doubt in the kid's mind just to pay Mummy back for gossiping. "Who was she talking to?" he asked abruptly, rapping on the open door.

"Auntie Kezia."

"And what did she say?"

"She said don't tell Christian I went looking—" John Jason looked at him, suddenly confused. "She said don't tell."

Christian hunkered down to his level. "Tell what, son?"

"John Jason!" The phone pressed to one ear, Marion swept down the hall like a dynamo, grabbed her son and hauled him into a one-armed embrace. "Where have you been!" She held him away from her, scanned him for damage and hugged him again. "It's okay, Kezia." She sighed her relief. "Christian found him…call you later."

She dropped the phone and squeezed her son. "I only realized he was missing ten minutes ago. Where'd you find him?"

Christian pleaded John Jason's case, then accepted lemonade he didn't want for the sake of getting the information he did. John Jason was sent grumbling off to the shower. "Don't push your luck," Christian advised him.

"I'll launder this." Marion picked up Christian's T-shirt. "Sit down while I find you another."

Ignoring his protest, she left the room, coming back with a man's faded blue sweatshirt. "Put this on."

It was too short, and tight across the shoulders and biceps, but one look at Marion's face and Christian kept his mouth shut. The last thing he needed was more tears.

Her embarrassment plain, she said, "I've been meaning to get rid of his clothes, but some have memories, y'know?"

A couple of weeks ago Christian would have thought she was crazy. Now he could only nod grimly. "How are you settling in?" he asked to make conversation.

"You know, I was scared about being on my own again but it's been good for me." Bringing a jug of lemonade and two glasses over to the table, she attempted to pour it but her hands shook too much.

Christian took over. "It's okay, he's home safe."

"What about next time? I'd die if I lost him, too!"

Her outburst startled Christian so much he reached out a hand to cover hers. "Muffet?"

"Ignore me, I'll come right." Still, her return grip on his hand made the bones ache. "It's just so hard raising him on my own. John Jason needs his father, and where is he? Probably drinking himself to oblivion in some hellhole."

"Let me give you money."

She laughed at that, released his hand and sat down. "What is it with you, Kelly, that you keep trying to buy off women?"

He grinned back reluctantly. "I don't know," he admitted. "It's only happened since I got back. Normally, I'm the one getting offers. I must be losing my touch."

Marion's expression sobered. "What you *can* do is tell me whether you intend to close the hotel if Kezia refuses to take it. Working there is the only thing keeping me sane." Seeing Christian hesitate, she added, "I can keep a secret."

"It will stay open."

"Thank God."

"Now tell *me* something." He repeated what John Jason had said.

Marion looked at him steadily. "I just said I keep secrets."

"Kezia implied that she came after me all those years ago, but I'd already left town. Later she told me she hadn't. Which one do I believe?"

Marion would never make a poker player. He pushed back from the table. "Thanks for the lemonade."

JOE UNPACKED HIS BAG AT the cheap Auckland motel that constituted his halfway house. *Alcoholic Anonymous' Big Book* came out first, along with details of a local AA meeting. No photos, no personal mementos. The night he'd run, sickened by what he'd done, Joe had only taken his shame.

He sat on the end of the bed, pulled a coin from his jeans' pocket and held it, remembering. The day after he'd hit his wife, still half drunk and more desperate than he'd ever been in his life, he'd sat in his car on a deserted byway with a loaded shotgun and tossed this coin to see whether he would live or die. The coin chose life.

And so he'd emptied the family's savings account and gambled it on one last chance at salvation—rehab. It was a selfish act, and whenever he teetered on the verge of giving up in those first bleak weeks he'd reminded himself whose money he'd be throwing away.

So he submitted to the physical hell of detox and to the psychological hell of holding a mirror up to his soul. Exposed as a loser.

Joe tucked the coin back in his pocket and walked to the window. Nothing to see but asphalt. "I'm an alcoholic," he said out loud. *Now I can admit it.* He looked at the phone.

Ironically, the better his recovery had progressed the worse he felt about who he'd been and the harder it became to make that call. He wanted the best for his wife, his child, and he wasn't it, not by a long shot. After all, he'd left them to exist on her meager earnings and the goodwill of a town that knew how to take care of its own.

For weeks Joe had convinced himself that the

selfless thing to do was get a good job and send money on. Stay the hell out of their life.

But it hadn't stopped him lying awake night after night, worrying about them, missing them. Until somewhere in the confusion he'd acknowledged his utter helplessness.

Then something amazing happened.

He began to believe that even though he didn't deserve another chance, someone might have given him one in the toss of that coin. He began to believe he might earn back his family.

He'd rung the bar she worked at and his luck had held—a stranger answered. The guy said she'd moved out and innocently gave Joe her new number. Except twice now his courage had failed.

He picked up the phone and dialed. Doc Samuel was right; his own fears meant squat against his wife's rights.

"Marion Morgan's residence." A male voice. His wife had gone back to using her maiden name and this sounded like the same man who had given Joe her new number. She had found another guy, maybe one who deserved her.

"Hello…anyone there? Muffet," the man called, "I think there's something wrong with your phone."

Muffet? Joe's knees buckled and he leaned against the wall. No, the guy had to be talking to someone else. Please God.

"I wish you'd stop calling me that!" Affection pervaded Marion's complaint. The man laughed.

Joe dropped the receiver, ran to the bathroom and threw up. Then he cleaned up and headed to the nearest bar.

"THERE'S NO ONE THERE." Marion said it lightly but Christian heard an undercurrent of distress as she hung up.

"You've been having crank calls?"

"Maybe. Actually, I thought…hoped…" She shrugged. "It doesn't matter."

The penny dropped. "You think it's your ex?"

She shrugged again. "Wishful thinking, probably."

"Wishful? You *want* it to be your ex?"

Marion avoided his eyes. "He's not my ex, he's my husband."

The hairs rose on the back of his neck. "Marion, you can't take him back. He's a drunk and a wife-beater."

"Once, Christian. He hit me once. And it was more of a hitting out than a hitting at."

He couldn't believe he was hearing this. "Next you'll be telling me he's a good provider who loves his family."

"He was," she said sadly. "I know this sounds crazy but taking our savings, abandoning us, is totally out of character."

"He took your savings?" Christian thought of John Jason, and a fierce protectiveness swept over him. He pulled out a chair and sat Marion down. Straddled another opposite it. "Look at me."

She raised her eyes reluctantly to his. Good God,

she still loved that asshole. "Don't do this. Don't cling to the happier memories, hoping he'll change and become the person you once knew. Don't buy into the excuses he'll make." Christian gripped the chair back.

"Guys like him look for someone to blame. In the end he'll even make you believe it's your fault—that he gets violent because you provoked him. It's bullshit."

"For the last time, he hit me *once*. Would a battered woman kick him out and tell him never to come back?"

"You did that?" His anxiety eased. "Good. Well if he rings you, call me and I'll make sure to reinforce the message."

She didn't answer, busied herself with standing and pushing the chair back under the table.

Christian stopped her with a hand on her arm. "It's none of my business, but I know what I'm talking about. Don't let that bastard screw up John Jason's life."

Her eyes widened. "Joe would never hurt our son."

He had to make her understand how important this was. "I bet you used to believe he'd never raise a hand to you, didn't you?" His voice was deadly serious.

"Your father beat you, didn't he?" she said suddenly. "You weren't just neglected."

Christian got to his feet. "If he shows up here, call me." He left before she could read the answer on his face.

JOE WATCHED AS THE BARMAN polished a shot glass then held it up to the whiskey bottle that hung in the middle of a gleaming row of spirits. Vodka, gin, rum. Faith, hope and charity. He saw the burp of an air bubble and heard the thirsty glug-glug as the bottle released its measure.

The barman put the drink in front of him. Without needing to ask, Joe handed him the exact money. Like a lover remembering his beloved's curves, his hand closed possessively around the glass. He breathed deep, inhaled the smokiness of peat.

"Good health," said the barman.

Joe nodded and stared into the tawny liquid, swirling it around to catch the light. And stared.

"Hey, mate," joked the barman, fifteen minutes later, pausing between customers, "if you find the meaning of life in there, let me know."

*Without my family there is no meaning in life.* Still the glass stayed on the counter, its contents warming in his grasp, releasing a pungent promise. *Let me ease your pain.*

Joe knew the promise was double-edged. His second chance would disappear with the first sip, replaced by a more pressing need to take the next sip, and the next. *If you've lost your family, what the hell's the point in staying sober?* The breath of defeat sent a shiver down his neck. Familiar, comforting. *Not your fault.*

With an exclamation of disgust he pushed back from the untouched drink and walked out, surprising both the bartender and himself. The sun was a brassy orange, low in the western sky and, after the dim confines of the bar, made him blink.

He might have lost Marion, but he still had a son who needed him. Joe climbed into his Holden and headed south.

# *CHAPTER TEN*

CLOSED UNTIL FURTHER NOTICE. White moths
danced in the streetlight that illuminated the sign. Joe
sat in his truck staring at the door of the Waterview
Hotel as he tried to formulate a Plan B, crushed by
disappointment.

Marion worked Friday nights. He'd planned to
wait for her after work and to find out whether he had
a chance in hell of staying in his son's life beyond
resuming financial support. His throat tightened on
the need for a drink. He couldn't lose his son, too.

His gaze fixed on the lone light in an upstairs
bedroom. Kezia would have looked after his family.
Joe had relied on that, though his conscience had
pricked him when he'd seen Muriel's death notice.
And Kezia had always been fair. If he could make
her believe he'd changed, she would tell him where
his family lived.

Joe got out of the car and walked toward the hotel.
A shape moved on the porch, there was the chink of
ice in a crystal glass and he realized someone had
been watching him all this time. A match flared, was
lifted to a cigar. For a moment he saw a pair of eyes,

hard as diamonds in a too handsome face. "I thought you'd show up tonight," said a voice he recognized.

"I don't know you," said Joe. But he did. His wife's lover. Jealousy and respect stabbed at him— at least the guy was looking out for her, which was more than he'd done lately. He stepped up onto the porch, out of the circle of light and waited for his eyes to grow accustomed to the darkness. The man sat holding a shot glass, with a bottle on the table in front of him. Joe recognized the shape. God, no, Marion, he prayed, not another drinker.

"She doesn't want to see you," said the man. His shape matched his voice, strong and hard.

"Is that your view or hers?"

"Hers." But the slight hesitation gave him away.

Joe stepped closer. The moths beat against the streetlight. "However Marion wants to play it, we'll play it. But she sets the rules, not you. I need to see her."

"So you can manipulate her into taking you back?" The ice chinked as he set the glass down on the table.

"How much do you drink?" said Joe abruptly.

The other man laughed, low and humorless. "You are some package. A drunk who hits his wife, cleans out the joint bank account, disappears for three months and still has the balls to challenge her friend about his drinking habits."

Joe's attention caught on the word friend. Could he have misread things? "At most you've been friends with my wife for a couple of months." He kept the word neutral. If this man suspected Joe's real fear, he might lie to get rid of him. "That doesn't give you the right to play God in our lives."

"Marion and I have been friends all our lives. My name's Christian Kelly."

Not Marion's lover but Kezia's. Relief made him laugh, before all the memories fell into place. "I've heard about you." He eyed Christian with amused contempt. "So the guy who deserted Kezia sees fit to pass judgment on me?"

"You're misinformed."

"So are you."

"Am I? I beg your pardon. Sit down, Joe, have a drink on me." The insult hung in the air.

"I don't do that anymore." Joe braced himself, for the first time admitting it to a stranger. "I'm an alcoholic. I've been in rehab these past three months."

"Uh-huh." Christian folded his arms. "Let me guess, and now you think you're saved?"

Joe ignored the skepticism. "I'll always be a recovering alcoholic, committing to sobriety a day at a time."

"Wow, you've got all the jargon, haven't you?"

Screw you, thought Joe. "No doubt you've heard it all before," he drawled. "Marion told me your dad was a drunk."

He saw the man stiffen, but Christian answered casually. "Yeah, the two of you would have had a lot in common."

"The big difference being that I've stopped drinking."

"The big difference being," said Christian in a

hard voice, "that I didn't have anyone to protect me from false promises. Marion and John Jason do."

Joe clenched his fists. "Leave my son out of this."

"Or?" The word was full of menace and Joe itched to break the guy's straight nose. But that would just play into the bastard's hands. "You'd like to provoke me into a fight," he guessed, "to convince Marion I'm still a loser. Does she know you've taken on the role of vigilante?"

"Crawl back into the gutter where you came from, asshole. You won't be dragging your family with you."

Disgusted, Joe turned toward the hotel door. "Let me talk to someone who doesn't have their own shit to deal with."

He lifted his hand to knock and found himself flying through the air, landing with a painful thud on his knees in the street.

Joe picked himself up. Slowly, deliberately, he brushed himself down with shaking hands. He faced Christian, who stood, fists raised, on the porch steps.

Squaring his shoulders, Joe took a deep, deep breath. "You just don't get it, do you?" he said. "I don't fight anymore. Like I don't drink anymore. Like I don't run away from my responsibilities *any-more*." Though he spoke quietly, his voice was steel. "I'll be back. Because there's nothing you can do to me that will stop me trying to make amends to my wife, and nothing short of killing me that will keep me away from my son."

He limped to his car and opened the door, glancing over his shoulder. "You know, we're not so different you and I. My father was a drunk, too." He gestured at Christian's glass. "I'd watch that if I were you."

Christian waited until the Holden's taillights swung left at the T-junction before he relaxed his fighter's stance. He sank into his chair, picked up the cigar. The aftermath of the encounter kicked in, fine tremors in his hands. He stubbed out the cigar, reached for his drink, then paused. *I'd watch that if I were you.*

Oh, yeah, Joe Bryant was good at deflecting attention away from his own behavior. Christian downed the shot in one swallow and refilled his glass. To hell with him. Even if he was sincere, in Christian's experience those with good intentions ended up doing the most damage. When they failed, the disappointment was worse than if the promise had never been made.

Like his mother telling him she'd beat cancer. Like his father, when sober, saying he'd forgiven Christian for her death. Like Kezia at eighteen promising that nothing would ever keep them apart. And every one of them had meant it at the time. Yes, indeed, he thought bitterly, savoring the whiskey, the world was full of people with good intentions.

Except this afternoon he'd learned that Kezia *had* changed her mind about going with him all those years ago. So why had she lied about it on Wednesday? He'd left Marion's house fully intending to confront her, but as the last couple of kilometers ate up his anger, Christian asked himself some difficult questions.

What difference could it make now to rake over old ashes? It was a bitter pill to swallow that he'd lost Kez through a twist of fate and his own impetuous nature but it didn't change anything. They were two very different people.

She was country, he was rock n' roll. And if the fight with his father hadn't erupted, if Kezia had left with him, what then? Would two eighteen-year-olds playing grown-ups still be together? He doubted it. But, oh, God, he had loved her.

He pushed himself up wearily and took his glass and the empty whiskey bottle into the kitchen. He dumped the bottle in the trash and his glass in the sink. She'd probably lied to him to save her pride. The very least he could do was respect that.

He wouldn't tell Marion of Joe's visit, it would only upset her. Come to think of it, better to keep it secret from Kezia, too. Feeling disturbingly virtuous, Christian went to bed, confident that despite Joe's defiance he'd scared the drunk away for good.

LONG DARK HAIR PILED LOOSELY on her head, wearing a strapless red dress, gold-tipped Manolos and an air of phony bravado, Kezia hesitated at the top of the stairs. She felt as though she was about to jump onto a funeral pyre. Hers.

She had intended to cry off the wedding until Christian had mused whether Suzie would interpret Kezia's absence as sour grapes.

Too bad, she'd retorted. Christian suggested he could probably mollify the bride by telling her about

Kezia's latest sexploitation of him. At which point she had asked, through gritted teeth, how much she owed him for her share of the salad servers. He had let her see but not touch them; perhaps her murderous intentions had been too clear.

Whatever lingering hope she'd held that Christian was bluffing had been shattered over the past twenty-four hours. He'd come back from his run in a distracted mood, remained distracted ever since. Twice she'd reminded him the banister needed fixing. Twice he'd reminded her there was no point in repairing a condemned building—unless Kezia had something to tell him?

His attitude had hardened her resolve to make him suffer as long as possible before conceding defeat. Now her time had run out.

"You look beautiful."

She hadn't realized Christian stood in the hall below, watching. Her heart began to race. That was why she was dressed to kill, to pretend her heart and pride weren't withering away. With controlled steps she started down the stairs, wishing the corset bodice of her dress allowed for deep calming breaths.

Christian's gaze met hers and Kezia's breath came faster. He looked gorgeous—dangerous and urbane in an expensive linen suit worn with the carelessness of a wealthy man and the confidence of a handsome one. And she'd hoped to score points wearing her Sunday best and a pair of borrowed heels. "I have something to tell you." Kezia reached for the banister.

"Don't lean on that, it's dangerous." Christian

was at her side in seconds, holding out his arm. "Lean on me."

Oh, God, she thought dizzily, I have no stomach for these games anymore. His forearm was strong and vital under her cold hand.

Even through the cloth, Christian felt her chill and unconsciously put his other hand over hers to warm it.

"You win." Kezia's voice was so colorless, so toneless that it took him a moment to understand. Then jubilation and relief flooded through him.

"You'll accept the hotel?"

"I'll accept the hotel."

"Thank you, it means a lot to me to be able do this for Muriel." He hesitated. Something didn't feel right. "And you, Kez. I've seen how much you've suffered through this."

"Really." She freed her hand and continued down the stairs, leaving him frowning after her. She moved like an automaton, without her usual flowing grace.

"Wait."

Kezia turned back, her face pale, her expression polite, and Christian's disquiet grew. "This was never about having the last word or revenge. It was about…" He stopped, unsure what his true intentions were. Yes, he wanted to free himself from this town, his past, from the power of this woman once and for all, but it was also about honor, a tenderness he couldn't articulate and didn't want to explore. As he searched for the right words he sensed her withdrawing further. It was almost a physical thing and it left him cold.

"It doesn't matter." She turned to the door. "You got what you wanted."

That being the case, why did he feel so terrible? In the car he glanced at her profile, remote and sad in the early afternoon sun—and got mad. Regrets were for losers. He jerked the car into gear and accelerated with a squeal of tires. She didn't reprimand him and Christian's anger grew. "Damn it, I want you to be happy about this!"

"My mood is the only thing left under my control," she answered coolly. "And now you want to own that, too?"

He pulled to the side of the road and slammed on the brakes. "Look, I know, all right? I know you came looking for me, so that blows your revenge theory out of the water because what have I got to punish you for? If anything, it's you who got the last word. And you know what's really funny? Since Marion let it slip, I've been driving myself crazy with what-ifs. Me, the hardened cynic. Does that make accepting the hotel more palatable to you?"

Kezia stared at him and for a moment she thought she would pass out. "What did she tell you?"

"Nothing. I guessed." He frowned, his impatience obvious, and she realized he didn't know everything. "My point is, you can rest easy about taking the hotel. Probably for the first time in my life, my motives are pure." His gaze flickered to her mouth. "Well," he conceded, "maybe not entirely pure."

He leaned toward her and Kezia panicked, pushing against his broad chest to hold him at bay.

But he was still close, too close. His eyes seeking answers she wasn't willing to give. He asked, "Why didn't you try to track me down?"

"I realized I'd made a mistake. Up and leaving someone doesn't give them a lot of faith in your ability to make a commitment." Kezia was amazed at how calm her voice sounded. "And if you recall, you didn't leave a forwarding address."

"No," he agreed with a bitter laugh. "At the time I was intent on hurting you."

She said nothing, staring blindly at his pale green silk tie. The hurt was less knowing he regretted it, but it didn't change the fact that in a fit of pique he'd abandoned her when she'd needed him most.

"I'm not trying to hurt you now." The sincerity in his voice weakened her. She had to be strong.

"Wait a minute, does this mean you were bluffing?"

He groaned. "If I say yes, will you still take the hotel?"

"Only if you agree to accept some sort of reparation when it starts making a profit." Christian shook his head and Kezia set her jaw. "I'll never be able to pay you back so at least let me pay a small percentage of what I owe you."

"You owe me nothing, but if you must give me something, give me this." He pulled her closer.

"You know what I really want?" With one hand he cupped the back of her neck, with the other he lifted her chin until she was forced to look into his eyes, intent and passionate. "One wild night with you." His voice, low and husky with longing, sent an involuntary response shivering down her spine. "I know we can't change the past but let's burn out every misunderstanding with a new memory."

He was already burning her, his body heat incinerated common sense, and Kezia ached to bring him closer, but she wasn't going to kid herself that she could handle another desertion. Not by the man she still loved.

She pushed him away gently. "And then you'll leave again."

"And you'll stay again." His gaze captured hers. "But this time we'll both know where we stand."

Kezia had never seen it from Christian's point of view, that he had suffered her loss yet was willing to take the risk again. But for her, suffering wasn't a risk—it was a certainty.

As she hesitated, he lifted one of her hands to his lips. "I never let myself have regrets, never acknowledged how much you meant to me, but when I learned you'd changed your mind..." He turned her hand over and kissed the pulse point on her wrist.

"Christian, I didn't." The words came from someone else's lips surely, for her own had barely moved, so devastating was the realization that his offer was based on a misconception.

"I don't follow." His gaze searched hers, cautious now, and she steeled herself.

"I wasn't looking for you to say I'd come with you." With exaggerated care Christian replaced her hand in her lap, and Kezia's heart sank. "It was to tell you why I wouldn't."

He restarted the engine, his profile carved out of granite. "You mean, there was an excuse I hadn't heard yet?"

Kezia gave him the choice. "Shall I tell you now?"

After a quick glance in his side mirror, Christian swung the sports car back onto the road. "Frankly, my dear, I don't give a damn."

THE WEDDING WAS HELD AT Everton's finest multipurpose function center. In the garden, under a bower of white roses. The ground, kept moist and green by sprinklers, sucked like quicksand and the ladies kept stepping out of their heels as they walked.

While the bride kept a nervous watch for bees—she was allergic—the groom sweated in his gray coat and tails in the eighty-degree temperature. And the flower girl ripped her chiffon dress jumping over the lily pond. Anticipating repercussions, she howled during the exchanging of the vows until she was placated with a soda.

Christian saw none of it, seething through the service and stalking to the bar the minute it was over. There he downed a neat Scotch. He put down his empty glass. "Another."

"Make that two." The stout woman who'd joined him was dressed in a daffodil-yellow silk suit with the sort of hat—all flowers and straw—a goat would love. "You look like I feel," she said. "I lost my son today."

"I'm so sorry." He was shocked out of his dark reverie. "And you still came to the wedding?"

"He's the one I lost." She grimaced at the first

taste of whiskey. "I should have stuck with champagne." There was the faintest slur in her words.

The penny dropped. "You're William J.'s mother."

"And you're Kezia Rose's latest conquest."

Christian scowled. "We're not together."

She took another sip from her glass. "Watch yourself. She comes across nice as pie but that one's a heartbreaker." The third sip went down without a face. "Though I hear you have a reputation in that area yourself. Lots of *Penthouse* playmates, Billy said."

"Did he?" Fighting irritation, Christian accepted the glass the bartender placed in front of him with a nod of thanks. "That just confirms that Kez is not my type."

"Good for you." William J. Rankin the Third's mother clunked her glass against his. "Everyone thinks she's kind and sweet but if I wasn't a lady I'd call her a ball-breaker."

Christian had been thinking the same thing, but hearing it voiced by someone else showed him it was patently ridiculous. Kezia was too honest to deliberately mislead anybody. "Maybe the fact that she ended the engagement is skewing your judgment."

"Maybe. And maybe you're already under her spell. Lordy, I think I'm tipsy." Mrs. Rankin sought the support of a bar stool and climbed on it with Christian's assistance even though he was more tempted to push her off it.

"One thing I will say for Suzie..." Mrs. Rankin wriggled around on the stool until her wide girth

## An Important Message
### from the Editors

Dear Reader,

If you'd enjoy reading romance novels with larger print that's easier on your eyes, let us send you TWO FREE HARLEQUIN SUPERROMANCE® NOVELS in our NEW LARGER PRINT EDITION. These books are complete and unabridged, but the type is set about 20% bigger to make it easier to read. Look inside for an actual-size sample.

By the way, you'll also get a surprise gift with your two free books!

*Pam Powers*

off Seal and

*Place Inside...*

LARGER PRINT
FREE BOOKS
EDITION

84

## THE RIGHT WOMAN

she'd thought she was fine. It took Daniel's words and Brooke's question to make her realize she was far from a full recovery.

She'd made a start with her sister's help and she intended to go forward now. Sarah felt as if she'd been living in a darkened room and someone had suddenly opened a door, letting in the fresh air and sunshine. She could feel its warmth slowly seeping into the coldest part of her. The feeling was liberating. She realized it was only a small step and she had a long way to go, but she was ready to face life again with Serena and her family behind her.

All too soon, they were saying goodbye and Sarah experienced a moment of sadness for all the years she and Serena had missed. But they had each other now, and that's what

She held

Printed in the U.S.A.
Publisher acknowledges the copyright holder of the excerpt from this individual work as follows:
THE RIGHT WOMAN Copyright © 2004 by Linda Warren. All rights reserved.
® and ™ are trademarks owned and used by the trademark owner and/or its licensee.

## YOURS FREE!
You'll get a great mystery gift with
your two free larger print books!

# The Harlequin Reader Service™ — Here's How It Works:

Accepting your 2 free Harlequin Superromance® books and gift places you under no obligation to buy anything. You may keep the books and gift and return the shipping statement marked "cancel." If you do not cancel, about a month later we'll send you 6 additional Harlequin Superromance larger print books and bill you just $4.94 each in the U.S., or $5.49 each in Canada, plus 25¢ shipping & handling per book and applicable taxes if any.* That's the complete price and — compared to cover prices of $5.75 each in the U.S. and $6.75 each in Canada — it's quite a bargain! You may cancel at any time, but if you choose to continue, every month we'll send you 6 more books, which you may either purchase at the discount price or return to us and cancel your subscription.

*Terms and prices subject to change without notice. Sales tax applicable in N.Y. Canadian residents will be charged applicable provincial taxes and GST.

was equally distributed. "She appreciates her good fortune. And she wants babies right away."

"There you go," said Christian dryly. "You can start thinking about a plaque for the nursery door."

"That's right." Her face brightened. "William J. Rankin the Fourth." She toasted him and threw back her head to empty the glass. When she straightened up her hat was askew. "I don't care what Billy says—" leaning over, she patted Christian's knee "—I think you're charming. Even if you do date centerfolds."

"There was only one, Mrs. Rankin." Despite his mood, he was amused. "I have also dated computer analysts, teachers, accountants...how come no one remembers the other professions?" Through the open French doors, he watched Kezia's cherry-red dress float against her slender calves as she approached the bride and groom with a congratulatory smile. He should be glad she hadn't changed her mind all those years ago. He could shake off the regret that had been plaguing him these past two days.

"So is it true implants make their breasts feel cold?"

With a sigh, Christian took Mrs. Rankin's glass away. "Bartender, how about a nice cup of coffee for the lady?"

Over the woman's hat he saw William J. sweep Kezia up in a hearty embrace and plant a big sloppy kiss on her surprised face. Suzie stiffened until there was as much starch in her posture as her bridal gown. "By any chance," Christian asked Mrs. Rankin, "did you and William J. share that champagne?"

"We had to open a second bottle," she confided. "To calm our nerves."

"Uh-huh," said Christian. A beaming William J. wrapped one arm around Kezia, the other around his bride. He looked to be sharing reminiscences in an overflow of tipsy affection. Suzie's expression grew pinched and though Kezia maintained her composure, there was quiet desperation in the way she scanned the crowd for an escape route. Her eyes met his and shied away.

The last of Christian's resentment evaporated as his conscience kicked in. "Mrs. Rankin, will you excuse me, please?"

Summoning his most charming smile, he slid off the bar stool and sauntered outside. He came within earshot in time to hear Suzie's pained, "You can't have two loves of your life, Bill." She turned on Kezia. "Speaking of which, where's yours?"

"Right here." Christian yanked Kezia out of William J.'s arm and into his, to kiss her thoroughly enough to lay the bride's doubts to rest and to punish Kezia for tormenting him at the same time. He forgot both intentions the moment their lips touched.

She made a protesting sound against his mouth and Christian lifted a hand to the nape of her neck and held her while he deepened the kiss, hungry for more, demanding an acknowledgment that she felt the same desire.

And for an instant he got it. Her surrender was sweet, a torture. With a moan, she broke the kiss and leaned her forehead against his pounding heart, trying to shield her expression. Dazed, Christian lifted a protective hand to her hair.

William J. was staring at him openmouthed. Christian thrust out a hand. "Congratulations."

William J. closed his mouth and took it. "Thanks." He had the grace to look shamefaced. "It's good to see you're taking the relationship seriously."

"We're deadly serious, aren't we, honey?" Christian felt Kezia take a deep, shaky breath, then slip out of his grasp and turn with an enigmatic smile that would make the Mona Lisa's transparent.

"Deadly," she agreed. Christian had never appreciated how well she could cloak her real feelings, and was intrigued.

"Wow." Suzie looked light-headed with relief. "How about a kiss like that for the bride?"

He obliged, lingering long enough to teach her new husband a lesson about territorial incursions. The bride thanked him with a squeeze of his forearm. The bridegroom pressed his new wife against his side so tightly she squawked and then he said gruffly, "I hear you're gifting Kezia the hotel."

"We're still in discussions," she answered before Christian could speak.

Astonished, he said, "Don't tell me you're backing out?"

Uncertainty quickened her reply. "No, but I thought you might have reconsidered, given our earlier—" she glanced at the bridal couple "—conversation in the car."

"I never renege on an offer. I might be disillusioned but I'm not petty." It occurred to him that Kezia could have said nothing when he was accepting the blame for ending their relationship. Instead she'd told the truth even when she believed it might jeopardize the deal.

Christian suddenly felt nothing but petty. So she hadn't loved him enough—at least she'd never pretended otherwise. It was time he grew up and got over it.

More relations converged on the happy couple, separating him from Kezia. Christian found himself hemmed in by well-wishers lining up to pepper Suzie's cheeks with different shades of lipstick and started backing himself the hell out of there.

Over a sea of shoulders, Suzie waved goodbye. "I think giving Kezia the hotel is so romantic," she said. "You must really love her."

Christian came to an abrupt halt in the middle of the lawn and the crowd swirled Suzie on, a meringue confection in the midst of color and laughter. God, no! He wasn't that much of a fool. It was Kezia's hot little body he craved. He caught sight of her standing under a magnolia tree, chatting with a couple of teenagers.

The sun gilded her bare arms and the dark strands escaping her French twist. When she smiled, tiny creases fanned out from the corners of her eyes. He could see where the wrinkles would eventually form—around her smile.

He could also see by the shadows in her eyes that she'd weathered loss and disappointment, and by the tilt of her chin that she hadn't been defeated by it.

For someone who considered his interest strictly physical he was finding it impossible to look past her face. Telling himself that Suzie knew squat—she'd married William J. Rankin the Third for God's sake—Christian stalked back to the bar.

## CHAPTER ELEVEN

KEZIA WATCHED HIM go, a scowl on his face. *And they call women moody and unpredictable.* She knew her confession had made Christian loathe her all over again—the punishing kiss had proved that—yet he still seemed prepared to give her the hotel. And she no longer believed it was some sort of revenge.

That was his real gift to her. Her dignity.

He hadn't chosen to know why she'd stayed and she was very glad of that because it meant she could return a gift of equal value. Blissful ignorance.

"Get over here!" Marion called across the garden, and thrust a glass of champagne at Kezia when she joined her. "I hear you've accepted the hotel, that's fantastic."

So Christian wasn't wasting any time making it impossible for her to change her mind. Well, two could play at that game. "Yes." She chinked glasses. "And he's agreed to accept repayments. They'll be modest, but it's something."

"I know," said Marion. "He told me."

Kezia stared. "He did?"

"He said he doesn't need the money so he wants it put into a community fund with me as treasurer."

"He did?" Kezia knew she looked as stupid as she sounded, but Marion didn't notice.

"Apparently all recipients are to be decided by—" her fingers drew speech marks in the air "—Kezia's bleeding heart." She turned and beamed toward the bar, gesturing for Christian to join them, and Kezia realized he'd been watching her reaction from the shadowy interior.

Dumbstruck would about cover it, quickly followed by a rush of love she was afraid she couldn't hide. She fumbled for her sunglasses and jammed them on. Christian stepped reluctantly into the sunlight, pausing to put on his own.

"Why, Christian Kelly—" Kezia kept her tone light "—are you warming to your old hometown?"

"No," he said bluntly, "I'm trying to stop it from falling down around my investment. But I'd appreciate it if you made the first project a tree house for John Jason."

Marion hooted and spilled champagne on Christian's jacket as she threw her arms around him. Christian said in a bored voice, "Let's not make a big deal about this, shall we?"

"I propose a toast." Kezia's voice was husky as she raised her glass. "To Waterview's reluctant philanthropist."

"Don't malign me." She could see nothing behind the sunglasses. "You're the only bleeding heart in this town."

"Then let's drink to that," suggested Marion.

Kezia raised her glass. "To my bleeding heart."

IT WAS JOHN JASON WHO STOPPED Christian drinking a fourth Scotch, tugging on Christian's jacket and asking politely if Christian wouldn't mind ordering him and his two friends some Cokes, seeing how it was a special occasion and seeing how he couldn't see over the top of the bar to ask.

"Can't you climb on the stool?" inquired Christian. He wasn't in the mood for cute.

John Jason informed him that he was too shy. "I don't get out much," he confided in a tone exactly like his mother's, and Christian weakened.

"Three Cokes, please, bartender." While they waited, he held his glass on his lap, strangely reluctant to take a sip in front of a child, and eyed the satin vest and bow tie. "So where's the Batman outfit tonight?"

John Jason scowled. "Mummy wouldn't let me wear it." He lifted his nose in the air and sniffed. "That stuff smells like what my daddy used to drink."

Christian sat transfixed. *I'd watch that if I was you.* "Mine, too." Slowly he put the full glass back on the bar.

People were being ushered to tables, and Kezia approached, looking as wary as he felt.

Glancing at John Jason noisily sucking Coke through a straw, he couldn't regret the impulse to start a community fund. Waterview needed the money; he didn't. Sentimentality had nothing to do with it. Very clearly he remembered Joe Bryant's face, raw with emotion, and was inexplicably angry. Neither, damn it, did guilt.

"Hi, John Jason, you look smart." Kezia playfully tweaked the child's bow tie. "Your mom wants you back at the table for dinner, honey. I'll help you carry those glasses." She glanced at Christian with the bright impersonal smile he hated. "We're at table ten. I'll meet you there."

"Humor the beast, it will be gone tomorrow," he said, and watched her blush. Annoyed at himself, he headed for their table.

Their deal had freed him to leave, but the realization that he still had unresolved feelings for Kezia—not love—was no freedom at all. It was fitting, he supposed, nodding to his table companions as he pulled out his chair, that a player like himself had been brought down by a woman whose attraction to him had only ever been physical. *And she can resist even that.*

"Old fogies and old lovers are at the back where we can't do any harm," Bernice May told him as he sat, and he had to smile. She patted his hand and did the introductions—an old boyfriend of Suzie's and his very pregnant wife, an elderly, deaf relative of William J.'s and Don, dapper as always.

"Leaving tomorrow I hear?" Christian detected disappointment in Don's voice that was difficult to interpret.

"There's nothing to keep me here."

"I'll bet you can't wait to get back to civilization," Kezia said behind him.

"It does have its attractions." He stood to pull out her chair, feeling anything but civilized where she was concerned. "A decent shower, a decent bed—"

"—and an indecent woman," she finished sharply. For a moment there was stunned silence. "I—I'm so sorry," she stammered, "that was an awful thing to say."

"But funny," approved Bernice May, and everyone laughed.

Not to mention enlightening, thought Christian. "Jealous?" he murmured, pushing in her chair. A stiff back was his only answer as Kezia turned to engage Don in conversation.

The MC called for silence and William J. stood, clutching a sheaf of pages that made the Gettysburg Address look like a Post-it note. A groan rippled around the room that was just short of audible.

The groom cleared his throat, took a sip of water and fixed his eyes on the audience over the top of his reading glasses. "Matrimony," said William J. Rankin the Third, "is not an institution to be entered into lightly…."

"Oh, my sweet potatoes," said Bernice May. "Pass the wine."

Christian thought, *This would be the day I give up serious drinking.*

By page three the guests' eyes were as glazed as the ham and even the bride looked bored. On page four, William J.'s mother got the hiccups and everyone else the giggles. The groom galloped through page five and finally conceded defeat on page six when John Jason's loud suggestion that Mrs. Rankin senior stand on her head and drink a glass of water sent the room into gales of laughter.

Yet he toasted his new wife with touching humility. "Thank you for making me the happiest man in the world. I'll do my best to deserve you. To my bride."

"To the bride!" chorused the guests with relief.

"You may escort me to the buffet before the rabble get there," Bernice May told Christian. "I want the pork crackling."

Kezia declined to join them. Unconsciously her gaze followed him as he led the old lady to the carvery. Bernice May was half Christian's height and he measured his steps to match hers.

"Muriel would have been very disappointed it didn't work out," Don said beside her, and Kezia explained the deal she and Christian had settled on. He gave her an enigmatic look and said he was going outside for a cigar before dinner.

"I'll keep you company, there's something I've been meaning to ask you privately."

They made their way down the wide brick steps into the garden, where they perched on a half wall that edged a flower bed of creamy azaleas. Don patted his breast pocket, found a cigar and lit it with the silver monogrammed lighter Muriel had given him last birthday. He saw Kezia looking at it. "We miss her."

"We do."

For a moment more they sat quietly, letting memories rise with the pungent smell of fine tobacco.

Kezia broke the silence. "Bernice May suggested Christian's father might have been violent."

Don looked at her, startled. "But you knew that."

Horrified by the implicit admission, Kezia immediately replied. "Why would I?"

He turned the cigar over in his fingers. "The night he left town, after the...episode."

"What episode?"

"He said he was going to see you and sort things out." Don frowned. "I always assumed...good God. What *did* he tell you?"

"That he'd had enough of the place. That he was too restless to hang around until his university scholarship kicked in. That he was leaving to find work in Auckland until it did. We'd already talked about me going with him but I thought I still had two months to decide. Instead he gave me an ultimatum—go with him then or forget it. I said no."

Kezia's breath caught in her throat. "In the morning when I went to the farm, his father yelled through the door that he'd gone for good." Her gaze pinned his. "What didn't Christian tell me, Don?"

The tip of old man's cigar glowed red as he dragged deeply on it, exhaling on a sigh. "The only reason I found out about the beatings—" Kezia gasped "—was because I nearly ran him over."

"It was a miserable night," he said, "raining hard, poor visibility. He was running down the middle of the road in a terrible state. Told me he'd killed his old man."

He paused to relight his cigar, took two quick

puffs. "We drove back to the farm together and on the way he blurted it all out. Said Paul had been beating him on and off for years, that he'd managed to minimize it by sleeping in the barn whenever he saw him hit the bottle."

Kezia stifled a moan. It was too horrible to believe. Her mind scrambled for a reason to make it untrue. "But I never saw any marks on him."

"The beatings stopped when Christian was seventeen, big enough to fight back. Paul Kelly was a hell of a big man, built like an ox. They'd had a standoff apparently, and the boy said he'd kill Paul if he ever touched him again. Things had been quiet for over a year but that night Paul pushed his luck and gave the boy a whack. Christian said it was like a volcano erupting inside him. The next thing he knew Paul was on the floor covered in blood and he was running for help."

He blew a ring of smoke and paused to watch it dissipate. "He'd hit him a good one all right," remarked Don with satisfaction. "When we got there, Paul was bleeding like a stuck pig but he'd recovered enough to shout that he was going to blow Christian's head off at the first opportunity. I was all for calling the police but Christian swore me to secrecy. He left to see you then, and was gone by morning."

Kezia couldn't hide her feelings, and the old man's eyes softened. "I can't believe the damn fool didn't tell you."

"Did Nana know?"

"Muriel thought she knew all his secrets but she didn't know that one, and I never told her. It would have broken her heart thinking she'd failed him. You see, she found out the rest of his home situation when he was fourteen, but the boy begged her not to tell Child Protection Services. He said he'd managed for two years, was nearly a man." Don snorted.

"Anyway, in return for keeping his secret he had to accept some practical support and let her keep an eye on him. She used to say to me, 'I've never met a kid so proud and so damn stubborn.'" Don's gaze fell on Kezia. "That was why he gave her the IOU, so one day he could repay her in kind."

Her anguish must have been obvious because he patted her hand. "Honey, I think Christian's independence was so ingrained he couldn't tell all his secrets even if he wanted to."

Kezia couldn't answer. *Never come to the farm, promise me.* Christian's bandaged hand, shrugged off as a farm accident. She recalled his uncompromising mood that night driven not by arrogance but by desperation. With sickening clarity she saw their past for what it was—a wasteland of missed opportunities.

Her pity died in the face of her anger. All those lost years they should have had together. If Christian had only trusted her. She stood. "We'll let him make his own excuses, shall we?"

Don jumped up and tossed his cigar into the flower bed. "Now, Kezia, remember we're at a wedding."

"I don't care," she said, and he appeared even more alarmed. Oh, yes, Kezia Rose always cared.

"Now you just stay here and calm down. I'll fetch him out."

While Kezia waited, she paced the garden, back and forth, back and forth, kicking off her heels when they caught in the damp earth, too agitated to stop. She balled her hands into fists.

But when a wary Christian finally arrived some ten minutes later, she was back sitting on the wall, legs crossed, sunglasses hiding her emotions. She didn't bother with preambles. "Don told me that the night you left Waterview your father attacked you."

His face became expressionless. "Don likes to exaggerate, you know that."

Kezia got up and took off her sunglasses. "You beat the crap out of your father for beating the crap out of you."

Christian winced. "We had an altercation. Yes."

She came closer until only inches separated them. "Tell me the truth about your childhood right now or I swear I'll make us this evening's entertainment."

He shrugged. "My father was a mean drunk and my mother's death made him meaner. The farm suffered; his health suffered, we had no money." Christian's tone was measured, almost indifferent, but Kezia watched his breathing change until it seemed he couldn't get enough air. "I started stealing what I needed because I knew if the state got involved I'd be taken into care."

"Oh, Christian." She watched the shields come up as he reacted to her pity.

"Actually, I kind of liked the reputation I got as a bad boy. It beat being sad and pathetic."

The same damned pride that stopped him from telling her. "I can't understand how you kept it secret so long."

"My father was careful where he hit me, so I could go to school and stay under the radar." A half smile touched his lips. "Until Muriel caught me stealing eggs from her henhouse."

"But she didn't know all the truth, did she?"

"About the violence? No. In hindsight, I know she wouldn't have turned me in. At the time, I didn't trust her."

Trust. "Why didn't you tell me that night?" she demanded. "You must have known it would have made a difference!"

"I wanted you to choose me for love, not pity." He made an impatient gesture when she tried to interrupt. "And don't tell me pity doesn't sway you. You spend your whole life following a kind heart."

If anything, the fact that he was so right and so very, very wrong heaped fuel on Kezia's anger. "How dare you assume that responsibility. I deserved to know the facts, all of them, so I could make a real choice."

"What the hell do you want from me? An apology after fourteen years? Okay, I apologize." His tone was bitterly sarcastic. "I'm sorry I wouldn't allow my sordid past to cloud your judgment when I asked you to leave with me. I'm sorry your decision wasn't in my favor but I learned to live with it, like I learned to live with my lousy childhood. Stop making such a big deal about a decision we both know you wouldn't change. You told me so not two hours ago."

"I told you I looked for you the next day because I figured you had a right to the truth—"

"Very noble," he interrupted, but she talked over him.

"Like I had a right to the truth, Christian, because of what we were to each other."

For the first time vulnerability flickered across his face and she realized she could destroy his peace of mind by telling him why she'd refused him. Like he'd just destroyed hers.

The words trembled on her tongue. Did she love Christian enough to leave the truth unsaid?

Yes. She did. Instead she said, "You know what hurts? That I never really knew you. You never trusted me enough to let me get that close."

He struck back with cool precision. "I always did have a good instinct for self-preservation."

Kezia buried her threatening tears under sarcasm. "Go back to the table and act like everything's just fine—you're good at that." She bent to pick up her shoes, but he didn't move. *"Go!"*

She pretended to inspect the damage to her shoes until he went inside, then shoved them on, snatched up her bag and ran. At the entrance, she asked the doorman to call her a cab.

"Where to, ma'am?"

"The Waterview Hotel." Only when the taxi was speeding away did she collapse against the seat, fragile and utterly exhausted. She would collect some clothes and drive back to Everton, hide out in a cheap motel until he left.

She never wanted to see Christian again.

CHRISTIAN SPEARED A PIECE of fresh asparagus, lifted it to his mouth and took a bite. It tasted like cardboard. Out of politeness he'd filled his plate when Bernice May had filled hers; now roast pork lay congealing in cold gravy while he toyed with the vegetables and made polite rejoinders to whoever spoke to him. Kezia still hadn't come back and frankly he didn't want her to. Enough already.

"Yes, delicious," he murmured to Bernice May who was cleansing her palate before dessert with a beer.

"Kezia will miss out on ham if she doesn't get a hurry on," she said. "Don, you find her while I go save her a slab."

Christian dropped his knife and fork and reached for his water, trying to swallow past the tightness constricting his throat and chest. He hated what had just happened. Hated it.

His father's threats hadn't driven him from Waterview that night—damn, he'd been living with those for years. It had been Don's discovery of his secret. Even one other person knowing made it unmanageable.

Seeing Kezia reel under the impact of the truth was worse than any physical blow of his father's. It made him acknowledge his childhood after his mother died for what it was. Sordid. Heartrending. Unbearable. And maybe a childhood he deserved.

The only honorable thing he'd ever done was keep the truth from Kezia that night. And he'd saved both of them a lot of grief. Clean, clear-cut choices. He'd lived by them; they'd saved his sanity.

Feeling a tentative hand on his back, he swung around to see Don's concerned face. More pity he couldn't bear. "Sorry, Don, I'm needed urgently in Auckland," he lied. "Will you tell Kezia goodbye when she shows?"

"She's already gone. Took a taxi fifteen minutes ago." Don hesitated. "Look, why don't you follow her and sort this out?"

So she had no desire to see him, either.

Inevitability washed over Christian. He and Kezia had come full circle. Ignoring Don's suggestion, he pulled out his checkbook and wrote out an amount that had enough zeros in it to ensure he never had to come back. "Give this to Kez. Tell her to use it to finish the renovations properly and to develop all the initiatives we discussed."

When Don hesitated to take the check, he forced it into the old man's hand. "Some things aren't meant to be," he said by way of apology. "This was one of them."

"I wish I hadn't kept your damn secret," grumbled Don, taking the check. "It only encouraged you to stay a loner."

Christian dropped a hand on his shoulder. "Give my farewells to the appropriate people, will you?" he asked, and left before Don could argue.

In contrast to the noisy celebration behind him, the reception hall was dim and quiet. Christian strode through it and into the golden freedom outside, wrenching off his tie. But he still felt suffocated.

To hell with it, once he was on the highway heading north he'd feel better. If he dropped by the hotel to collect his belongings he might run into Kezia and he couldn't handle another scene. She could forward them later.

Children were playing tag around the ornamental garden; one of them peeled off and raced toward him. John Jason. "Hey!"

"Hey, yourself." Christian kept walking and the little boy trotted alongside.

"Where are you going?"

"Back to the city." It occurred to Christian he wouldn't see John Jason again and a sharp pang of regret stopped him.

"Are you coming back?"

Christian kept his answer deliberately vague. "Maybe one day." *Sorry, kid, I'm just not made that way.*

"You have to kiss me goodbye." John Jason lifted his arms to be picked up. The boy smelled of talcum powder and strawberry shampoo but the cheek he presented was sticky with gravy. Christian kissed it anyway, then went to lower the child to the ground. Chubby arms wrapped around his neck. "Mummy said I mustn't tell secrets, but I didn't, did I?"

"No, you didn't," Christian assured him. "I guessed, and then Auntie Kez told me."

Satisfied, the child allowed himself to be put

down. "I 'spect she found it." Christian, digging in his jacket pocket for the car keys, gave a preoccupied shrug. "They cry a lot," John Jason insisted, "so it would be easy to find."

"What would?" The boy was obviously looking for some sort of reassurance so Christian tempered his impatience.

"The baby," said John Jason. "The baby Auntie Kezia lost."

# CHAPTER TWELVE

COUNTING TO SIXTY under her breath, Kezia swung the hose from the bean plants and watched the strawberry leaves bow under the arc of water. Shallow watering only encouraged roots to the surface. Damn Muriel's indoctrination! She couldn't leave without watering the dry garden.

Her throat tightened and she lifted the hose and gulped at the streaming water, sending it splashing down her beautiful red dress. No, she couldn't fall apart now. She turned the hose on the lettuces. Later.

Later, when the solid walls of an anonymous motel muffled the sound.

The lettuces grew waterlogged but Kezia didn't notice, lost in a bitter truth. She wasn't still single because she was discerning. It was because since Christian, she'd subconsciously dated men she didn't love. Because if she didn't love them, they couldn't rip her heart out.

She turned the hose on to the corn. How ironic that by dating playmates Christian had shown more self-awareness than she had. He knew he was damaged goods.

Would our baby have lived if we'd trusted each other more? She bent to turn off the tap with exaggerated care. No, that was madness. Her unhappiness after he'd left hadn't caused the miscarriage.

Even with Christian's revelation, three truths remained the same. They would have lost their baby. He hadn't loved her enough. She hadn't moved on with her life.

But she would now.

Turning, she walked smack into Christian's broad chest. Terrified, her knees buckled and his hands closed around her arms.

"You gave me such a fright," she said weakly, and waited for him to release her.

Instead his grip tightened. "The real reason you stayed. What was it?" Kezia went cold and still inside. He knew. And only one person could have told him.

"What did Marion say?"

"It was John Jason."

Kezia inhaled a sharp breath.

The grip on her arms became painful. "He said you'd lost a baby. Was it fourteen years ago, Kez?"

Very gently she shrugged out of his hold. "Yes."

Christian's eyes closed briefly, then he walked to the other end of the garden. Kezia sank onto an iron-framed bench and waited. The sky had faded through the colors of sunset into night before he returned to sit beside her. "Tell me."

"I miscarried three weeks after you left. It wasn't meant to be." Our refrain. "Nobody's fault," she added softly, and a little of the torment left his face.

"I hadn't told Muriel and the miscarriage meant I never had to." To Kezia's surprise her voice caught on the next words. "Hardly a pregnancy at all really."

She thought she'd made her peace with those awful days when terror at the prospect of being a single mother had given way to a profound sadness that she had nothing left of Christian.

"Why didn't you tell me that night?" The words sounded wrenched from his heart. This was what she wanted to spare him, the final price of his secret.

"You said you couldn't imagine anything worse than having kids."

"Oh, God, Kez." He still considered himself too scarred for fatherhood and the loss he felt for the baby frightened and confused him. "Even if it was true, you should have told me."

Her silence held some kind of accusation. "My secret has nothing to do with us. Damn it, I had a right to know, it would have changed everything." No, he was digging himself into a bigger hole, reinforcing the case she'd made earlier.

"I'd only just found out I was pregnant," she said, her voice devoid of emotion. "Marion and I had been on the bus to Everton in the morning to buy the test. We sat outside the shop for twenty minutes before Marion gave up on me and went in and bought it. You see, I knew it would be positive even though we'd only been careless once."

She didn't look at him, but he knew when she meant. "I was going to tell you that night but…" She shrugged. "Well, you know what happened next.

After you stormed off I knew I should have told you, so the following day I went to the farm. You'd already gone and..." Her voice trailed off.

"I'd already gone," Christian echoed.

HE SAT SILENT BESIDE HER, but Kezia sensed Christian's monumental struggle against vulnerability, which his childhood had convinced him was a terrible thing. She knew he needed to lose that fight.

She found herself praying as she waited, then icy cold reality doused her when he rose and walked away to the far end of the garden, back into the safety of his shadows.

That was when she knew she'd have to let him go.

Christian had lost her because he hadn't trusted her, but Kezia knew she'd been equally wary or she would have told him about the baby that night.

She'd grown up in an environment where she had to earn love through acts of service, and Christian had never been dependent enough for her. Probably, she would have turned him down anyway, regardless of the baby, because she had no more trusted him to keep loving her than he had her.

She still didn't.

Unable to bear the relentless waves of self-revelation any longer, she stood up. Christian looked back at her, his expression unreadable in the dusk. "Our child, what was it?"

"Too early to tell." Over time she thought she'd reached a stoic acceptance. But seeing the father of her child suffer the loss renewed her grief.

"God, Kez, I'm so sorry."

For years she'd waited to hear those words, thinking they would heal her, make things right. But what she'd wanted wasn't really an apology, what she'd wanted was happy-ever-after. She wrapped her arms around herself. "I'm sorry, too."

His next question startled her. "Where do we go from here?"

"This doesn't change anything." She couldn't bring herself to suggest friendship. Better a clean break, a chance to move forward unencumbered by the past.

"Doesn't it?" He moved nearer and Kezia stepped back, came up hard against the garden bench.

"No. It doesn't."

Christian put a hand around her waist and pulled her to him. Kezia planted her hands against his chest. "It's too late." Under the fine cotton of his shirt, pliant muscle scorched her palms.

"Then why do we still feel this?" Christian leaned into her restraining hands and brushed his lips along the curve of her clenched jaw. Warm lips on skin still cool from the hose water. Kezia dropped her hands and his mouth moved down to the pulse that leaped in her throat.

"No one hurt me like you did," he whispered. Words she thought she owned. "No one loved me like you did, either."

She swallowed. "But it still wasn't enough, was it, for you to trust me?"

"I trust you now," he said against her neck, and she knew he believed it.

It was futile; still she gave him the chance to prove her wrong. "In that case, tell me why you haven't visited your mother's grave."

Christian froze, then slowly straightened. "That's my business."

"Don't you see? You'll never let me get close."

"I don't go to dark places, Kez. Not even for you."

"Even if I could help you light them?" His expression remained closed and she struck out in bitter frustration. "Life might have branded you a loner, Christian, but it's your choice to stay that way."

His eyes narrowed. "Says someone who only feels safe when she's in credit on some emotional balance sheet. I've never been needy enough for you and I'm not going to start now."

Kezia's humorless laugh rang out across the garden. "See how easily we can still hurt each other? The prosecution rests her case."

For a moment there was silence, then Christian groaned. "Why the hell does everything have to be so complicated with you? Can't it be enough right now that we still feel something for each other?"

Miserably, Kezia shook her head and began to turn away. Christian caught her by the elbow. "You haven't heard the case for the defense yet," he said grimly, and loosened her hair from its chignon.

Then she was in his arms and his mouth was on hers. There was desperation in the way he held her, yearning in his kiss, and Kezia yielded, helpless, while his tongue stoked hers into a response and common sense scattered like fireworks somewhere among the stars overhead.

Recklessly she kissed him back, promising everything, withholding nothing, and he answered in kind. Her fingers flew to undo his shirt buttons and one soared loose as she tugged it open, craving the feel of his skin.

Christian pushed away long enough to peel down the bodice on her dress, then hauled her back against his bare torso. Their second kiss was wild, hungry with lust, and Kezia knew from the way her nipples swelled into the lacy fabric of her strapless bra, from the way he pressed his erection against her belly, that they teetered at the point of no return.

His hand slid under her skirt, and the night air was cool on her bare bottom as he pulled her panties down. They caught at her knees and she kicked out of them. Madness, this was madness.

Kezia wrenched her mouth away and cupped Christian's face in both hands, breathing hard, intensely aware of the fine scattering of hair on his chest tickling her sensitized skin. "If we do this," she said fiercely, "it's goodbye. Promise me."

Christian turned his head to kiss her palm and a sensual shiver worked its way up her arm and through her body. She dragged his head forward again. "Promise me!"

In the moonlight, his eyes were a shadowy, unreadable gray. "If you want it to be goodbye, it will be goodbye," he said finally.

She nodded, knowing this was insanity yet unable to send him away with anything less than passion.

But the mood had grown somber. In silence Christian caught her hand, led her through the garden and into the empty hotel, flicking on only enough switches to light their way and retrieve condoms. Upstairs, in her room, he released his hold and pulled back the drapes.

So much of the time he wore a mask of lazy affability, a wry grin that said he knew he was too handsome for his own—and any woman's—good. But the moonlight stripped all that away. She saw the strength of character evident in the set of his jaw, the shadows in those startling eyes. His victories had been hard won.

And, she thought, tomorrow I'll square off against reality. Tonight is a dream and who has power over their dreams?

Christian's face was grave as he came back to her, grave as he removed his remaining clothes, and Kezia swallowed her panic. No, don't take us seriously. Mustering her best Mae West voice, she drawled, "I guess we'll have our one wild night after all."

"One wild night it is, then." His voice gave no hint of disappointment as he drew her down to the bed, onto the expanse of white like a fall of virgin snow in the moonlight. He rolled onto his back with Kezia on top of him and unfastened her bra with one expert hand.

With the other he tangled his fingers in her long, silky hair, fitted his mouth to hers and let his tongue make deep, sultry promises of how he intended to love her.

She yielded with such sweet softness that he went

as hard as the teenager he'd once been with her. As close to exploding under the same rush of uncontrollable lust.

Her hand reached down to touch him and he caught it, breaking the kiss. "If you want this to last," he suggested in someone else's voice, "let me do the touching."

Holding her unfastened bra in place, Kezia sat up and Christian groaned as her lush firm bottom, bare under the red silk dress, pressed against his erection.

Equally distracting was the spill of ripe breasts above the white lace and the glimpse of taut nipple. Just when he thought nothing about this could get any harder, it did.

He watched her eyes widen as she felt his intense physical reaction, then darken with an elemental need that he leaped to assuage. Kezia glided against him and he suffered her slippery readiness.

With her lids heavy with passion, her skin lightly abraded from his stubble and her mouth swollen from his kisses, she was impossible to resist.

"No." He ground out the word. "Not yet."

Kezia leaned forward and her bra fell in a lacy heap. "We've wasted enough time," she said in a husky whisper. Her hair tickled as she brushed her lips across his. "I want you now."

For answer, Christian caught her other wrist and pulled her up and forward until her breasts hung above his face. Then he made love to them until her breath came so fast that each nipple rose and fell against his teasing tongue.

He freed her hands so that his could stroke and fondle. So that he could reach between her smooth legs astride him.

Kezia spread them wider and, unable to resist the invitation, he slid farther down the bed and under her dress. Ignoring her gasp of protest, he used his mouth and fingers to pleasure her.

She tensed, resisting the intimacy, but Christian persisted until she let him take her beyond all restraint. When at last she cried her release, he reveled in the rhythmic spasms against his finger inside her, in the wetness against his mouth.

He turned his head and kissed the softness of her inner thigh, glorying in the scent of her woman's heat mingled with the starched silk dress. He had always loved to corrupt Kezia, seduce her into abandoning herself to the passionate nature her conservative upbringing would have her reject.

This woman who was—in all the ways that mattered—incorruptible.

Gently, Christian rolled Kezia's languid form over to her back and began to kiss his way up her sweet curves on a voyage of rediscovery. Her hands tangled lazily in his hair, stopping him each time he reached an erogenous zone—her navel, the fourth rib, the underside of one creamy breast. He felt all the primal possessiveness of a man reclaiming his birthright.

Except she wasn't his to keep.

His tongue circled her nipples, peaked and moist from his earlier attention, but it was her mouth he lingered on, losing himself in her taste and texture.

In the aftermath of her orgasm, her response was indolent and inviting, and made Christian want her so badly he could only roll on a condom, nudge her legs apart and thrust into her swollen wetness.

He stilled, closing his eyes against a sensation almost intolerable in its intensity. As he struggled for self-control he felt the butterfly softness of a kiss on his closed eyelids. It had the reverence of love.

Intrigued, his lids flew open and Kezia hastily lowered hers. He moved inside her, slowly out, slowly in, stopping well short of full penetration, forcing Kezia to lift her gaze to his. Even in the moonlight her pupils flared with a hunger so raw it fanned his white-hot.

His jaw dropped on a groan and she took advantage, plundering his mouth as he'd so often plundered hers, until neither of them cared what happened tomorrow, only what was about to happen now. Right now.

With a sob, Kezia lifted her hips to his and Christian bore down like a man possessed. Up she lifted again, inviting even more of him, and he drove so deep inside her he knew he was lost forever with no hope of return.

He still loved her.

God help him, he loved this woman who wanted him to let her go. She lifted her hips again—provocative, demanding—and Christian gave her everything he was capable of, all of his body, most of his guarded heart, none of his soul.

Dimly he heard Kezia cry out and he exploded inside her, lost and found, emptied and renewed.

When he came to himself again he was lying with his full weight sprawled across her, their heartbeats slamming into each other.

Christian rolled to one side. "Did I hurt you?" She could only shake her head, but her eyes told a different story. "I did hurt you."

"I knew this would make it harder to let you go."

He tightened his arms around her. "You have as much of my heart as I can give anybody," he said fiercely. "Why can't that be enough?"

"I love you." Her whisper vibrated with intensity and he gathered her even closer, weak with relief. After a moment Kezia loosened his hold and slid up the bed until her face was level with his.

In the moonlight her eyes were luminous and wise but the sadness in them impaled him with dread. "I love you, but I'm thirty-two years old and I know myself better than I did fourteen years ago. I need this community and this community needs me."

"We'll split our time between here and Auckland." He was suddenly in the most important negotiation of his life.

She kissed him yearningly and he knew they could make it work. But she pulled back. Her gaze, unflinchingly honest, seemed to search his soul, and Christian fought the urge to break eye contact.

"I would compromise a lot to keep you in my life," she said quietly, "but I won't compromise this. I need a man who trusts me with his weaknesses as well as his strengths. No more half measures." Despite himself, Christian blinked first. "And I need a man who wants children as much as I do." Kezia paused, waiting, but he couldn't speak past the lump in his throat.

Her voice was strained as she continued. "I've wasted a lot of years sabotaging relationships because I so badly wanted to be with you. I still do."

Her fingers touched his face. "But if you can't be that man, then keep your promise and leave tomorrow because I've run out of strength to send you away." Her next words came as a whisper but they struck Christian like a powerful blow. "Love me that much, at least."

# *CHAPTER THIRTEEN*

IF ONLY SHE hadn't said that. *Love me that much, at least.* The risk-taker in Christian wanted to say, "Yes, I can be that man for you." But her honesty compelled his.

"I want to give you what you need," he said. "But I can't believe in a house full of children and happy-ever-afters." Not when his memories smelled of death and terror and dust-under-the-bed where a twelve-year-old still cowered on his belly and listened to his bereaved father scream that it was Christian's fault that his wife had died. "Kez, I just can't."

"It's okay," she said, though plainly it wasn't, and Christian forced himself to say nothing. He'd never love her more than he did at this moment of letting go.

"It's okay," Kezia repeated, and reached out a hand to smooth away the lines of strain on his face, to memorize its contours. He was a man who couldn't let himself be vulnerable. She'd forgiven him the past. Now, she forgave him the future. "I knew what your answer would be."

Denial flashed in Christian's eyes and was gone,

replaced by a steely resolve. His hands cupped her buttocks, brought her closer. He was hard again. "Tomorrow I'll leave as promised." Savagely he claimed her mouth. "But tonight, by God, you're mine."

Hunger, equally insatiable, rose in Kezia. He wanted to conquer her but he couldn't because she was reckless in her willingness to surrender everything she had. And by her passionate compliance, forced him to surrender to her.

With Christian she journeyed to places rich with erotic pleasures. He evoked needs she'd never acknowledged, needs no good girl should ever have, then absorbed them, transformed them and gifted them back to her shiny and new.

When there wasn't an inch of their bodies that hadn't been sated they lay facing each other on the white bed, physically and emotionally spent. Kezia had a sense of resting in the eye of a storm. She knew the worst was still to come but the disillusion that had kept them at war with themselves and each other was gone and a fatalistic acceptance filled the vacuum.

Her eyelids began to droop; she forced them open.

"You need sleep." His voice vibrated out of the dark.

"So do you."

In answer, Christian began to stroke her, starting at the nape of her neck. His palm, warm and sure, slid down her back to the slope of one buttock, before skimming lightly across and up the curve of hip, waist and shoulder back to her neck. And he did it again. And again.

He stroked her as though they'd spent every night of the intervening years together—with a tender familiarity. He stroked her as though they had years ahead of them instead of a precious few hours. Relax, his hands told her, let go. Rest in me.

And despite her resolve to make every last second count, Kezia felt her body soften and melt into his. Her eyes closed, she fantasized that all the obstacles keeping them apart no longer existed, imagined that his arms were home. His hand swept up and down her back with slow, rhythmic caresses. Deeper and deeper she sank into the oblivion of his chest, warm and dark and safe.

CHRISTIAN LEFT WATERVIEW BEFORE dawn, while Kezia slept. The main street looked like the movie set for a ghost town and the bleak isolation suited his mood. At the crossroads he waited while a stock freighter passed with a hiss of air brakes.

Still Christian sat there, letting the engine idle. The last time he'd been here at this hour he'd had a thumb out for a ride and a duffel bag slung over one shoulder. Winter had crystallized the roadside grass, and it crunched underfoot as he'd jogged on the spot trying to keep warm, while the knuckles on his right hand burned and stung.

The last time his eyes had been dry and he hadn't looked back. This time he was braver than that.

KEZIA WOKE UP HOT WITH THE SUN in her face. Rolling away from the glare, she felt paper crackle under her cheek. She opened her eyes, saw the note on Christian's pillow and shut them again. Too late. Her heart had already started pumping adrenaline. She sat up and reached for it.

I read somewhere that long goodbyes prolong the parting, not the being together. Love. Always. Christian

Kezia refolded the note carefully, recalling that any square piece of paper could be folded in two up to seven times, and folded it again. And again. On the fourth fold tears blinded her.

He was gone.

Kezia blinked them back and got out of bed. She showered, dressed and ate breakfast—two pieces of buttered toast and a cup of coffee—then sat at her grandmother's writing desk and looked at her list of things to do.

A fly buzzed erratically, calling her attention to the window. It struggled in a web that fanned across a lower pane and as she watched, a spider materialized and began to swaddle the fly in silk with an almost military efficiency.

With an effort, Kezia looked at her list again. Tradesmen needed to be called—the sooner the hotel was back in business, the sooner she could set up the trust. Apologies needed to be made—God knows what Suzie had made of her sudden flight from the wedding. She had to get busy.

Another hour went by while she watched the sun

creep across the carpet like a tide. She looked at her list again then tore it up into little pieces and flung them on the carpet. Lying across the desk with outstretched arms, she gave in to wrenching, agonized sobs.

Tears poured down her cheeks and into her mouth, her nose began to run. Gulping and gasping she tried to stem the flow of grief with tissues, with logic—she knew it would hurt—with stern admonitions to be brave, unselfish. Nothing worked.

In desperation she held her breath, but the giant fist holding her heart squeezed tighter and tighter until she capitulated with another sob. Slumped across the desk again, she could only wait for the grief to run dry.

It took a long time. When the sobbing had dwindled to sporadic shudders, she lay exhausted, the mahogany cool against her cheek, the scent of lemon polish soothing her blocked nose. Her eyes felt puffy and swollen; wearily she closed them.

Okay, it would take longer than she thought to get over him. Acceptance of that fact would be her first step toward recovery. It seemed to be the only step she could manage today.

"Are you here, Kez?" Marion's voice echoed up the stairs. Kezia's eyes flew open as she jerked upright, then nearly passed out under a wave of dizziness. Carefully she rested her elbows on the desk and cradled her aching head.

"Wait here, John Jason, and don't touch anything, do you hear me?"

A child's murmur of assent, the sound of Marion's tread on the stairs. In a panic, Kezia scrambled for the French doors, edging them shut behind her. On the deck she stepped out of view and pressed her body back against the weatherboards. She couldn't cope with sympathy right now; she had to believe she could bear this.

"Kezia, are you in here?" She heard her friend open the door to Muriel's bedroom, then the creak of floorboards as she came down the hall. "Kez?" A silence suggested Marion stood at the doorway, scanning the empty office.

Kezia's heart jumped as her friend started talking under her breath. "Where *are* you? I need you!" There was a catch in Marion's voice and Kezia stirred, pricked by her conscience.

Things must be getting back to normal. Someone needed her. Still she hesitated, rooted to the spot by a weariness that went bone-deep. Right now, she had nothing left to give.

Marion sighed.

And although she knew it was selfish and unfair, Kezia's exhaustion smoldered into resentment. Couldn't someone else carry the load for once? Did it always have to be her? She listened as her best friend's footsteps receded, crossing her arms to stop herself from going after her.

Marion could find another shoulder to cry on for once. Or better yet, toughen up and sort out her problems herself. She was better off without that loser of a husband anyway.

The horror of her thoughts made Kezia drop her face into her hands, but some part of her broke free. *I'm sorry but I can't ignore my own needs anymore. Otherwise I would have given Christian up for nothing.*

"I said, stay down there, John Jason!" Marion sounded fraught. "I'm just getting that last box from your old room...Wow, this is heavy, what'cha got in there? Blocks?" Now her tone was conciliatory as if to make up for her earlier sharpness. "No, honey, that's okay. I don't need you to carry the other end. But you're my big strong boy, aren't you? Let me just feel where the stair is...."

The banister.

Kezia wrenched open the French doors, raced across the room and hit the hall running. She was opening her mouth to shout a warning when the rug shot out from underneath her. Instinctively she threw down a hand to save herself and muffled a scream as agony splintered through her wrist.

"You count the stairs for me, I can't see them." Through a red haze of pain she could hear Marion burbling. "One, two, three...Wait, let me adjust the box, get a hand free."

Kezia shoved to her knees in an instant and was on her feet in another. "Marion!" The word came out as a croak, desperately she cleared her throat as she hurtled down the hall. "Don't touch anything!"

Unable to stop herself in time, Kezia slammed into the wall at the top of the stairs. Marion turned in surprise, one hand reaching for the banister. "Leave that," Kezia cried, "it's not safe!"

Marion dropped her hand, her brown eyes startled as they peeped above an enormous box. "Where did you spring from?"

Kezia's knees gave way; she sank to the floor.

"Can I try that, Auntie Kezia?" John Jason sounded impressed. "Run into the wall, too?"

"Sure," she said, light-headed with relief and pain. She cradled her throbbing injury. "My wrist is killing me."

"You hurt yourself?" Marion started back up the stairs.

More than you'll ever know, thought Kezia.

Then everything happened really fast. Marion's foot missed a step and she overbalanced. She dropped the box to save herself and the bottom blew out under the impact, sending blocks cascading around her feet. Kezia scrambled upright. Instinctively, Marion grabbed for the banister and a sharp crack rent the air. The wood gave as Kezia jumped a couple of stairs and caught at her friend's blouse with one hand. Started to topple forward. Pain knifed through her injured wrist.

And she let go.

Screaming, Marion fell backward down the remaining ten stairs, hit the bottom with a thud and lay still.

In the sudden terrible silence John Jason began to shriek, "My mummy's dead! My mummy's dead!"

"WHO DIED?"

"What?" Christian looked at the redhead blankly. A frown marred the smooth brow of Miss Congeniality, her affability waning under the lack of attention. "Sorry. What did you say?"

Thrusting out breasts she'd probably paid a great deal of money for, she repeated the question. "I asked, who died? You were miles away and the look on your face…"

"No one died," he said shortly. "Look, I'll go chase that drink." He was on his feet before she could answer and heading for the bar where his business partner had disappeared earlier, ostensibly to buy another round. Now he realized he'd been set up with the lovely Michelle. Or was it Rochelle? He honestly couldn't remember.

It was a Friday night and the Auckland bar was packed, but Jordan King's height and the long blond hair falling over quarterback shoulders made him easy to spot as he sat on a bar stool holding court. The females jostling around him were all of a type, Christian noted, show ponies with taut rumps, glossy manes and lots of jingling gold. A fortnight ago he would have found them attractive. Now he changed course and threaded his way to the other end of the bar. If he had to look at one more set of bleached teeth he'd go blind as well as mad.

At the gleaming metallic counter he shouted his order over the football commentary blaring from the big-screen TV. "A champagne cocktail for the lady in booth five." He handed over a big bill. "You can keep the change if you deliver it."

Across the bar, Jordan saw him alone and raised an eyebrow.

Christian shrugged and said, "All yours." He received a disgusted look in return. The unspoken message was easy to read: What the hell is happening to you?

Kezia Rose, that's what. Christian had been back a week. Or more precisely—he glanced at his Rolex—four hours short of five days. And was driving himself and Jordan crazy by doing what he'd never done in his life—vacillating over a woman.

Monday, he'd done the noble thing in leaving Kezia to find a better man.

Tuesday, he'd kill any better man who came near her.

Wednesday, so she didn't want him, fine, there were plenty of women who did.

Thursday, why the hell would anyone want to be monogamous anyway?

Friday, maybe he should call her to make sure he hadn't misunderstood. Or did Jordan think that was too pushy?

"Cut this emotional crap, tell her no isn't an option, and screw her into submission." Jordan King had inherited more than looks from his Viking forbears, and witnessing Christian's man-of-steel in meltdown had stripped away his veneer of civilized male. "Thank God, Luke is back in the country. I'm through with being Dear Abby."

Christian couldn't blame him. He was heartily sick of himself.

"Damn it, Kelly." Jordan had slammed his fist on the board table. "Why are you pining for one mulish woman when there are so many beautiful weak-willed ones out there?"

"Good point," Christian had agreed. "Let's go find some."

They'd gone to The Bar, where Jordan had ordered two beers.

"Actually—" Christian had been determined not to look sheepish "—I've quit drinking."

Jordan had sent him a withering look.

Christian scowled back. "Screw you. This has nothing to do with her." And the night had gone downhill from there.

A hand grasping his shoulder brought Christian back to the present and he steeled himself for Miss Congeniality's breathy tones. The grip tightened beyond a woman's strength. "If you're buying, I'll have a double."

Christian heaved a sigh of relief. "Man, am I glad to see you." He changed the order, then turned with a welcoming grin, which faded almost immediately. In his youth Luke Carter had been a world-class athlete and he still had the physique and vitality of someone whose blood pumped at optimum efficiency.

Tonight, however, he looked like hell.

His tailored suit must have been slept in, his gray eyes were bloodshot and he was white under his tan, but what really shocked Christian was the look on his friend's face. He looked… defeated.

Luke's expression tightened. "You don't look so hot yourself." He cast a glance across the bar at Jordan, a Viking afloat in a sea of Chanel and pheromones, and shook his head. "I see our boy is busy. Let's find somewhere quiet."

By its nature the sports channel had created a female-free zone; Christian led the way into the room's dimmer recesses and found an empty booth, his mind working overtime. Luke had been in Europe for a week, back last night. He and Jordan had expected him in the office this morning but figured he was making up for lost time with his wife.

Luke threw back his Scotch, caught sight of Christian's orange juice and raised a brow.

"I met a kid who made me realize I was following too closely in my father's footsteps." Christian kept it short, knowing Luke, who'd had a similar childhood, would understand the shorthand. The other man nodded and Christian cut to the chase. "What's up?"

"Amanda's left me for someone else." Luke's delivery was short and brutal, but his hand shook on the glass. "I came home last night to an empty house." He shook his head in disbelief. "She ended our marriage with a goddamn note."

Christian censored his first reaction—"You're well rid of her"—and tried to imagine how Kezia would approach this. "How do you feel about that?" he said carefully.

Luke stared at him. "I feel like shit, thanks for asking. And whatever you've substituted alcohol with, I'll have some."

Embarrassed, Christian dispensed with Kezia's approach. "You want to know what I really think?" He took a sip of orange juice. "You poor bastard."

"Damn right." Luke signaled for another drink.

"I mean the guy who's taken Amanda on," said Christian.

THERE WAS ABSOLUTE SILENCE while he watched Luke struggle against the urge to knock him senseless. As he braced himself for the blow, his friend suddenly dropped his head between his hands and laughed.

"I knew I could count on you to put this into perspective." Luke sat back and raked a hand through his disheveled hair. "So what if my marriage of twelve years is breaking up? So what if my wife says she's found true love with someone else? It comes down to you feeling sorry for the other guy." His tone grew bitter. "And all these years I thought you liked her."

"I gave her the respect due my best friend's wife." Christian studied Luke's reaction closely as he added, "And I will again if you two reconcile." He caught Luke's instinctive recoil and was satisfied. Still, best to be sure. "Do you love her?" It wasn't a question any of them had ever—would ever—ask. Sourly attributing this new empathy to Kezia's influence, Christian wondered if his friend knew what had become so evident to his partners—that he didn't love Amanda.

Luke's folly, Christian and Jordan called Amanda privately: beautiful, intelligent and spoiled, enamoured with the trappings of wealth. Luke had married young, when he was naive enough to mistake lust for love. At least that was Christian's take on it and he'd always congratulated himself on avoiding a similar fate with Kezia. Now the irony bit deep.

"Yes. No. I don't know. I feel responsible for her." Luke's reply was pained and Christian stopped pushing. "I do know it's time I reassessed what I want out of life, and that means pulling back from the business."

This was more shocking than Amanda's defection. Luke lived and breathed the business. Seeing his reaction, Luke's expression hardened. "How much more damn money do we need to make, Kelly? Where's the meaning in it now?"

"Wealth has its uses." For some reason, Christian started talking about the community trust fund attached to the hotel; saw the interest in Luke's eyes. They discussed it for some time, along with which manager could assume some of Luke's responsibilities while he took a break. The lines of fatigue on Luke's face deepened.

"You need sleep."

"You're right there." Luke massaged his temples. "And I'll need all my wits about me when I meet Amanda at the lawyer's tomorrow." Still he didn't move.

Christian wondered if he was reluctant to return to his empty house. "Why not stay with me for a while? It'll be like old times."

"Isn't there somewhere else you need to be?" The cryptic remark stumped Christian. He looked more closely at his friend and saw a glint of his old devilment. "C'mon," drawled Luke, "you didn't think I was going to let you dunk me in the deep stuff and not return the favor, did you? I've heard all about her."

"Jordan's got a big mouth."

"I'm sure you want to tell me all about this Kezia Rose—" the glint grew more pronounced "—seeing as how you like everyone to be in touch with their emotions now."

"Screw you."

"What I want to know is, since when does Christian Kelly let someone tell him when to quit?"

"It's more complicated than that." Damn he hated this.

"It always is," said Luke without sarcasm. "Does she love you?"

Surprised by the question, Christian answered. "She said so."

"Then get back there and let love conquer all. Isn't that how it's supposed to work?" This time, Luke's tone was full of cynicism, and pain.

Christian realized he'd known his marriage was a sham all along and was hurting. "You don't believe that shit." He said it to console. Not just Luke, but himself.

"No, but I have no reason to. You do."

"We lost a child—a long time ago." Where the hell had that come from?

# CHAPTER FOURTEEN

LUKE SIMPLY WAITED. The silence stretched between them, until Christian had to fill it. "I would've made a lousy father." Not with that! He rushed to qualify it. "Hell, I don't even know how to play."

"Mate, you don't know how to do anything but play. Your challenge is to stop once in a while."

Okay, Christian thought, let's change the subject before this gets embarrassing. "I'm scared," he heard himself say instead. "Not for me—for her. I don't know how to do this crap. What if I stuff it up?"

"You're asking me?" Bleak humor glimmered in Luke's eyes. "I'm heading for divorce, my wife is screwing a man who can give her emotional security, and I don't know who I want to be anymore. But I won't be a guy who never tried to find out. I won't be a whiner, a loser, a coward." He glanced at Christian's clenched fists. "Want to hit me yet?"

Christian unclenched his hands and his jaw. "Okay, you've made your point. I'll be her better man." He stood and Luke stood with him. "Come on, asshole. I'm taking you home to bed."

"I always wondered what your line was, Christian," Jordan said from behind him. "Now I can see why women fall over themselves."

"Wise guy," Christian said without heat. "Where's the harem?"

"Ditched." Jordan grabbed Luke's hand and pulled his mystified friend into a bear hug. "I'm sorry you had to come home to this."

Christian winced. "Have I been that pathetic?"

"Yes." Jordan released Luke but kept a light hand on his shoulders. "But I was talking about Amanda."

Luke narrowed his eyes. "How the hell do you know that? I've only just told Christian."

His expression pained, Jordan turned Luke toward the big screen and, with a sinking premonition, Christian looked, too. News had replaced sports. The sound had been turned down to a mumble, but behind the newscaster was a big picture of Luke and Amanda's wedding. The happy couple had been separated by a stylized rip and, across the top, a headline proclaimed Tycoon's Wife: Marriage Over.

"Oh, my God." Instinctively, Christian stood in front of Luke and, with Jordan running defense, shepherded him past the curious stares of the few looking at the broadcast. They were out and heading for the car park before the gossip could catch and spread.

Luke jerked to a stop as soon as he realized they were steering him to Christian's Ferrari. His face had set like granite, impossible to read, but his tone exuded suppressed violence. "If I need baby-sitters, I'll ask for them." He turned and stalked toward his own vehicle.

Behind his back, Christian exchanged glances with Jordan. "Let me drive," he coaxed Luke. "You've been drinking."

"Not nearly enough." Luke kept walking.

"Then come home with me," Jordan tried, "and we'll have a session."

"Another time." He pointed his remote control and the locks clicked.

They came up behind him as he opened the driver's door. Jordan pushed it shut and leaned against it. "You're not seeing her tonight, buddy, and you don't have to go through this alone."

"In fact—" Christian seized the car keys "—we won't let you."

"That's sweet of you, girls." Luke's tone was pure poison. "But if you don't step away from the car and give me back my goddamn keys I'm going to smash your faces in."

"And we have such pretty faces," Christian remarked to Jordan, who shook his head, causing his long blond mane to shimmer under the streetlights.

"Next he'll threaten to pull my hair."

Luke's punch caught Christian in the solar plexus and knocked the breath out of him. He bent double, cursing himself for being caught off guard when Luke had so obviously been ready to explode.

Luke grappled for the car keys but he hung on to them and butted headfirst into his friend's concrete midriff, hearing a satisfying whoosh of air as he sent him backward into Jordan. He stood up wheezing, to see Luke straining to break Jordan's bear hold.

"Takes you back to our old arm-wrestling competitions, doesn't it?" Christian gasped conversationally. "I'm just trying to remember who won."

"I did." Both men ground out the words simultaneously. With an immense groan, Luke wrenched one arm free, reached back to grab a handful of Jordan's hair and pulled.

"Aaaaah!" Jordan's surprised bellow rang through the car park. "That hurts!" He released his hold and pushed back just enough to bring a knee up hard into Luke's tailbone. Luke let go, dropping his hands to his injured rear, and Christian made the mistake of laughing.

The next thing he knew, he was on the ground clutching his balls and trying not to be sick. Luke was kneeling beside him apologizing profusely. "The worst thing you can do to a guy…I lost it…I'm sorry."

"Well, that solves the fatherhood dilemma anyway," Christian whispered when he could speak.

They hauled him up. Still nursing his affected parts, Christian leaned against the car and looked first at Luke, gingerly massaging his ass, then Jordan, wincing as he rubbed his scalp with one hand and clutching a handful of long golden strands in the other.

And he began to chuckle. The chuckle turned into a laugh that combusted, until all three men were roaring.

"That was pathetic," Christian managed, cradling his aching ribs with one hand, his balls with the other. "These days, we couldn't fight our way out of a pair of Levi's."

Jordan was nearly sobbing with laughter. "You pulled my hair," he accused Luke.

"Hey, it was your idea. I just used it." Rolling his head helplessly, Luke tried to sit, which set them all off again. "What the hell was that kick up the rear?"

Tears streamed down Jordan's cheeks. "I was trying not to hurt you too much."

"Forget your ass," Christian interrupted, "how am I supposed to keep Kezia satisfied after what you did?"

Jordan gave a whoop. "You're going back?"

"Guess so." The thought sobered Christian. He cast a doubtful look at Luke, who shook his head.

"Oh, no, you don't. You're not using my problems as an excuse. Jordan will cover for you another few days."

"Yeah, go ahead." Jordan opened his hand, regretfully watched the strands of his hair fall. "You've been useless to me this past week anyway."

"And despite you two clowns doing the musketeer act," Luke warned, "I'll fight my own battles." Christian exchanged glances with Jordan again and, sighing, Luke added, "Tomorrow." He pushed away from his car in a concession of defeat. "Tonight I'm getting drunk with Jordan."

"I'll watch," said Christian.

Jordan snorted. "If I ever let a woman reduce me to his state," he told Luke, "shoot me."

Christian threw an affectionate arm around Jordan, his mood buoyant. "And I'll watch that, too," he promised. "Got any cocoa?"

DAWN WAS CHILL AS CHRISTIAN drove the last twenty kilometers into Waterview, but he had the top of the sports car down anyway. Happiness rose in him like cream on new milk.

A cattle truck rumbled past and he laughed out loud. Jordan was right. He had to be certifiably crazy if even the smell of cow shit added to his sense of well-being. Who would have thought commitment could feel this good?

Okay, he and Kez still faced hurdles—he had no intention of baring his soul. But hell, his heart was no mean gift and he'd bare his body as often as she liked. Oh, baby, please still be in bed and not up and about do-gooding. Let's do some do-badding first.

Six on Saturday morning and the main street of Waterview was deserted as the car purred through. Only the bakery showed signs of life, its open door shielded by a fly screen. Driving past, Christian breathed deep the aroma of baking bread. It smelled like home and hope.

On an impulse he did a U-turn, parked outside and bought six warm apple donuts, fragrant with cinnamon sugar, and a couple of sausage rolls. He still had a kid's taste for baking and he knew it, but damn, this represented wealth to him—money to buy what he liked at the Waterview bakery. At least he'd resisted the gingerbread men with their raisin eyes. Next time.

The hotel looked just the same, which surprised him. Scaffolding still framed the southern side of the building, some of the window frames didn't have even an undercoat. Surely the painting could have been finished by now? Maybe Kezia was concentrating on the inside renovations.

Parking the car, he smiled as he made his way to the entrance. It would be just like her to work from the inside out, saving the best till last. He would have done it the other way 'round but then, as she'd once told him, he was all style and no substance. Well that was about to change.

Whistling, Christian used his key to let himself in. The hall was stuffy with stale air. Nothing had been done here, either. What the hell was going on?

His footsteps slowed as he approached the stairs and saw yellow tape printed with Danger! Hair prickling on the back of his neck, Christian lifted his gaze. Close to the top, the banister hung at a crazy angle. In one place a section was missing.

He jumped the tape, took the stairs two at a time. "Kez!" The shout echoed off the wood paneling. "Kezia!"

Shoving open her bedroom door, he scanned the room. Bed made. Empty. There was a sound from the guest bedroom; he spun around with relief but the person who peered out, bleary-eyed from sleep, was Don.

"Well, well," Don said, tying the cord of his dressing gown. "The prodigal returns."

"What are you doing here? Where's Kezia?"

After the briefest hesitation, he replied, "There was an accident. Marion injured her cervical vertebra."

"God, no!"

"Kezia's been staying near the spinal unit in Auckland since Sunday with John Jason."

"That's six days ago! Why the hell wasn't I told?"

"You tell me." Don sounded like the lawyer he was. "Kezia got hysterical at the first mention of it. Something about the banister giving way."

"The banister..." Realization dawned on Christian, as gray and ominous as an impending cyclone.

Watching him, the old man's face softened. "You'd best sit down, son, I haven't told you the worst yet."


THIRTY MINUTES LATER CHRISTIAN walked back to his car. His fault. *Not again.* He pressed his palms against the smooth, cool metal of the bonnet until the sensation of falling receded, then caught sight of the baking lying forgotten on the passenger seat.

Bile rose at the sight of the luminous grease spots on the brown paper bag. In one movement he picked it up and hurled it over the fence into the fields.

In the car he gunned the engine, then sat, hunched over the steering wheel, staring sightlessly.

Marion had loss of function in her hands and legs, which could be permanent, Don had said. "The banister gave way when she tried to stop her fall, but she knew it was broken.... One of those things and nobody's fault... Kezia will come around."

No. She won't.

If Christian knew anything, he knew that. They were finished. The low rumble of Consolation's engine vibrated into his consciousness. He shot the car into gear and reversed onto the road.

A horn blasted and an SUV swung past, narrowly missing a side mirror. The wake-up call sobered him. What the hell was he doing mourning a future with Kezia while Marion's still hung in the balance?

*Selfish, you've always been selfish.* His father's words rang clear as the past blurred with the present. *Your mother would have lived months longer if you'd stayed away from her. I don't care what she said.... Don't you shirk responsibility for killing her, you little bastard. Don't you dare!*

The guilt brought it all back. The helplessness, the grief and loss. At the end of Waterview's main street Christian turned north, struggling to contain his emotions with logic.

A child gave his dying mother influenza and became a scapegoat for a grieving man. The child accepted the burden unquestioning, until he grew into reason. He'd been twelve years old, for God's sake. Twelve. His mother had asked for him, he'd gone. He'd needed to see her, to be hugged and comforted. He'd known she'd come home to die.

The speedometer crept up; ten kilometers flew by. Except pneumonia killed her, not cancer. Her death certificate had reiterated the bald, unpalatable truth ten years ago when he'd received all her things, boxed up and sent to him on his father's death. The old man had been right all along. Selfish. Selfish. Selfish.

Christian's hands were shaking on the steering wheel so badly he had to pull over. The car skidded in the loose gravel, swung to a stop in front of the wrought-iron gates of Waterview's cemetery. The perfect place to abandon hope. The song of a skylark rose and quivered in the morning air.

Why hadn't he repaired the damn stairs? Why had he pawned safety to score points against Kezia? What kind of loser kept hurting people he cared about?

The same loser rushing back to help where he wasn't wanted, that's who. If he really loved Kezia, wouldn't he respect her wishes and stay away? Or would that be ducking the judgment he so richly deserved?

And what about his responsibility to Marion and John Jason? Sending money felt like a cop-out. Or was he trying to salve his conscience by forcing a sick woman to acknowledge his culpability?

In his agony he got out of the car and paced the tree-lined avenue that led through the graveyard. His mother was buried here, among the soft shady green. Many more graves had joined hers since he was last here, yet he still knew where to find her—if he had the guts to look. Maybe confronting an old guilt would help him deal with this new one.

He began walking in the direction of her grave and the years fell away with every step until his grief was so raw and new he ached with it. A nameless terror stopped Christian in his tracks, turned him blindly back toward his car, a sinner desperate to leave hallowed ground. He knew now why he cried at funerals…because he wished he'd cried at hers.

He sat in the Ferrari for a long time before coming to a decision. He could never make amends with the dead but he had to try with the living. The engine roared into life as he pulled out onto the empty road. With nothing to gain and less to lose Christian headed north.

"WHAT'S THAT ON YOUR HEAD?"

"It's called a halo. It keeps my head still while my back gets better."

"Like angels have?"

Supine in the hospital bed, Marion smiled at her son through a mirror set up for the purpose. "Yes, except theirs isn't made of metal."

"They'd be too heavy to fly," John Jason said, an authority since the emergency helicopter flight.

He moved in for a closer look and Kezia threw out a restraining hand. The other was useless, in a fiberglass cast from hand to elbow. "Not too close, honey, remember what I said."

He scowled at her. "You go 'way."

"Don't talk to Auntie Kez like that." Marion's voice revealed the strain of the visit, John Jason's first since the accident. Kezia held the little boy's mutinous gaze, her own flashing a warning, a plea. *Please, please, please be good for your mummy's sake. Hate me later all you like.*

He turned away and buried his face in his aunt Sally's skirts. "This is my real auntie," he muttered.

Marion's sister, Sally, three hours off the plane from Australia, looked over his head at Kezia. "I told you it was counterproductive to let him see her like this."

"Who's her? I may be flat on my back but I still have an opinion and this was a great idea." The forced cheer in Marion's reply made Kezia ache for the effort it must be costing her. Surely, Sally could see her sister needed things made easier, not harder?

"Besides—" Marion reached out a clumsy frozen hand, feeling for her son's soft hair "—I wanted to see my boy."

John Jason grabbed her hand and held on. "I thought you were dead, Mummy." He wailed into Sally's skirt.

Over the previous week none of Kezia's reassurances had carried any weight. To John Jason she was still the monster who had dragged him away from his unconscious mother, shoved him into the bar and locked the door. Abandoned him to terror. To save Marion's life, she had forfeited her godson's trust.

"No, baby." Marion's voice was tender. "Not dead, just too sick for visitors."

"I want to go home," he cried. "I want my rat." He and Kezia were staying at a motel within walking distance of the spinal unit.

"Hasn't Roland been writing every day?" In the mirror Marion smiled at Kezia, who forced herself to return it. *Don't thank me for small favors. Not when I'm the reason you're lying here.* But all that mattered now was shielding Marion from every anxiety.

So her friend didn't know that her son loathed his godmother and accepted her ministrations under sufferance. She didn't know that Kezia was using the money Christian had left for the hotel's renovations to pay for a private room and the best specialists. And she didn't know her partial paralysis might be permanent.

The only reality Kezia had allowed into that quiet hospital room, redolent of the jasmine she'd entwined around Marion's pillow, was that John Jason needed to see his mother.

"Roland is having bad dreams," he told her now. "He wants me to go home and play with him." Roland's so-called nightmares had helped Kezia to finally persuade Marion to let her son see her hooked up to drips and monitors with a traction halo drilled into her skull and her right ankle encased in plaster.

"But, honey, Auntie Kezia said you liked the hospital day care." Kezia stiffened, knowing the mention of her name would provoke resistance. It did.

"I hate it," he said, and glowered at his nemesis, who bit back a denial. It would only stoke the little boy's opposition. Instead she opted for guerrilla tactics.

"Let's go to the vending machine," she suggested brightly. "You can have whatever you want."

John Jason cast her a hostile look but the lure was too strong. "Two things," he demanded. At her nod, he skipped to the door with a wave to his mother.

"He's fine," Kezia reassured Marion in a low voice, but though her friend smiled, her eyes were full of anxiety. "Really. He likes day care and the staff spoil him at the motel."

"How can you look after him with your arm in plaster?" Sally challenged from the other side of the bed. She'd been like this at school, too, verging on antagonistic.

"We manage." Kezia kept smiling at Marion, giving no hint of how difficult that managing had been while her arm still needed a sling. Only when her smile was returned did she face Sally. "And this is fiberglass—much hardier and lighter." Holding up the arm encased in virulent flourescent pink, she tried to break the tension. "John Jason chose the color. Like it?"

Sally wouldn't play. "Now that John Jason has family here to look after him, there's no reason for you to manage any longer. In fact, the sooner you leave, the better off we'll all be."

Marion gasped. "Sally!"

"She's the reason you're in this state." Sally eyed Kezia with contempt. "And she's terrified you'll sue so she won't let the doctors tell you you're facing permanent paralysis. Well—"

"Shut up, Sally." White-faced, Kezia stared at Marion.

"It's all right," her friend said quietly. "I already suspected, so you can stop trying to protect me."

"Protect you!" Sally's tone was incredulous. "Are you crazy? Her negligence is responsible for—"

"Auntie Kez!" John Jason swung impatiently between the double doors. "Come, come, come!"

"—you being here. And if you think I'm going to let someone with her safety record look after my nephew—"

Marion interrupted the tirade, her face tight and drawn. "Don't force me to choose, Sally. You won't like my choice."

"Come with the money," called John Jason from the door. "Mun…e…e. Mun…ee."

"You don't have to choose, Marion," Kezia said, forcing herself to speak calmly. "We're both here for you, aren't we, Sally?" No answer. "*Aren't* we?" Put your sister first, *now*.

"Yes," Sally conceded, but her eyes promised retribution.

John Jason flew back into the room, seized Kezia's good hand and towed her to the door.

"I'm coming, I'm coming. I have a few errands, so I'll come back later," she called as cheerfully as she could over her shoulder.

Marion murmured her assent; Sally said nothing.

When they reached the vending machine, Kezia's hands trembled so much, she had to give her purse to John Jason. As she watched him press his face against the glass front, trying to make his choices, she wished her own were as simple.

Sally was right. It *was* Kezia's fault. Yet she knew she could be of most help to Marion and John Jason if she stayed and weathered Sally's antagonism.

Pulling up a greasy green vinyl chair, she sat, exhausted by the cumulative strain of the previous week. Had it only been—she glanced at the date on her watch—six days since the accident?

In this intense limbo of fear and hope, she couldn't even recall her old life. An image of Christian flashed into her brain; viciously she tamped it out. The collaborator in her crime.

One of the specialists walked by on his rounds and

smiled in passing. On impulse, Kezia reached out a hand and stopped him. "You said the spinal swelling should have gone down enough by now to determine—" she glanced at John Jason, but he was absorbed in the vending machine "—whether Marion's condition is permanent?"

To her surprise, his eyes shied away from hers. "I'm sorry," he replied formally, "but Marion's sister has instructed us to restrict our briefings to family. Why don't you ask her for information?" With an embarrassed nod, he strode away.

John Jason motioned her over. "I want a packet of M&Ms and a Coke." He paused, obviously waiting for her to veto the Coke, but still dazed, Kezia helped him put the money in the slot and punch the right buttons.

She was being pushed out and there wasn't a damn thing she could do about it without embroiling Marion in more unpleasantness.

They walked back to the motel where Kezia made John Jason eat a sandwich and fruit before she opened his chocolate. Lost in thought, she patted his head as she gave him back his treat. He jerked away, reminding her that two people hated her guts. If she included herself, that made three.

Their room in the Ambassador Motel was on the ground floor. Sliding doors opened onto a trellised concrete patio and Kezia flung them wide, suddenly desperate to release the pungent odor of motel cleaning products and breathe fresh air.

The trellis was overgrown with jasmine, lending

a welcome dimness to the room's seventies decor of tangerine, tan and purple. She picked a fresh replacement for Marion's pillow, knowing she'd hate the smell by association for the rest of her life once this was over, then put a protesting John Jason down for a nap and made herself a coffee.

She should eat but she was too tired. She should nap, except every time she closed her eyes she was back in Waterview, hiding when Marion called, "Where are you? I need you!"

Wearily she sat at the round Formica table and tried to think of a way around this latest dilemma. The fact that Marion would choose her over Sally only exacerbated her guilt.

*You let go. You let go. You let go.*

Why hadn't she held on? Over and over, Kezia replayed the accident with its new ending. Herself, holding on.

She ached to confess the whole thing to Marion and be vilified, as she deserved. But Marion had enough to bear right now without Kezia's remorse.

The habit of routine saved her from the circular madness of what-ifs. John Jason was napping. It was time for Roland the Rat to write his daily letter. Getting up, she went into the bedroom and opened her suitcase, found a pen and the colored paper hidden among her clothes. Back at the table she started to write.

*Dear John Jason, please don't hate me.* Kezia took a deep breath, screwed up the paper and reached for a fresh sheet. *Dear John Jason, today*

*Bernice May gave me a very nice piece of cheese for
my breakfast. I know you're still cross with Auntie
Kezia for keeping me away from your mummy when
she fell, but—*

Bang, bang, bang. Marion was at the door, desperate for shelter. Kezia tried to get up and answer
it, but she couldn't. She sat imprisoned in the chair,
caught in a spider's web.

Bang, bang, bang. Frantically, Kezia struggled to
free herself, opened her mouth to scream. This time
she had to answer. Had to. Sticky fly-filled web
choked her off. The spider was near—poised, ready
to spring and devour—she could sense it.

She woke with a strangled cry as John Jason clam-
bered onto her lap, his dislike forgotten with the
advent of a new terror. "Someone's at the door."

She heard the knock again, even more urgent.
Heart hammering, Kezia got up and staggered to the
door, John Jason clinging like a sleep-dazed limpet.
"I'm coming, I'm coming."

At the door she tried to put him down to free up
her good hand, but he hung on tighter. "What if it's
the bogeyman?" His confidence had been another
casualty of the accident.

"It's not the bogeyman." Kezia tried to sound
calm. She struggled with the doorknob, telling
herself not to panic. Like John Jason, she was now
conditioned to expect disaster. The door swung
open. The bogeyman stood there, gorgeous and un-
obtainable.

"What do you want?" she choked out past the lump in her throat.

Christian took a deep breath. "I'm here to be your better man."

She slammed the door in his face.

# CHAPTER FIFTEEN

NO ONE SAID this would be easy, Kelly. You can only put yourself in the firing line and take the bullets. Squaring his shoulders, Christian knocked again.

There was a sharp murmur of voices, a fumble at the door then it swung open a second time. Beaming, John Jason flung his arms around Christian's knees and held on tight. "I told her we need a daddy to keep away the bogeyman." Anxiety settled on the small upturned face. "You will, won't you?" Behind him, Kezia cradled a bright pink arm cast, holding it across her body like a shield.

Christian picked up the child and hugged him. "But John Jason, you're the scariest dude I know," he said. It was true. This kid toppled his defenses as if they were a toy fort. "And what about Batman?"

"I left my cape at home. *She* bought me a new one. I don't like it." The child turned his head to scowl at Kezia. Hurt flared in her eyes, quickly doused. There were undercurrents here Christian didn't understand, and she looked so damn sad and fragile he could hardly stand it.

"Can I come in? Please?"

She lifted her chin. "I expect you've come about the hotel money I've been spending on hospital bills. Settlement on my land is next week, then I'll pay you back." He didn't answer, just looked at her steadily until she blushed and stepped back. "Okay, a few minutes."

John Jason turned an ebullient face to his. "You can even have some of my Coke."

"Thanks, buddy, you keep it. I'll take a coffee, though." That should buy him more time.

Carrying the kid, he followed Kezia into the dim interior, noting its shabbiness, the forlorn cleanliness. Dishes were soaking in the sink. He guessed her cast would make washing up laborious. Other than a few childish paintings stuck to the fridge with magnets, the place was impersonal and tidy. Its inhabitants obviously spent little time here.

Still holding John Jason, he took one of the two orange bucket chairs at the Formica table. Immediately, the child slid off his lap and went to the tiny fridge. Glancing defiantly at Kezia, he took out a can of Coke. Without a word she pulled the tab and filled a glass. John Jason snatched it back.

"Say thank-you," Christian reminded him but the boy's mouth set in a stubborn line. Christian frowned. "John Jason?"

"Please!"

"That's fine." Kezia turned back to the tiny kitchenette and switched the jug on. "Hey, why don't you show Christian the car I bought you, the one like his...what's it called again?"

God, I love this woman. Christian exchanged a male look with John Jason before the kid scampered off to get his toy. He saw her struggle to unscrew the lid on the coffee jar. "I'll make that."

"I can manage."

Ignoring her, he came up behind her, close enough to touch, to torture himself with what might have been. "You don't have to."

"I want to."

A toy Ferrari tore across the lurid carpet, driven by a heavy hand and some fearsome broom-brooms. Reluctantly, Christian sat. John Jason careered around the Formula One lounge circuit while Christian applauded his driving skill, equally aware of Kezia's one-handed independence in the kitchen.

He was in love with a woman who would rather die than accept assistance. To help her, he'd have to submerge his feelings and be tougher than she was pretending to be. John Jason extended his circuit into the bedroom and Christian took advantage of his absence. "What's the latest on Marion?"

"She might make a full recovery, she might be left with permanent paralysis. We should know soon."

"I want to pay for the best specialists."

"You already are." She shrugged, awkward and defiant. That was one battle he didn't have to fight.

He tried to keep the next question neutral, didn't quite manage it. "Why didn't you call me?"

"Why would I?" Face averted, she busied herself pouring milk into his coffee, adding one sugar with an unconscious familiarity that made her coldness more painful.

"It's not just you I care about!"

She stopped stirring, stared into the cup. "Then you must feel like I do—guilty as sin."

"What the hell has this got to do with you?"

"If I'd taken the hotel when you offered it, this never would have happened. If I'd been *thinking* instead of playing mind games with you, I would have got the carpenter back to repair the stairs. Now my best friend might be a cripple!" Her laugh was bitter. "And you wonder why I didn't call you."

Still grappling with this new revelation—of course, it made sense that she would shoulder some of the blame—Christian tried to keep his emotions out of it. "I'm told the banister wasn't the cause of the accident—"

"How like you to minimize your share of the responsibility."

"—but contributed to Marion's fall," he finished, accepting her need for a punching bag. Kezia's self-worth relied on her success as a safety net for the people she loved, and Marion's accident represented a devastating failure. "I stopped the repairs, not you, so keep your thieving conscience out of my liability." That startled her into looking at him. He held her gaze. "You're not going to carry the can on this one, Kez. I won't let you."

For a fleeting moment he saw the weight lift from her shoulders. "You don't understand."

"So make me."

"She came hunting for me, and I wouldn't answer. I knew she needed me and I hid." Her voice caught. "I hid, Christian. She had the accident because I wanted to wallow in self-pity over losing you." He started to rise; she waved him down. "I forgot duty, loyalty, compassion—pretty much every value I hold dear. Having you around made me selfish."

"And now you're atoning for being human by donning sackcloth and ashes and playing the martyr," he said, understanding suddenly how her penance would work. In two strides he closed the gap, grasped her shoulders. "Don't you get it? You're not punishing yourself for ignoring a friend, you're punishing yourself for being human and wanting a life."

She looked at him as if he were laying out the seven temptations on a picnic blanket. "I don't expect you to understand."

"Oh, I understand too well. I know your parents didn't bring you up to believe this, but being a good person doesn't have to mean always stifling your own needs." Hell, on the basis of his track record why would she listen to him?

"The coffee's getting cold."

Engine spluttering, John Jason charged back into the lounge and demanded a tire change. "I burned rubber." Christian took the proffered toy and sat. There was no point in discussing this further anyway. Kezia had clearly retreated behind defense mechanisms that only dynamite could breach.

Grimly, he shucked off the tires and dropped them onto the table. A sheet of purple writing paper caught his eye. Bringing over his coffee, Kezia caught the direction of his gaze and removed Roland's letter but Christian had seen enough to fill in the puzzle. "John Jason—" he replaced one tire "—I'd sure like to see that Batman cape your auntie Kez bought you."

"I hate it."

"I just wondered if it was one of those new magic ones." In the middle of handing Christian the next tire, John Jason paused to stare at him. "You know about the magic ones, don't you?" The child shook his head. "Go get it and I'll check it for you."

The boy crawled under the couch, pulled out the offending object and brought it over. Christian examined it, praying for a distinguishing mark. "Ah! See that?" He pointed to the label—Made in Korea—and received an awed nod. "This means it's a magic cape. Makes its wearer invincible." John Jason looked blank.

"That means nothing and no one can ever beat you." Kezia clarified, and the child's eyes widened.

"Then I should give it to Mummy," he exclaimed.

For a moment Christian couldn't answer. Out of the corner of his eye, he saw Kezia turn away. "It's really kind of you to think of doing that, but you know, the doctors are using their own magic on her." He held out the cape. "So what do you say?"

"I want to put it on."

Christian helped him, pulling the shiny black hood over the child's head, adjusting the oval eyeholes and straightening the crumpled ears. As he tied the shiny ribbons under John Jason's chubby chin he foresaw a potential problem. "You know, the magic in this cape is so powerful that you should really only wear it some of the time, a few hours. The good thing is, the magic still works when you take it off, say, to have a bath or go to bed."

When the cape was secured, Batman stood back, his eyes button-bright behind the mask. "Am I in'cible now?"

"Invincible? Yep." Christian nodded seriously. "One more thing about that cape, you have to be nice to whoever gave it to you, otherwise the magic won't work."

Kezia turned back sharply.

"Oh," said John Jason. His lower lip pushed out, then his small fingers tugged at the bow.

Recognizing this was no easy fix, Christian backed off. "That means, saying 'please' and 'thank you' and using your manners."

"Then the magic will work?"

"It will work," he promised.

"Okay." The child glanced at his godmother. "Thank you for the cape, Auntie Kez." Spoken grudgingly, it still made her brown eyes glow.

"You're welcome."

"I'm gonna see how I look in the mirror." Batman disappeared into the bedroom.

Reluctantly, Kezia's gaze met Christian's. "Thank you." Could he count that as progress? She moved to the door. "I'll see you out." Guess not.

He followed her without protest. "You didn't ask me how I found out. I went back to Waterview."

That surprised her. He watched her eyes widen as

she took in his proximity, realize he'd blocked off her escape route. "I came back to try to be that guy you wanted. To see if I could change." He put his hands on the wall on either side of her body, watched her face pale.

"Christian, don't."

"When I heard about Marion I knew I didn't deserve another chance. So I came here to make amends and leave."

She made no protest. He'd known she wouldn't, but her eyes were luminous with regret. Christian leaned forward and kissed her, knowing full well she'd kiss him back if it was intended as a goodbye.

Not knowing he'd changed his mind.

Still, he wouldn't be Christian Kelly if he didn't take advantage of the last willing kiss she would give him for a while. Her kiss was warm and sweet and sad until he caught her face in his hands and breathed fire into it. She broke free.

"That was my plan when I came here. Then I find you intending to sacrifice your life to guilt. So I figure I'll marry you." Kezia made a strangled sound. Christian paused politely but she couldn't seem to get any words out. "Because if you're set on throwing your life away on one error of judgment, then, babe, it's going to be me."

"HI, SOLDIER." IGNORING THE MEDICAL paraphernalia, Christian laid a hand on Marion's cheek, and got a wan smile in reply.

"I was hoping you'd show," she said. "We need

some comic relief. It's all too mighty serious around here."

"Can we be serious just a little longer?" He stood where she could see him without the aid of mirrors. "I'm here to confess. It was my fault the banister wasn't fixed."

"And Kezia's fault she fell and needed help, and my fault for packing blocks in a flimsy box." She was obviously weary of the subject. "I don't see any point in playing the blame game, Christian. Being human is an imperfect business. When I'm better, remind me to slap you around."

He felt he'd gotten off too lightly; she sensed it. "It was an accident, a bad hand. From the same deck as your lousy childhood, my broken marriage and the mess Muriel left Kezia. All we can do is make the best of the cards." Tears trickled down her face. "I haven't been doing that, but I need to be a survivor now—not a victim."

Something shifted inside Christian, something big and important. He took a tissue from the box on the bedside table, gently wiped away her tears, and swallowed a couple of his own. "How can such a wise woman be scared of spiders and not rats?"

She half laughed, half sighed. "Thanks for giving me another reason not to lie here helpless longer than I need to."

Christian scanned the ceiling, declared it spider-free, and pulled up a chair. "Talk to me or nap, it doesn't matter. I'm company."

Over the next hour Marion did both. Through their

drifts of conversation, he learned a lot—some of it from what she said. He learned Kezia had been her rock, but Marion was ready to deal with the specialists directly now if her overprotective minder would just back off. He learned that Sally had been stirring the pot; Kezia had taken it off the boil, but Marion was worried about future confrontations. He learned that while Kezia had Marion's loyalty, she really didn't want to lose her sister, the only family she had left.

"How did a man like you get so good in the sickroom?" she wondered sometime in the second hour as he adjusted her mirrors so she could see the jacaranda flowering outside the window.

"My mother was sick for a long time before she died."

"I remember your mother," said Marion as though his admission was unremarkable. "She was a nurturer like Kezia but…" Her voice trailed off.

"But?"

"These silly painkillers loosen my tongue."

"Finish what you were going to say."

"But too passive. My mum always said she should have left your father."

Christian had never considered that. The beatings had only started after her death but Paul had always been a difficult man—moody, unpredictable. Theirs had never been a happy home. He changed the subject. "I saw John Jason this afternoon. You've got a great kid."

"I'm worried about him. This is no place for a little boy."

Christian agreed with her. "How about if Kez took John Jason home and brought him back weekends to visit?"

Marion's eyes lit up, then the worry lines reappeared. "I know Kezia, she'll see it as banishment. And what about her wrist? She's managed this past week because she's had to, but…"

Suddenly he saw a way forward for all of them and it involved jumping off a cliff. "I'll go with her, share the child care."

"I want to shake my head in disbelief right now but I can't. Is this where you tell me I've been asleep for a hundred years?"

Christian relayed the highlights of his conversation with Kezia and Marion's eyes went as wide as saucers. "How did she react to the marriage thing?"

"I left before the shock wore off." He grinned. "Let's just say I'm not expecting her to fall into my arms crying, 'You're right, I'm wrong and I really, really love you.'"

The tissues were called for again. "God, I needed to laugh so badly," she gasped. "But no running away this time, promise."

"No running away this time—except to see you."

Her expression grew thoughtful. "You can restart the hotel renovations."

"That's the least of our concerns right now."

"You two might not care about the hotel, but I do. I'm still going to need a job when this is over." She swallowed hard. "If I'm able."

Christian touched her where she could feel it, on her shoulder. "You'll get the best treatment."

She gave him a wan smile. "I think prayers at this point might be more useful."

"You've got those, too."

KEZIA PAUSED IN FRONT OF the beige door to Marion's private room, and pasted a smile on her face.

Since Christian had left her standing gob-smacked on the doorstep, her emotions had gone from incredulity to a profound hurt that he would play her like this. So he would sacrifice himself for her, would he? Be the martyr he accused her of being. At least she didn't have to marry anyone to salve *her* conscience.

With an effort she pulled herself together and knocked on the door with her good hand. Later she'd deal with Kelly. Right now he was distracting her from what was really important. She pushed the door open with a cheery, "It's me," saw Christian standing by the bed, and the smile fell off her face. For the life of her she couldn't retrieve it.

Instead she managed a croaky, "Hi," crossed to the bed and kissed Marion. "John Jason sent this picture for you. I have to warn you, it looks like you're hanging from a clothesline." Ignoring Christian, she busied herself with pinning the picture where Marion could look at it.

"We've just been discussing him," Christian said.

"I want you to take John Jason home." Marion's voice was stronger than Kezia had heard it in a week. "You can bring him back weekends to visit."

Kezia's mouth went dry. "Look, I know he said he hated day care this morning but he was cross with me. And I can't leave you until we know...until you're in the clear."

"I'll make sure Sally rings if there's any news." Marion's voice softened. "Kezia, you're the only one I'd entrust my baby to. You desperately need a break, and with Sally here, you can take one."

A suspicion occurred to Kezia. "Did Christian say that?"

"No, he let me say that—and without arguing." Suddenly her friend sounded exhausted.

Stricken, Kezia stroked Marion's arm. "Sorry." With a massive effort she dredged up another smile. "If that's what you want, then of course I'll do it."

"I knew you wouldn't let me down."

"I'll ring Don tonight to come get us."

"No need." Christian cleared his throat. "I'm going with you, to help out with John Jason."

*"What?"*

"You have no idea," said Marion, closing her eyes to signal an end to the conversation, "how that puts my mind at rest."

Kezia bit down on her tongue until she tasted blood.

"Another thing." Marion opened her eyes a crack. "Save on motel bills and stay at Christian's tonight."

Christian's blink of surprise saved him from certain death but Kezia's forbearance had reached its limit. "He's more than happy to pay for the motel, aren't you?" Her murderous tone suggested he concur; he murmured assent.

"Yes, but I don't want to be indebted to him more than I need to be." Lids closed again, Marion's features assumed a Madonna's peacefulness. "You of all people would understand that."

By the time Kezia thought of a comeback, her friend was asleep—or pretending to be. Frustrated, she jerked a thumb toward the door. Outside! she mouthed to Christian.

In the corridor she grabbed the front of his expensive shirt and swung him against the wall. "You lousy son of a bitch. Manipulating Marion to push us together."

"I can see why you'd think that," he conceded, passive in her grasp. "It isn't true."

"Whose idea was it I take John Jason home?"

Hesitation. "Mine but—"

"Bastard!" Releasing her hold, she stormed toward Marion's room. Christian grabbed her by the shirttail.

"She's worried about you…have you looked in a mirror lately? You're exhausted. Yet she knows her kid would be better off at home and you're the one she trusts. She's ready to deal directly with the doctors now. What would you have suggested?"

She hated self-pity, but she was too tired to fight it. "I really tried to make things easier. Now you're telling me I've failed."

"No." He reeled her back, grabbed her unresisting body and held tight. "You succeeded. Relying on you has made her strong enough to reclaim some independence. And to look out for the people *she* loves."

The only reason she leaned against his long, hard body was that she needed the rest. "I've got to tell her how John Jason feels about me."

"No, you don't. That's one of the reasons I'm coming with you, to act as a go-between. That, and to make sure you look after that arm." His tone grew gentle. "Let's face it, you've been putting out one fire after another since Muriel died."

Not all the fires were out, though. The thought galvanized Kezia to shrug free, address the real issue between them. "I'm not marrying you, Christian. Let me be quite clear on that."

"You're clear." His face gave nothing away, making Kezia even more nervous. She desperately needed a renunciation.

"You only want to marry me to ease your conscience."

"I hadn't thought of that." He considered. "Nope, that's bullshit."

Too tired for this, she changed the subject. "I can't leave Marion yet. Not until I know her prognosis."

"And if Sally picks another fight? Yeah, I heard about that one, too. Do you really want Marion to lose her only sister? Because she will choose you, Kez."

"Oh, will she?" The female voice bristled with hostility. Kezia looked around to see Sally, arms folded defensively, blond hair drawn into a ponytail as tight as her expression.

Kezia went to stand beside her. "We don't know who Marion would choose," she admonished Christian. "And Sally and I have already agreed not to force the issue."

Sally stepped away. "You mean, you fell back on emotional blackmail. Well, be warned, when Marion's well enough, I'm going to encourage her to sue you for every cent you've got."

"Here, take them now." Kezia opened her purse, shook out some coins. "Two dollars and twenty-five cents."

"Very funny. I know you own the Waterview hotel."

Kezia looked to Christian. "Do I?"

"I sent the deed through on Wednesday."

"You know I haven't thought about it in a week." She looked at Sally. "If you're sure you want it…I'm sorry, I'm forgetting my manners. You remember Christian Kelly, don't you?"

Sally blushed. "Are you trying to be funny?"

"Don't you remember?" Christian prompted Kezia. "I…we used to…know each other. It ended badly, didn't it? Sorry, Sal. And I'm the person to sue, not Kez. I was the owner of the hotel at the time and I stopped work on the renovations. I've already told Marion I accept all responsibility. Meanwhile I'll cover all costs, including your flight and hotel expenses."

For a moment Sally stood nonplussed. "Screw you," she said and went into Marion's room.

Christian stared after her. "Didn't I just do the right thing?"

"Wait here." Kezia followed Sally into the room, saw her bent over Marion, love and concern in every line. Then Sally caught sight of Kezia and her expression hardened.

Kezia steeled herself. "I've come to say goodnight." She kissed Marion tenderly. "And goodbye, until next weekend."

"You're leaving?" Sally couldn't hide her satisfaction.

Marion spoke for her. "I've asked Kezia to take John Jason home."

Sally said nothing and Kezia breathed a sigh of relief. Maybe Christian had done some good then, in accepting responsibility. From her bag she took out a scrap of paper, scrawled all her numbers on it, and handed it over to Sally. "Will you call me if there's news?"

"Of course she will," Marion answered.

Kezia waited until Sally reluctantly nodded. "Okay then, see you in six days." She touched Marion's cheek, took a deep breath and walked away.

Behind her, Sally moved out of Marion's line of sight and dropped the piece of paper in the bin.

# CHAPTER SIXTEEN

"NICE PLACE." Realizing the understatement would alert Christian to her nervousness, Kezia tightened her grip on his house key until it bit into her palm. Tried again. "Actually, it's fantastic." And not what she expected. Not stark, minimalist or sterile.

The entry foyer opened into a generous living room and the last of the sun's rays glowed on butterscotch walls and warmed the terra-cotta floor tiles. Luxurious sofas were set off by textured drapes and deep Turkish rugs. Beyond floor-to-ceiling windows, the Auckland Harbor stretched to a violet horizon. It was exactly like looking at the Plains, except in blue.

She opened the oak door wider and stepped aside to let Christian pass, a sleeping John Jason cradled in his arms. She quashed an impulse to jolt the child awake. Kezia hated being alone with Christian on his turf.

"You can come in, you know." Kezia became aware of Christian watching, and stepped forward, pulling her battered suitcase. The ancient wheels gave voice to her reluctance.

She'd delayed this moment as long as possible,

lingering at the restaurant he'd taken them to for dinner until the waitress had mentioned how much their son looked like his mother.

"I thought you and John Jason could sleep through here." Her tension eased—and that annoyed her. Given her emphatic rejection of his proposal, he was hardly going to expect to share a bed, now was he? The room she followed him to was a neutral canvas of whites and blues with no imprint of its owner. Good.

She pulled back the duvet on one of the two single beds then slipped off John Jason's trainers. Christian laid him down gently and, with a sigh, the child burrowed under the covers. Across the bed they shared an involuntary smile and Kezia's nervousness came back. "I think I'll turn in, too."

"At eight-thirty? Relax, Kezia. I can't make you do anything you don't want to." Strangely she didn't find that reassuring. "And we need to talk—"

"It's still no, Christian."

"About practicalities."

"Oh." Feeling a fool, she followed him through the living room and into a kitchen, more like the one she'd imagined for him. Beautiful, clear of clutter and obviously barely used. Christian opened a cupboard and pulled out a battered copper saucepan, switched on the gas hob. "Hot chocolate?"

"Sure." She watched him measure in the milk, the powdered chocolate, gently stir the contents. "Mugs to your right, marshmallows in the pantry in front."

Okay, maybe he had one or two domestic skills. The pantry held more than she expected, including a few herbs she'd only read about in cuisine magazines. "You cook?"

"I'm competent."

"Who taught you?"

"I dated a chef once."

"Figures." Kezia took a seat at the marble island that separated the kitchen and dining room. "Do you even have any male friends?"

He poured the hot milk into the mugs, added marshmallows. "I've known my two business partners since university. What are you telling me, your boyfriends never taught you any life skills?"

She thought about that. "Chess, how to change a tire and do my own oil change. Bill was very knowledgeable about wine."

"See, there's a positive in every relationship, even with William J. Rankin the Third." Kezia didn't rise to the bait, simply took the hot drink he passed over. He came around and took the stool beside her. Hardly threatening behavior, yet she stiffened. "You know what your legacy was?"

She regarded him warily over the rim of her mug. "Bitterness? Mistrust?"

"Self-belief," he said quietly. "You were the only person who bought into my dreams and made me believe them." His gaze flicked around the room, came back to her. "In a real sense I owe all this to you."

The gift, unexpected and generous, compelled an honest response. "Because you had no expectations of how I should behave, I could play at being different people, find out who I wanted to be…an uptight, orderly chocoholic."

He didn't laugh, simply opened a drawer in the island and passed her an open bar of Toblerone. She took a piece. "You see, before I came to Waterview I was used to people who expected—"

"Sacrifice."

"Support," she corrected. A lifetime of practice meant she could skirt around sore spots blindfolded. Still she slipped off the stool, putting some space between them. "Of course, it was easy for you to encourage my independence. You didn't need me."

"I pretended not to."

Annoyed, Kezia tipped the rest of her drink into the sink. "Strange you couldn't say any of this last weekend."

"I needed time to get my priorities straight. I came back to try again before I heard about Marion's accident."

"For all I know you might really have been coming back to check up on renovations. Hell, you might have forgotten a pair of socks." Her mug hit the counter with a sharp crack. "Excuse me if I don't trust your sudden change of heart."

"What about yours?" he challenged. "Last week you loved me, this week you don't?"

"Last weekend I was dreaming and Marion's accident was a wake-up call. There are a hundred reasons we wouldn't work out."

"Name them."

"Our history is heartbreaking."

"Our future doesn't have to be."

"I'm country. You're city."

"We'll have the best of both worlds."

"I want a man with no shadows. You live in them."

"I'll buy sunblock."

He wasn't taking this seriously. She took a deep breath. "We caused Marion's accident."

"I caused it and she forgave me." The blue of his eyes was clear all the way down to his soul. "You could forgive me too."

Kezia started to feel desperate. "I want to be a good person. You make me selfish."

"I want to be selfish," he said slowly. "You make me a better person."

"I want lots of kids."

"After I've grieved for the one we lost."

"No, Christian." Kezia could hear her voice getting panicky. "*No*. I don't like the person I am with you."

"I love you, Kez, and I'm not losing you again."

Her hands gripped the edge of the counter. She had no faith anymore—not in him—not in her own ability to make a difference. "I don't trust your love."

He didn't even flinch. "Why would you? I've never given you cause to. You know what's always stopped me in the past? Fear of failure. Well, I'm tired of losing you to that."

As she stared at him helplessly, a wail came from the bedroom. "I wet the bed!"

Later Kezia watched night tick away on the luminous green dial of the bedside clock and worked on her strategy. She'd play up her injury, load Christian down with responsibilities, drown him in the minutiae of her day-to-day life. Having to perform good deeds would snap him back into reality quick enough.

Her thoughts turned to Marion. She wondered if her friend was sleeping or lying awake in the darkness, too, scared and lonely. Full of self-loathing, Kezia buried her face in the pillow.

"SO HOW'S YOUR WOOIN' DOIN'?"

Christian jammed the mobile phone between his ear and a shoulder and reached into the back of Kezia's old station wagon for two insulated containers, one from the lunch pile, one from the dinner pile. "She's still trying to shake me off with the twelve tasks of Hercules."

On the other end of the line, Jordan laughed. "What are you doing today...strangling lions or killing a nine-headed monster?"

"Delivering golden apples to the ancients. Meals-On-Wheels."

Christian had to put down the containers and hold the phone away. With the other hand he waved an acknowledgment to Bernice May who sat on the love seat on her front porch. "Give me a minute," he called.

Her foot began to tap impatiently. "You're already twenty minutes late," she yelled back. "My blood sugar's lower than a politician's IQ."

"Blame Kez's rust bucket!" He returned the phone to his ear. Jordan was still laughing. Christian punished him by ringing off, picked up the containers and made for the porch.

"Where's your fancy car?" the old lady demanded.

"Not enough boot space."

"Humph. All that money for no storage."

"Bernice May, you don't buy a Ferrari for its storage capacity. Besides, you think I want it smelling of breaded chicken with mushroom gravy?"

"Mushrooms! I hate those damn things."

"Pick 'em out."

"What's for dessert?"

He grinned. "A fig bar."

"Isn't it enough that they take out the salt and fat without trying to make me regular, as well?"

Christian's phone rang, saving him from having to answer that one. "Excuse me a minute."

"Give the food here," she grumbled, taking it from him. "I'll put it in the kitchen and fix a drink. Cup of tea?"

"Sounds great." He waited till she left. "Okay, Jordan, I know I have to put up with some ribbing while you cover my job and Luke's, but give me a break."

"It's me," said Luke. "Jordan's still laughing. And I'm back at work—at least until you get the girl. Then, well, I need to talk to you about that. We thought we'd drive down tomorrow."

"Sure." Christian's interest was piqued. "But make it evening. In the morning I'm dropping Kez off at a town council meeting, then delivering

Meals-On-Wheels. In the afternoon there's pre-school with John Jason, site supervision and building a tree house. After dinner I've got bell-ringing practice at church." He sighed. "I've booked extra training. I refuse to be lousy at pulling a goddamn bell rope."

Luke started laughing. Christian cursed him and he laughed harder. Jordan came back on the line. "Is she worth it?"

"I'm starting to wonder." His voice was grim. "In the four days here she's kept me so busy doing good I've hardly seen her. Listen, Jord, I need a favor... yeah, I know—another one. Our friend in hospital, there has to be more news on her prognosis by now but we're getting stonewalled by her sister. Looks like we'll get nothing until we visit this weekend, and we're both climbing the walls."

"You want us to call in on our way down, visit the patient?"

Christian gave him the details. "Thanks, man, I owe you."

"Line me up a hot date. I love country girls."

Bernice May came on to the porch with two mugs. The steaming tea slopping over the sides didn't seem to bother her.

"You want a hot date?" Christian asked her.

"Is there any other kind?"

"I'm onto it," he told Jordan. "How's Luke doing? I've been watching the news...the media's giving him a hard time."

Jordan lowered his voice. "Bitter. I'm hoping this new project will help. Gotta go."

"What new project?" But Jordan had already hung up.

THE SMELL OF THE HOSPITAL—impersonal and sanitary—reminded Joe of the rehab center. Walking toward Marion's room, he wondered whether he should have run this by Dr. Samuel first. Except if he'd advised against it, Joe would have ignored him. For once in his life he had no doubt about the right thing to do.

Which was just as well, he thought as he spied Sally Morgan coming toward him, because there were still a few obstacles to overcome. He crashed into the cleaner who was bending over her trolley and caught her as she lost her balance. "I'm so sorry, ma'am." He waited until she was steady, then released her. "I wasn't looking where I was going."

"No harm done, I guess," she grumbled.

Sally spotted him. "Uh-oh." Joe sidestepped the trolley and went to meet her.

As soon as he was within earshot, she started. "I thought I told you to get lost. You are *not* seeing Marion."

Joe stood his ground. "I know. I'm here to see you."

"Me?"

He took advantage of her momentary confusion. "I've been thinking about what you said, that the accident makes it even more important I put Marion and John Jason first. So——" he cleared his throat "——I'm moving to the South Island."

"Good riddance."

They'd once been good friends, which was probably why she was being so hard on him now, Joe reflected. He had hurt so many people. "I'll get a job and send back every dollar I can."

Sally didn't soften. "Make sure you do."

"In the meantime, I have something I want you to give Marion."

She waved a dismissive hand. "I'm not telling her you're here, Joe, I've already told you that." She pushed past him.

"It's your mother's wedding ring," he called, "the one she left to Marion." He saw the moment Sally was caught, conflicted, and breathed an inward sigh of relief.

Reluctantly she came back. "How did you get that?"

Joe shrugged awkwardly. "I took it when I left, thought I might have to hock it for booze."

Her fists curled. "You bastard!"

"The thing is, I didn't. Will you return it to her for me?" She hesitated and he added quickly, "You don't have to say where you got it. Make something up."

"Let you off the hook, you mean." Her expression tight with contempt, Sally held out her hand.

Joe reached into one jeans' pocket, then the other. "That's strange…." He fumbled in the back pocket. "Oh, I remember. I put it in the glove compartment of my car for safe-keeping."

"In this neighborhood…? Where's it parked?"

Joe hung his head. "Out back."

"Well, let's go get it."

She marched ahead of him toward the entrance. "Sal—" his tone was humble "—there's a shortcut." He held open a side door. With an exclamation of impatience she came back. Joe led the way through the labyrinth of corridors he'd explored earlier. They walked past the hospital laundry, where workers talked loudly to each other over the rumble and hum of a dozen commercial washers and dryers. Turned a corner, then another.

"This can't be a shortcut," Sally complained.

Joe stopped, scratched his head. "I think I took the wrong turn."

"Damn it, Joe!"

"No wait, it's through here." He opened a door to his left, gestured for her to go first.

Sally walked into a utility room full of buckets, mops and cleaning products. "How could you turn into such a loser? I don't know—"

"When you've been had." Joe slammed the door behind her and locked it, then pocketed the key he'd lifted from the cleaner. He just hoped the skeleton set was hard to find. "Sorry, Sal, I know you're only trying to protect her," he called through the door. "But for the record, Marion keeps the ring in her jewelry box. Some things are sacrosanct, even to me."

The door vibrated as Sally started hammering on it. "Let me out! *Now,* Joe!" Her tone grew imperative. *"Right now!"* Smiling faintly, Joe strolled down the hallway.

The hammering resumed, louder and angrier. "Somebody! I've been locked in here! Help!"

Joe turned the corner and the din Sally was making lessened. Satisfied, he picked up his pace. He didn't know how long his reprieve would last.

Only when he hit the main hallway did his footsteps slow and start to falter. He came to a stop in front of Marion's door and squeezed a hand to his throat. It felt as though his heart was about to jump right out of it. Sending a silent prayer heavenward, Joe turned the handle and went in.

"Hello, Marion," he said gently to the slight form lying in the bed, and because he was so damn scared, added unnecessarily, "It's me."

# CHAPTER SEVENTEEN

"CAN I TALK to Sally, hon?"

"Here's Auntie Kez." John Jason swept his Batman cape aside and handed Kezia the phone. "Only until I get Roland—Auntie Sally wants to say hello to him."

Kezia curbed her irritation. It was obvious where she stood in Sally's pecking order—after the rat. Calm, she had to be calm and get information. Shots reverberated through the building as the carpet layer started using his nail gun.

"Sally? Hang on...Rusty!" The nail gun stopped. "Take a break for a minute, will you?" Kezia waited until he was out of earshot. "Sal, what news?"

"I'm afraid I can't talk now, Kezia." Sally's voice sounded stilted and formal. "Can I ring you back?"

"No you can't, because you won't." Four days of playing diplomat had got her nowhere. "What's been happening?"

There was silence on the other end and Kezia's heart plummeted. "Sally? What's Marion's condition?"

"The same." There was a peculiar note in Sally's voice that Kezia couldn't decipher. "Look, I really have to go. Tell John Jason I'll call him tomorrow. 'Bye."

Chilled, Kezia dropped the receiver back in its cradle, leaned her forehead against the wall and closed her eyes. "The same was not good. If Marion were to make a full recovery she would be feeling more sensation by now. The specialists had been very clear about that. Please God, don't do this.

"Auntie Kez?"

*"What!"* Her eyes opened in time to see John Jason's recoil and her conscience took another blow. "I'm sorry, honey, I shouldn't have yelled at you. What is it?"

Eyeing her warily, he flicked back his cape and kept his distance. It killed her. Nothing would go right until she told Marion what she'd done. This weekend.

"I can't find Roland."

"Remember Christian put him in your room so he could clean out Roland's cage." Despite her torment, Kezia's mouth lifted in a ghost of a smile, remembering Christian's face when she'd given him *that* task.

"I do it twice a week," she'd insisted, straight-faced. As with every job she'd tripled her workload.

Except he'd simply given her a look and grabbed a clothes peg and some rubber gloves. "It won't work, you know," he'd said. "You're stuck with me."

Kezia shook off her doubts. He'd left her twice; he'd leave her again. That was one thing she could count on.

John Jason stamped his foot, his eyes glittering through the slits in the mask. "My rat's not there!"

He was right; Roland wasn't in his room. Wasn't

anywhere else in the hotel or the grounds. Kezia searched and re-searched. By dinnertime, John Jason had worn Kezia out with his tantrums and tears, and she suspected Roland had escaped or been flattened under the newly laid carpet.

She didn't tell John Jason her suspicious, keeping up a running commentary on the adventures the rat was having and helping the boy lay cheese trails so Roland would be lured home. "Don't worry, he'll be back."

"You promise?" It was a measure of the child's need that he was prepared to put his faith in her again.

Wishing with all her heart she could give John Jason the answer he wanted, she cupped his chin in her good hand. "I promise to try my very hardest, but if he doesn't want to be found…"

John Jason sagged against her in relief. "Then you'll find him because he wants to be found. He'd never leave me." Now she was in serious trouble.

"Who'd never leave you?" Christian was in the doorway. "Me?"

"Roland's gone missing," John Jason blurted.

"I'm sure he'll turn up when he's ready, don't worry about it." Christian patted the little boy's head with an almost forced heartiness. "So, what's for dinner? Please tell me it's not breaded chicken and mushroom gravy."

A suspicion occurred to Kezia. "Don't you want to join the hunt?"

He looked away. "Let me go wash up first. I won't be long."

She stared after the rat-hater's departing back. He wouldn't have...would he? "John Jason, how about watching a video?" She settled Batman in front of the television and marched down to the bathroom, not bothering to knock before opening the door.

It was full of steam. Really, they needed an extractor fan in here. "What do you know about—"

The shower curtain swept back and Kezia momentarily forgot what she was going to say. Her gaze slid over Christian's naked body, slick under rivulets of water.

"The rat?"

"Yes...the...the..." Discomfited, she turned her back, felt foolish for showing him how much he affected her, then turned back to show him she wasn't. Affected. Through the steam she fixed her gaze on his eyes, blue as heaven, knowing as hell.

"The rat?" he prompted again, and she flinched, spoke more sharply than she meant to.

"What have you done to Roland?" Realizing she'd raised her voice, Kezia shut the door.

He shook his head in disgust. "You really don't trust me, do you? Pass the damn soap."

Kezia held out the soap and he jerked her forward against his wet chest. Water sprayed her face like rain. "My cast!"

"It's fiberglass," he reminded her, and hauled her all the way in, ignoring her yelp. Hot water pummeled against the denim of her jean skirt, which grew sodden and heavy. "Do you know how many old ladies hit on me today? Do you know how much

I hate your car? Do you know how hard I'm trying to fill your Goody Two Shoes and prove you can trust me? And you ask me if I've killed that goddamned rodent? Screw you!"

So he was buckling under the pressure. "I guess that's a no, then," she said calmly. Dread mixed with her relief.

Christian's eyes narrowed, then one hand pressed the small of her back while the other tangled in her hair. Very slowly he tilted her face up to his, exposing her throat. "Screw you," he said again, a threat and a purr combined. "Two can play mind games."

He bent his head and his mouth was hot on her neck. His tongue followed the water droplets down, all the way to where they disappeared into her pink camisole top. Kezia shuddered as his mouth closed over a nipple, clearly outlined under the wet cotton. She pushed him away. "Stop."

"That's not what your body's telling me." He caught her arms, splayed them against the shower tiles to hold her still and took his time, teasing her nipples to tight need.

"Stop it!" Her voice shook. She tried to put more authority into it. "I said—"

He caught her lower lip lightly between his teeth and his tongue slid into her mouth, cajoling hers into a response while he ground his lower body against hers. And Kezia felt herself get wetter and hotter and more desperate.

Desperate for what?

She couldn't remember but it had to be this: to

drown with him under the pummel of water, to drown in him. Christian yanked her skirt up to her waist, his hands everywhere, tantalizing and teasing, and it still wasn't enough.

It wasn't enough to run her hand down his ridged abdomen to the smooth, velvet hardness, to make him groan and grow harder. Not enough to lick the water droplets off his chest and rake the fingers of her good hand down the sleek muscle of his back. Water trickled inside her cast; she didn't care. Steam billowed around and between them, but she could still feel him, oh, yes, and crave him.

She let Christian pull off her panties. He cupped her bottom in his searing hands and lifted her up. With a moan, Kezia clung to his neck for support, wrapped her legs around his waist and impaled herself on him. He thrust and she countered, both clumsy and panting in their need, too hungry for grace. This coupling was like no other they'd shared. Impassioned, raw, almost painful in its intensity.

Kezia's climax seized and shattered her. As she clasped Christian closer in the throes of his own release she knew with utter certainty she would never get over this man. And she hated him for bringing her down to this level of need. "Put me down."

Still shaken by what just happened, Christian heard the anger in her voice. It had been mutual...hadn't it?

Gently he pulled out, slid her along his body to the floor. "That wasn't meant to happen, I'm sorry." He felt like a heel, an animal rutting in heat. "We didn't even use any protection."

Her expression was unreadable. Her voice fierce. "Don't worry, I've just finished a period. There won't be any consequences you can't handle."

"That's not what I meant!" With a shock he realized he wanted her to be pregnant. She'd have to marry him then. Crazy thinking. "Are you all right?"

"I'm furious." She slapped away his helping hand, winced slightly as she pulled the sodden skirt down around her thighs.

Christian handed her a towel. "I hurt you."

She didn't deny it, wrapping the towel around her body sarong-style. "How can you make me feel like this—say one thing and do another?" She turned on him like a caged lioness. "I hate this, this…"

"Need?" Relief made Christian dizzy. He had a chance.

"*Weakness*. My own weakness."

Someone's cracking, babe, he thought as she slammed the door behind her. But it's not me.

The door flew open again. "What did you do to Roland?"

He wrapped a towel around himself. It was infuriating how quickly Kezia could rebuild her defenses. "I hid him."

"You hid him?" Her face was a study in shock. "I've been searching the hotel for hours, John Jason's been crying…What the hell do you think you're playing at!"

"Think about it. The rat disappears, John Jason is inconsolable. You find and return the rodent and are back in his brilliant books. I thought it was a pretty good plan myself. I did mean to call but you kept me so damn busy I didn't get a chance."

A range of expressions flitted across her face. "It's a plan," she conceded. "But where is he? I searched everywhere."

"In a shoebox, bottom of the wardrobe. Go put some dry clothes on and then get him."

Back in his bedroom Christian dressed quickly in jeans and an Italian shirt, his spirits rising. Their lovemaking had removed any lingering doubts he had that Kezia had stopped loving him. She was scared to trust—hell, so was he—but if he held fast to his promises she'd see that he meant to stand by her. And the idea of hiding the rat was inspired. As he opened the old wardrobe he allowed himself a self-congratulatory grin.

The shoebox was light. Too light. Christian saw the reason—a ragged hole chewed in one side of the cardboard. "Sonavabitch, don't do this to me." He opened the box anyway, saw food pellets, the lid of water, a few droppings. No Roland.

The dirty rat had escaped.

HANDS—DOZENS OF HANDS—grasping and letting go. Marion falling, hitting each step with a dull thud. John Jason, mouth open in terror, keening beside his dead mother. Kezia woke with a shout, her heart pounding. His scream had been so real. Sweat saturated her nightdress and she kicked off the covers. Another nightmare, that's all, she told herself. Calm down.

A hair-raising wail pierced the dark.

Heart rocketing into overdrive, Kezia leaped out of bed and grabbed for the lock on her bedroom door. As her fingers closed over the metal, the wail came again and she dropped the key. Swearing, she fell to her knees and scrabbled around until she found it, jammed it back in the lock and jerked the door open.

At the end of the hall a sliver of light escaped under the door of John Jason's room. She heard the murmur of voices—one young and querulous, the other deep and soothing—and her panic subsided. Christian was there.

She pushed open the door and he raised his head, sent her a reassuring glance. He was sitting on the bed in a pair of jeans and the rotating night-light dropped stars across his bare torso. John Jason lay cradled in his arms, his face buried in Christian's chest. Every now and then the little boy gave a deep shuddering gasp and tightened his hold on one bicep.

"He's okay now," Christian said quietly, and John Jason lifted his tear-stained face.

Seeing Kezia, his eyes brimmed with tears again. "Don't let her lock me away," he sobbed, and clung tighter to Christian.

Kezia stumbled back. "I'll leave," she managed.

"No." Christian patted the bed, his eyes a compelling silver in the lamplight. "Come over here. Let's sort this out."

Torn, Kezia took a perch, then tentatively reached out a hand to stroke the crying child's sturdy back, warm through his thin cotton pajamas. John Jason squirmed away.

"I hated taking you away from your mummy," she began, and the stars playing across their bodies made it easier to speak. "Can you remember I cried, too, when I did it? But you were so upset and I was scared you might try to touch her."

John Jason's sobs abated. He was trying to listen and Kezia took that as encouragement. "When someone hurts their back, you're not supposed to touch or move them. Only the ambulance people are allowed to do that. I had to look after her first, honey, but I'm so sorry it's given you bad dreams."

"Kezia has bad dreams about it, too," said Christian, and Kezia stared at him. "I hear you. I'd come and wake you," he added dryly, "but for some reason you lock your door."

John Jason lifted a cautious face. "What happens in your dream?"

"I try to stop your mummy from falling," she said carefully. "But I never do." She sensed Christian watching her intently. "What happens in yours?"

"She won't wake up."

Kezia risked another caress. This time the child let her push back his damp fringe. "She's not going to die, honey. I promise."

"That makes two promises," he reminded her. "Have you found Roland yet?"

She and Christian exchanged pained looks. "Not yet." She did have an idea though, which meant sinking even lower than she had done already. But desperate times...

"When you do," John Jason murmured, settling into Christian's warmth with a drowsy sigh, "we can be friends again."

The remnant of a last shuddering sob shook his small frame and Kezia couldn't help herself. She bent and kissed him. "I love you, JJ."

"Hmm." He clutched her hand and fell asleep. Kezia sat up and her gaze collided with Christian's, mere inches away.

"That dream of yours," he said. "What didn't you say?"

"Nothing." She started to move away, but John Jason's hand tightened reflexively on hers.

"Secrets can be destructive."

"You should know." Kezia loosened John Jason's hold and stood.

Christian looked down at the sleeping child in his arms. "After my mother died, the only time my father held me was to stop me running away while he beat me." Abruptly, Kezia sat again. Slowly his gaze came up to hers. "He blamed me for my mother's death."

Kezia's stomach knotted in fury. "She died of cancer. How could you possibly be responsible?"

"She wanted to live." Christian's irises were steel-bright. "From the time she was diagnosed with cancer she fought to stay alive. Every hour, every minute, was precious to her and I stole that time from all of us."

"Did she know you were sick?"

Christian looked at her blankly for a moment. "Yes, she gave me one of her tonics."

Kezia struggled for the right tone. "The time she was fighting for was to spend with you—her child," she said with calm conviction. "If she'd waited for you to get better she would have lost a week or more with you. She didn't know if she had that to spare, so of course she chose to see you." When he shook his head, she insisted, "Any mother would." She hesitated. "I visit her grave sometimes."

Christian's expression darkened. "Who the hell gave you permission?"

She ignored the smoke screen of righteous anger. "I planted flowers last time. Purple pansies. Bernice May said they were her favorite."

Under the anger, she could see how much he wanted to believe her.

John Jason stirred in his arms. "Jump through the hoop," he commanded.

Kezia watched Christian tuck the child back into bed. It would be a tragedy if he never let himself experience fatherhood because of Paul Kelly.

"Let's get back to what you're not telling me," he suggested in a tone that said his subject was closed.

"Nothing," she said huskily, and headed for the door.

"I didn't tell you about my mother for pity." Kezia stopped. "I told you because one of us has to start trusting the other."

The temptation to lean on him was sudden and

strong and frightening. For five long seconds Kezia wavered. Then she thought about how many troubles he'd already borne in his life and knew she couldn't burden him with hers. "Good night."

## CHAPTER EIGHTEEN

BREAKFAST WAS A minefield of things left unsaid, camouflaged in civility. Exhausted from a restless night, Kezia toyed with her food and noticed Christian did, too. Beside her, Batman wolfed down his cornflakes, keen to start the next search-and-rescue mission.

"My business partners are arriving after dinner." Christian pushed his plate away. "Some proposal that needs discussing. I suggested they stay the night."

"All the bedrooms are finished, that shouldn't be a problem." In a mild tone she added, "It'll be good to have some feedback before we start taking paying guests." In truth she couldn't care less about the hotel since the accident, though she feigned an interest for her staff.

The bar was next in line for renovation but improvements would happen outside drinking hours to avoid a wholesale riot. As it was, Bob Harvey still hadn't forgiven Christian for its temporary closure.

Peach bustled in with coffee and noticed their untouched plates. "What sort of example are you setting the boy?" she scolded—then looked at their faces. "Come with Peach, darling," she said, and took John Jason away with her.

Watching him skip off, Kezia's heart sank. The odds of finding Roland were getting less by every hour.

"Well—" Christian got to his feet "—off on another fruitless day of trying to prove I'm good enough for you."

"It's not about that and you know it," she said sharply. "I'm not saying yes to a proposal motivated by guilt." Because when that wears off, you'll leave.

"If guilt's clouding anybody's logic, it's yours." His expression of exasperation softened as he looked at her. "Sure you haven't got anything you want to tell me?"

Her throat suddenly tight, Kezia shook her head. "No, but…thanks. I am grateful."

"How grateful?"

"You never give up, do you?"

"At last," he said, "you're getting it." He dropped a kiss on the top of her head and left.

The kiss still burned like a brand when Kezia phoned the hospital ten minutes later. "Marion's sister will ring me back, yes, I know, I've heard it all before." She'd long given up trying to wheedle information out of the receptionist.

Disconsolate, she rang off, hesitated a moment, then phoned Everton's pet shop. Feeling like Judas, she ordered a white male rat, about Roland's size, to be delivered before lunch. The thirty pieces of silver went on her credit card. "Sorry, Roly," she whispered as she hung up.

John Jason's face, when she presented the substitute at lunchtime, almost made her duplicity worth it. Almost.

"Roland!" He shoved aside his peanut butter sandwiches, seized the rat and stroked between the tiny ears. The rat's whiskers even twitched as nervously, as Roland's. "Where'd you find him?"

"Outside. He, um, walked over when I was watering the garden. Probably thirsty." Okay, Kezia cautioned herself, don't overdo the lies. White lies, she amended.

"You look funny," said John Jason. He tried to coax the rat into eating some peanut butter. The rat balked. "That's weird, normally he loves peanut butter."

"Does he?" She dragged her voice down from the rafters. "Maybe he's full of…hayseed and the other stuff he's been eating."

"Hi, honey, I'm home." Christian's voice came from the hall, a timely diversion. He was back for a quick lunch, then taking John Jason to playgroup. "And look who I found poking his nose out of Kez's car…."

Oh, no. No, no, no, no! Kezia's coffee cup clattered in the saucer as she sprang to her feet, but she couldn't move quickly enough. Christian stood in the doorway beaming, gingerly holding a towel wrapped around a—

"Roland?" John Jason sounded puzzled. Kezia subsided back into her chair.

Christian caught sight of the rat cupped in John Jason's hands and his mouth fell open. "I'll be damned," he said. His gaze flew to Kezia and she couldn't help herself. She blushed. Christian's eyes widened, then he started to laugh.

The blush scorched to the roots of her hair but she managed to look surprised. "Wow, *two* white rats!"

Christian couldn't play ball; he was laughing too hard. Deep down a similar tremor shook Kezia. Oh, no, one of them had to be sensible, carry this off for John Jason's sake. The child looked completely bemused. She took Christian's rat out of the towel and inspected it. Amazing, his clone was as good as hers. Almost.

She couldn't suppress an explosive snort of laughter. It felt as if a detonator went off inside her, vaporizing the trauma of the past ten days. She laughed until she howled, until Christian stopped laughing and stared at her, until tears ran down her cheeks. Picking up a napkin, she wiped her eyes and said weakly, "Don't mind me. Do carry on, Christian, you obviously know what you're doing."

He looked from one rat to the other and blanched. "I think it's great we have two rats."

"Yeah," said John Jason, "but which one's Roland?"

Kezia played up her smugness. "The one you're holding."

As expected, Christian bristled. "What makes your rat Roland, Miz Smarty Pants?"

Kezia started laughing again. "Because yours is a girl."

"Oh, shit!"

"Christian said *shit*." It was obvious John Jason's

day couldn't get any better than this. "You can be my friend again," he told Kezia magnanimously, and insisted on taking both rats to preschool with Christian.

Kezia napped while they were gone, a deep, heavy sleep of utter exhaustion, and woke feeling better.

"DOESN'T ASKING FOR VOLUNTEERS imply choice?" Christian complained as they finished an early dinner of Peach's beef stew and mashed potatoes. "I had an idea for a preschool fund-raiser and suddenly I'm chairing the subcommittee."

"I hope you told them you won't be here."

He scowled. "Very funny. And speaking of yanking my chain, time for the bells, Esmeralda."

"Esmarella. That's what I'll call the mummy rat," John Jason said. It didn't help Christian's mood but made Kezia smile.

As she pried John Jason out of his Batman outfit and got him bathed and ready for bed she remembered that at the town council meeting that morning everyone had sung Christian's praises, too—not all of them women, either. It bothered Kezia that his popularity bothered her.

Christian had shaken them all out of a rut by challenging systems that could be improved. Which was about half of them, she acknowledged wryly.

Kezia flexed her fingers inside the cast. Still another month to go before it came off. Then Waterview could get back to normal. But deep down she knew normal had changed in some indefinable way for everybody, forever.

Absentmindedly she took the rats off a protesting John Jason and put them to bed in separate cages.

"They want to sleep together," he complained.

"Tough." The phone rang in the middle of their argument. "Breeding prevention center."

"Kezia?"

She leaned against the wall for support. "Marion!"

"Listen, I had a couple of visitors earlier, friends of Christian's." Marion's voice sounded strained. "They said you haven't been getting any news."

Kezia clutched the receiver. "Sally said yesterday there'd been no change."

"That's nonsense. I've been getting sensation and movement back since the day you left. The specialists say I'll make a full recovery." Kezia opened her mouth, but couldn't speak. "Did you hear that, Kezia? I'm going to be fine."

"Fine," she choked out at last. "You're going to be fine? John Jason, Mummy's going to be fine." Laughing and crying, she grabbed him with her cast arm and danced him around in a circle.

"I know that. Why are you acting funny?"

"Because I'm so happy! Oh, Marion." She sank to the floor in relief. "I'm so happy."

Marion started crying. "I can't believe Sally put you through this...she told me she was keeping you updated. I'm sending her away."

"No, don't. She's family. Just make her grovel. Now tell me again!"

"Actually, there's something else Sally didn't tell you." There was a pause. "Joe's been visiting."

Kezia sobered immediately. "Marion, be careful."

"I knew you'd say that and I am. Joe's been in a rehab center all this time. He thought we'd be better off without him, but when he heard about my accident he came straightaway. He's not expecting another chance but...I want to give him one. I think we've both changed enough to make it work this time. I want John Jason to see him on home ground so I've suggested he come visit you in Waterview this weekend."

"But that will mean not seeing you for another week. Look, there's something I need to confess—in person."

"It can wait, can't it?"

"No." She heard disappointed silence on the other end. "Yes. Just tell me the good news again."

"I'm fine, Kezia, I'm going to be fine. Now let me talk to my son."

"You want me to prepare him for J-o-e?"

"I'll tell him now, but yes, that would help."

Kezia's first thought while she waited for the child to finish was, *I've got to tell Christian.*

"'Bye, Mummy, I love you." John Jason hung up. "My daddy's coming to see me!"

They shared another celebratory dance, then Kezia grabbed the phone and dialed Christian's mobile. It was switched off. She scooped up John Jason. "We're going to tell Christian your mummy's good news." She buckled the child into the passenger seat, climbed into the driver's side, and looked at her cast. Glanced at John Jason. What the hell, the church was only two kilometers down the road. "Let's practice changing gear."

As Kezia drove, while John Jason graunched between first gear and second, she broke down in tears of relief. "It's okay, honey," she reassured him. "This is happy crying."

His face scrunched up. "I don't like it. You stop!"

Swallowing the tears gave Kezia the hiccups, and they were both laughing when they pulled into the churchyard. If only she didn't have the confession still hanging over her head.

When she lifted John Jason from the car he clapped his hands over his ears. "What's that awful noise?"

"A beginner," she said smugly as another discordant clang rang through the air. At last something Christian Kelly *wasn't* good at. Though to be fair, it took at least twelve lessons to control a bell well enough to adjust its speed and stop it at will before you even started learning to ring rounds with other people.

Of course Christian didn't know that, or he wouldn't be attempting to replace her at next Sunday's service. Kezia quashed a niggle of conscience.

She followed John Jason, running ahead up a narrow spiral staircase that led to the tower's small ringing room below the belfry. Near the top she held him back, put a finger to her lips. "Let's listen first, shall we?"

The six bell ropes, each woven with a colorful tuft of wool to mark where the ringer caught the rope, hung through holes in the twelve-foot stud. Four ropes had been hooked out of the way, leaving two for Christian and his tutor.

Bob Harvey was dressed for church in a bright

blue suit, circa 1970. In deference to the stifling air of the tiny room, Christian had abandoned his shirt and the faint sheen of sweat on his tanned back was disturbingly pagan. Kezia felt her own temperature rise.

Muscles bunched as Christian pulled the bell rope. "Too bloody hard!" bellowed Bob. "Lightly, lightly." The rope slithered upward as the unseen bell swung through its full circle to the up position. Christian pulled again to send the bell through another 360 degree spin in the other direction—mistimed, thought Kezia, counting automatically, a view confirmed when Bob sucked air through his teeth in noisy disapproval.

"Stand!" he ordered, and Christian tried to park the bell. It clanged through another turn and his curses turned the air blue and John Jason's ears pink.

"Halloooooo," Kezia called to drown them out, and his swearing stopped abruptly.

"How the hell did you get here?"

"I drove," said John Jason proudly. "And you said shit again! And hell."

"Watch your mouth, young man," Bob growled. "And stay away from the ropes—these bells can pull a grown man into the air." He glanced at Christian and received a warning glare. Bob's mouth twitched but he said no more.

Looking at Kezia, Christian's expression grew anxious. "It's good news," she reassured him, but her tears were already welling again. "Marion's going to make a full recovery." Unable to help herself, she grabbed him and held tight. "I had to tell you as soon as I could."

He stilled, then pushed her away and left the room. She took no offence, hugging Bob instead, who smelled of yeast and hay and Old Spice after-shave. "That's grand news, grand…" He patted her back awkwardly. "Bloody hell, I'll start bawling myself if I don't watch it." He pulled away, his eyes wet. Kezia pretended not to notice.

"Where's Christian gone?" John Jason wondered.

"He'll be back, young fellow. Why don't you come up the tower with me and I'll show you the bells, eh?"

Though she longed to follow Christian, Kezia stayed where she was, too emotional to trust herself. He wasn't gone long—his self-control was too good for that—but his eyes were red. He hesitated when he saw her there, alone. "I can't touch you right now," he said awkwardly, "or I'll make a fool of myself."

She nodded and his expression grew rueful. "Ah, to hell with it." He pulled her into his arms. His ribs expanded in a deep tremulous sigh and Kezia buried her face against him. Only when they heard footsteps clobbering down the stairs did they pull apart.

"Your friends," Kezia said awkwardly. "I'd better get back before they arrive."

"I'll come with you."

"No, you bloody won't," contradicted Bob, John Jason at his heels like an eager puppy. "Not until you can stand that bell."

"I'll never be able to stand that bell," Christian muttered, but there was no heat in it. Grinning, he ruffled John Jason's hair. "And you need to be in bed, little guy."

"My daddy's coming back."

The good humor vanished from Christian's face. "I don't think so," he said, looking to Kezia for confirmation.

"We'll talk later," she soothed.

"Bob, can you amuse John Jason for a couple of minutes?" Christian put a hand under Kezia's elbow and propelled her toward the stairs. "We'll talk now." A single bell tolled behind them, musical and haunting.

"It's none of our business," she insisted outside.

"Of course it's our business. The sonovabitch is taking advantage of Marion when she's down." Christian paced in his agitation, his shoes crunching on the gravel driveway. The bell rang again, momentarily distracting him. Why couldn't he get the damn thing to ring like that?

"She says he's changed...AA, counseling."

Christian snorted. "That's exactly the line he spun me when he came to the hotel a couple of weeks ago. I sent him packing."

"What?" Kezia stared at him. "And you didn't tell me?"

"I didn't tell anybody, figured he wouldn't be back. Guess I underestimated his nerve."

"And *over*estimated your authority." Kezia looked as mad as a hornet. "Who the hell do you think you are?"

"I did what I thought was best. You should thank me."

"*Thank* you?" Okay, mad as two hornets. "You had no right to keep this from me, let alone Marion." Her brow furrowed. "She never mentioned it on the phone, I don't think he's told her."

"Maybe he's ashamed of backing down." Except honesty compelled Christian to admit Joe hadn't backed down, not really.

"Maybe he's giving you the benefit of the doubt because you were trying to act in Marion's best interests," retorted Kezia.

"*Him* giving *me* the benefit of the doubt—"

She cut him short. "You don't know him, Christian. I do. And I believe Joe is capable of changing. Anyway, what you and I think is immaterial. Marion's a grown woman, able to make her own decisions without your paternalistic interference."

"We'll see about that," he said grimly.

"Look!" Kezia grabbed him by the biceps, forcing him around to look at her. "She hasn't done this lightly but she loves him and she's willing to give him another chance so—"

"If she wants to kid herself, fine," Christian interrupted, "but there's more at stake here than her fantasy happy ending. She has John Jason to consider."

"Joe never struck John Jason. Never. The incident with Marion was a one-off."

He shook free. "And that excuses him, does it?"

"No, of course it doesn't." She wasn't cowed in

the least. "But he had the sense to leave before he did any more harm. This is not your fight."

Christian moved away. "I'm not prepared to sit by and watch John Jason get screwed over because Marion is in denial."

"I don't want to say this, but your attitude is forcing me to," she said in a low voice. "Joe is not your father and John Jason is not you. Some people deserve another chance."

So much for trusting her with his secrets. "Are you going to help me talk her out of this or not?"

"I'm reserving judgment. So should you."

Christian shook his head in disgust. "You know, I will stay here with Bob. I can't stand being anywhere near you right now." The hurt in her eyes made him feel better—for about a millisecond. But his pride wouldn't let him take it back.

"Ditto," she retorted. "Let's hope your friends have better manners, because I've had it with pig-headed men!"

Christian thought of what they could tell her, and blanched. "Just don't listen to anything they say about me," he warned.

Kezia gave him a withering look. "Why the hell would I want to talk about *you?*"


"IN ALL THE YEARS YOU'VE KNOWN him, has Christian ever mentioned me?" Kezia put her glass of whiskey down harder than she'd meant to and some of the liquid spilled onto the table. Didn't matter, the bar closed at nine-thirty on a Wednesday, she didn't have to behave herself. She squinted at the grandfather clock. Nine forty-five and still no Christian. Okay, she was officially miserable.

"No," Jordan admitted. "We didn't know you existed until a few weeks ago."

"Essactly." Kezia stopped dabbing the spill with a napkin and stabbed one finger into his chest to emphasize her point. At least it was supposed to be one finger; if it would just keep still she'd know for sure. "Nice pecs." Distracted by his resilient muscle, she poked again. "Course not as nice as Christian's."

"In his defense—" Luke brought her back to the subject "—who did you tell about Christian?"

Kezia tried to think. "Nobody."

"And I hate to disagree with a lady," said Jordan, "but this nicer pecs thing is debatable."

"Now see, there you go calling me a lady when I'm not." Kezia propped her head in her hands; it was getting sooooo heavy. "I used to be good before Christian came back and then I forgot to be good and things started going wrong, which was a shame because sometimes it's so good to be bad…"

She lost the point of her story and gazed at them while she tried to recollect it. Boy, they were some lookers, the sort of guys—like Christian—who were so fun to be bad with. "Now what would you say if I was a bad girl?" she wondered, then realized she'd spoken the words our loud. "No, really—" she took another swig of her drink "—go ahead."

Jordan looked at Luke. They both grinned. "You have nice pecs too," Jordan offered.

Kezia recalled Miss September. "And they're not cold to the touch, either. Wanna feel?" She fumbled with the buttons of her blouse. Jordan and Luke caught a hand each.

"Unfortunately, Kez," said Jordan, regret in his tone, "we're obliged to take your word for that."

"Okey doke, then." They were such nice guys. Gorgeous and wickedly funny and charming, even when they'd suggested that a third glass of Muriel's fine whiskey might not be wise. Perhaps Marion's recovery had been toasted enough?

"Nonsense," she'd said, feeling damn fine by that stage. "I don't know why I don't do this more often."

"You will in the morning," Luke said dryly, but other than putting a jug of water in front of her, hadn't argued with her. Not like Christian!

Kezia scowled. "An' who the hell does he think he is, being better than I am at helping people. Whass' his motivation, huh?"

The men looked at her affectionately. "Now there's a question we can answer," Luke said, but she waved him to silence.

"The oldies love him. So do the preschool mums—well, okay they're women, but the mayor isn't and he wants him to stand for council. 'Cept for me, the only one who sees through him is Roland." She'd told them all about the missing Roland.

Jordan seemed to be having trouble with his face. "The rat?"

"Sssssactly. Very sound judge of character is

Roland. Only thing he's hopeless at is ringing bells. Yeah, he sucks at that."

"The rat?" Luke choked.

"No, Christian. Pay attention!"

"Oh, Kez." Jordan burst out laughing. "He's gotta keep you."

"He intends to," said a dry voice behind them.

"Christian!" The men got to their feet.

Kezia rolled her head back to check. "Nope," she corrected. "The rat."

Christian helped her lift her head. "How much have you had to drink, babe?"

"Not nearly enough, you f....fff...flock-stealing wolf in sheep's clothing! You insulting, secret-hid-ing—"

"Four whiskeys," Jordan volunteered.

"Straight," added Luke.

Kezia frowned in their general direction. "I refuse to drink with tattletales." Gathering her dignity, she tried to stand but sank back in her chair. "Hey, this floor's ssstill out of level. I thought we had it fixed?"

"Uh-huh." Christian hauled her up and she found herself hanging over his shoulder staring at the of-fending floor.

"Even the floorboards aren't straight." She yelped and grabbed a hold as Christian swung around and headed for the door.

"Say good-night, babe."

She pushed against Christian's butt to bring the guys back into view. Grinned. "G'night, babes."

"Good night, Kez. See you in the morning."

But she was already distracted. "Now you can't tell me," she called back, her hand still curved around that deliciously rolling rump, "that anyone's got a nicer ass than this."

Jordan glanced at Luke. "You have," he replied, and both men grinned when Christian missed his stride.

"I'll be back." He threw the words over his shoulder.

Luke waited until Christian was out of earshot. "Kez's invitation…"

"Breast kept between us?"

"That's what I admire about you, Jord. Your sense of the proprieties."

In the bedroom, Kezia found herself propped up by one of Christian's hands while he pulled back the duvet with the other. "I'm fine," she insisted, pulling out of his hold and toppling into bed.

He took off her shoes. "You are so ripped."

"This is what it would be like to be married to me," she warned him. "You'd be stuck at home wiss kids and I'd be out getting drunk evreee night."

"Uh-huh." He pulled off her skirt, unbuttoned her blouse.

Even in her drunken haze Kezia noticed his care. That would never do. She stuck out her lower lip aggressively. "Thought you couldn't stand the ssssight of me?"

He sighed and sat on the bed. "That was a lousy thing to say and I'm sorry. I don't trust Marion's judgment but I trust yours, so I'll try to give this Joe a chance."

"Is that why you didn't come home, cause you were mad at me?"

He hesitated. "No, Bob and I had business. Incidentally, I don't have to play bells on Sunday, do I?"

"Nope, jus try'n to put you off marrying me."

"So how am I doing on this ridiculous test of yours?"

"You're passing," she wailed. "People like you more'n me."

Christian stroked loose strands of hair away from her face. "Why don't you want to marry me, Kez?"

She rolled away from him and thumped her cast against the wall. "I just wish I'd answered when Marion called!"

"And I wish I'd repaired the damn stairs. But she's going to be fine, so dump the guilt and let's get on with our lives."

"I can't, not until she knows. You see, I le' go," she whispered. "When she fell, I grabbed her. But I le' go."

"Kez, you had a broken wrist." He reached out a hand and she flung away, shunning the comfort she didn't deserve.

"I didn't grab her with that hand."

His momentary shock was enough to supercharge her shame. "Oh, Kez—"

"Don't say anythin'." She rolled onto her stomach and put a pillow over her head. "If you really love me," she said from under it, "you'll leave me alone."

It was a dirty trick, but it worked.

# CHAPTER NINETEEN

CHRISTIAN SHUT KEZIA'S door and hesitated, reluctant to leave her. But she wasn't in any fit state to see sense tonight—to understand that Marion's momentum and greater weight would have made it impossible for her to hold on.

Still, he couldn't leave. Didn't he know that misery intimately? Only Kezia's suggestion that his mother knew what she was risking by seeing him had eased his conscience. And only Kezia's confession to Marion, would ease hers. At least he hoped it would.

Hurt soul to hurt soul, he understood her so well. He had no doubt Marion would forgive her, but Kezia's intolerance of her own failings bordered on pathological. She refused to hear a word against her parents, but they'd set the bar too high. Muriel—irascible, accepting and loving as she was—had relied on the young Kezia more than she should have. So, for that matter—he'd noticed this week—did everyone else in Waterview.

It was time Kezia had someone to lean on. Guess he had to grow up to realize how much he wanted—needed—the job of protecting the protector.

Unable to help himself, he opened her door. She lay sprawled across the bed asleep, flushed and disheveled. The bedroom smelled like a brewery. Christian opened the window then straightened the rumpled sheet and covered her with it. "I love you, Kez."

She answered with a light snore and he grinned. He kissed her forehead, breathed her in. Feeling more optimistic, he headed back to his guests. It was a good thing all the cards were finally on the table. Now they'd get somewhere.

KEZIA WOKE UP WITH A MOUTH so dry, she could taste sand. She rolled over, shielding her eyes against the shaft of light slicing through the drapes, and her stomach rolled with her.

Maybe if she didn't move it would— Tumbling out of bed, she dashed for the bathroom and threw up, then changed into a nightdress and crawled back into bed. Aspirin and a water jug were on the bedside table. She took two pills, chugging the water straight from the jug.

Lying down, she tried to think. Marion okay... good. Too much whiskey...bad. Two gorgeous men, one dark, one fair... She drifted back to sleep.

Kezia jerked upright two hours later with one thought. *I can never ever see Christian's friends again.* While she'd been sleeping, she saw, someone had delivered dry toast and a cup of tea. Beside them, were two dozen red roses in a crystal vase with a gilt-edged card propped against it. "Sorry if we made fools of ourselves last night. Drank so much we can't remember a thing. Your fans, Jordan and Luke." Relieved, Kezia hid the toast with a napkin and sipped the cold tea. That was one problem solved. But there was another, something terrible trying to wriggle into her consciousness. It was…it was…

*You told Christian about Marion.*

Droplets of tea splattered across the white sheet and Kezia stared at them, unseeing. *I told Christian about Marion.* Racking her brains to recall details, she remembered his shock. Remembered telling him to leave her alone. Remembered…he did.

She heard the door open and Christian stood in front of her as if raised by her clamorous emotions, his expression holding a challenge that made her instantly wary. "Still feeling sorry for yourself?"

She didn't like his tone, either. "Don't tell me you've never had a hangover."

"I was talking about that guilt you've been nursing since the accident."

Under the sheet, Kezia brought her knees up to her chest and clasped them. "I'm sorry I unloaded on you—"

"I'm not," he interrupted. "It explains a lot. Why haven't you told her?"

Kezia picked up the edge of the sheet and began fretting with it. "At first she was too sick, then Sally was always around, then you showed up and we brought John Jason home." She paused. "Where is he? And your, uh, friends?"

"John Jason is with Bernice May for the morning.

I figured you weren't up to child care. Luke and Jordan are—" he glanced at his watch "—halfway home by now. We're setting up a charitable trust. Luke will run it."

"That's fantastic!" For a moment Kezia forgot her problems. "Tell me which causes you'll support."

He folded his arms. "First, your excuses for not telling Marion."

Kezia squirmed. "They're not excuses. I intend telling her the first chance I get."

"If that's all that's stopping you…" Christian tossed her his mobile. Kezia dropped it as though it was hot.

"Are you crazy? I'm not telling her over the phone."

"Call her now, Kez," he ordered. "You know she'll forgive you." Seeing the dread she couldn't hide, his expression softened. "Please. Put us all out of our misery."

Her eyes shied away. "I'll call her when I'm good and ready, and my misery has nothing to do with yours." Except they both knew that wasn't true. Her shame erupted into anger. He knew everything now, every sordid secret she had, and he still kept trying to raise her hopes.

Well, she was sick of it. Sick of never being strong enough to resist him, sick of waiting for him to abandon her. "You want to be put out of your misery?" She glared at him. "*We have no future.* When are you going to get that through your thick skull?"

Christian threw up his hands in disgust. "You

know your problem, lady? You really believe you can be perfect, if you just try hard enough."

"That's not true, I—"

"That's why you can't forgive yourself for Marion's accident. That's why you don't call her and confess. Because you don't want to accept that you're fallible like the rest of us poor sinners. No, you'd rather sit on your little saint's cloud, wringing your hands, than live a real life with me!"

"You sanctimonious bastard!" Enraged, Kezia flew out of bed and tried to shunt him out the door. "Don't you dare preach to me about self-forgiveness until you've visited your mother's grave!"

She regretted the words instantly, more so when Christian went very still. "I'm sorry, that was…" she wanted to say "unforgivable," but that word had become too loaded. "Thoughtless."

His eyes flashed. "You're the second person to accuse me of not dealing with my issues and I've had enough." He turned and left.

Kezia bit her lip to stop herself calling him back. Better to let tempers cool before she offered another apology. *Yeah, for telling the truth.*

Slowly her irritation abated. She showered and put on a summer-green dress she knew Christian liked and stripped the tea-stained sheet off the bed. His cell phone fell to the floor and she stood in an agony of indecision. *What if he's right?* At last, with trembling hands she dialed the number she knew by heart and asked to be put through to Marion.

"Hello?" A man's voice.

She let out the breath she'd been holding.

"I'm sorry, I've been put through to the wrong room."

"Kezia, it's me, Joe."

"Oh. Joe...hello." There was an awkward silence.

"Thank you for looking after my family," he said simply. "I'm sorry you needed to and I swear you won't need to again."

"Christian told me what he did when you came back. Why didn't you tell Marion?"

"How can I squeal on a man who was trying to look out for my son? Plus I owe you. You still love this guy?"

She closed her eyes. "Yes."

"That's what I figured. Marion's getting physio, so I'll put you on speaker phone."

"No, don't bother, I'll call la—"

"Kezia!" Marion sounded bright and breezy. "How's my boy?"

"He's visiting Bernice May and probably baking inedible cookies. I rang for a private chat but..."

"You want to call back?"

Kezia sat on the bed. Did she? Took a deep breath. "Christian said I shouldn't put this call off any longer."

"Does that mean you've accepted his proposal?"

"No! How'd you know about that? Look, never mind. We won't be getting married."

"You know, if I can forgive him for the stairs, you can forgive him for leaving you."

"I do, I have! It's not Christian I can't forgive,

it's me." *Hadn't he said that?* "I—I have something to tell you."

"You could never have held on to me. Don't you know that?"

Marion *knew* she let go? "Do you also remember," she said slowly, "that I grabbed you with my good hand?"

"No, but it makes no difference. If you hadn't let go when you overbalanced, we would both have fallen down those stairs and taken out John Jason. All three of us would have been injured."

"There's more." Kezia made a full confession before she lost her courage. "I—I heard you calling me and I ignored you. If I'd answered, the accident would never have happened."

Marion laughed. "I was such a cling-on after Joe left, wasn't I? It's a wonder you didn't hide more often."

Kezia persisted. "You're my friend. I should have been there for you." Maybe Marion was high on painkillers?

"You know, you forgive other people anything— yourself nothing." Marion sounded annoyed. "Have you ever thought how condescending it is that my forgiveness counts for less than yours?"

Kezia froze. "Christian said I have double standards."

"You let us all get away with murder, except for Christian." Marion's tone grew thoughtful. "I guess it's a measure of how much you love him that he has to meet your standards."

"And a measure of how much he loves you," Joe added, "that he tries." For a moment there was silence.

"Oh, God." Kezia dropped her head into her hands. "I've been such a fool."

"Welcome to my world," said Joe, and she knew Marion had been right to give her husband a second chance.

"I've got to see a man about a proposal," she blurted. "I'll call you back later." She dropped the phone and ran.

Christian wasn't in the office, the kitchen or the garden. The garage was open; light filtering between the torn boards. Empty. She forced back the rising panic. He'd gone for a drive to burn off some anger. He'd come back. Act normal, she told herself, do some chores.

Instead she found herself wandering out to the front veranda and staring down the main street, which was bustling with market-goers. What if she'd pushed him too far this time? Distracted, she only half noticed Don's jalopy pull into the hotel's car park. What was the last thing Christian had said? *I've had enough.* Suddenly the words sounded ominous.

"Hail the victor." Don commanded her attention, dressed impeccably for golf, a Panama hat pulled low on his brow.

Kezia tried to think. "You won the tournament!"

"No, just my match with Bob. The old cheapskate has to buy drinks. Showed up yet?"

"Who? Oh, Bob. No, I haven't seen him." Kezia

gazed down the road, but there was no sign of Consolation.

Don rubbed his hands together. "Excellent, I'll have time to put a few on his tab. Damn shame Christian's left. I'd have asked him to join us, just to rub old Bob's nose in it."

Kezia's attention snapped back. "You've seen Christian?"

"Passed him on the highway north, driving too fast, as usual. Business dragged him back to the city, has it?"

Kezia's heart skipped a beat, then kicked in fast and hard. "He's gone for good." She stumbled, near fainting.

Don grabbed her arm, shepherded her to a seat and fanned her with his Panama. "What's all this about?"

"I deliberately drove him away...I don't know why...it's all my fault."

"That makes the solution easy then, doesn't it?" Kezia looked at Don uncomprehending and he said patiently, "What does an honorable person do when they've made a mistake?"

"Fix it."

"Well then." Don tilted his hat to a jaunty angle. "Off you go."

Confused, Kezia looked into the old man's eyes, then she was running, up the stairs, scrambling in her handbag for her car keys. Except she couldn't drive without John Jason shifting the gears. She flew downstairs and raced across the road to the doctor's rooms where the nurse sat filing her nails. "Get your buzz saw and cut my hand free."

"I can't do that…you're not due."

"Please." Even in her agitation, Kezia remembered her manners. "Just trim off enough to let me change gears. It's life or death." My life or your death.

Ten minutes later she sat in her station wagon with a modified cast. The old girl started with the first turn of the ignition—a good sign surely—and with a squeal of wheels Kezia was on Main Street. And straight into market day. Calm down, she told herself, we're meant to be.

The numberplate on the vehicle in front bore the legend Bob4Me from Bob Harvey's unsuccessful mayoral campaign five years earlier. Its taillights flashed red and it pulled to a stop, blocking the main street.

Kezia slammed on her brakes as Bob's wife climbed out, straightened her floral dress and exchanged a few words with Bob. C'mon! Kezia's hand hovered over the horn, but manners prevailed. Instead she bounced out her frustration on the vinyl seat. Move it, woman! At last Bob put on his indicators and waited for an opening to perform an illegal U-turn. Toward the hotel.

Kezia's fist hit the horn. She wound down her window and screamed, "Move your bloody vehicle *now!*"

The citizens of Waterview stopped to gawk; she didn't care. Bob got out of his cab, moving slow and sure like a gunfighter at the OK Corral. Recognizing her, his jaw dropped.

Kezia thrust her upper body through the window. "*Now,* godamn it, or I'll ram this up the rear of your pride and joy!"

Bob scrambled back in the driver's seat and—possibly in shock from having obscenities shouted at him by Waterview's sweetheart—stalled his car. There was a smattering of clapping and catcalls, led by his wife and Bernice May.

"Oh, this is ridiculous." Kezia pulled out and passed him on the wrong side, blaring her horn to warn approaching traffic. Fifty meters ahead the traffic light turned amber. She gunned the accelerator and blasted through it. The speedometer hit sixty kilometers, labored to seventy-five. Who was she kidding? She'd never catch Christian. Kezia gritted her teeth. So, she'd die trying.

On the long road heading north, she coaxed the engine to ninety even though the car shook so much she had to cling to the steering wheel with both hands. The arrow on the water gauge quivered into the red. Please let it be broken, like everything else on this heap. Still she eased her foot off the accelerator. The speed dropped to eighty.

Wisps of steam seeped out from under the hood. Kezia thwacked the steering wheel. Shit. Shit! Abruptly she took her foot off the accelerator. Seventy, forty, ten. She swung onto the gravel.

Kezia got out. There was no one to hear, nothing to stand between her and despair but desolate fields of harvested corn. Fists clenched by her sides, she screamed her frustration until her voice went hoarse.

Now what? *How many signs do you need that it wasn't meant to be?*

"To hell with fate," Kezia croaked into the blue sky. "You've screwed me around for the last time."

In the glove compartment she found a rag, wrapped it around her hand and pried open the blistering hood. The radiator hissed. It would have to cool before she could refill it. Kezia got the water can from the boot and gulped a couple of mouthfuls while she waited. It tasted sour and warm but was better than dehydration.

With no shade on offer, she climbed back into the stinking hot car, staring along the ribbon of road to where it faded into the horizon. Christian would be miles away by now, probably thanking his stars for a lucky escape. *Admit it, you're as afraid of deep emotion as Christian is.* He had been her baptism by fire—and he'd left her. Worse, she'd expected him to, maybe because she'd always fallen short of her parents' expectations no matter how hard she tried.

Kezia started laughing at a joke that was so not funny and covered her face with her hands. By demanding to know all Christian's secrets, insisting he pass her tests before she trusted him, she had practiced the conditional love she despised. Why had he put up with her for so long?

Opening her fingers, Kezia spotted a speck of red shimmering in the distance. Then heard the faint hum of an expensive car's engine and knew exactly who was coming. And he'd find her here, doubting him yet again. Shame paralyzed her. *How many times can I screw this up and keep him?*

The car materialized in a blur of speed and Kezia sat frozen as Consolation stopped alongside.

"Aren't you going the wrong way?" Christian asked.

"Actually, I might finally be heading in the right direction."

"And that is?"

She swallowed. "Toward you."

His teeth flashed white against his tan. "Is that so," he drawled, and swung Consolation off the road.

Kezia grabbed the oily rag and wiped her sweaty palms dry, then climbed out of the car, pulling at the creases in her dress and feeling eighteen again.

Christian leaned one shoulder nonchalantly against the station wagon. "You thought I'd left, didn't you?"

"We had a fight and I said some terrible things and you were seen driving out of town and…" Her voice trailed off.

"And?" he prompted. So, he wouldn't make this easy.

"And if you still want to get married, I'd like to." His sunglasses reflected her hot and embarrassed face. "Or we could live in sin, it really doesn't matter because I think I need to stop trying to change you and just…love you the way you are." There was a catch in her voice. "I love you," she said, and the words sounded like freedom. "I love you."

"About bloody time," said Christian, and then she was in his arms and they were trying to kiss except he was laughing and she was crying and they made a pretty poor job of it.

He took off his sunglasses and dropped to one

knee on the hot sticky tarmac and Kezia bit her lip because she so nearly said, "You'll ruin those pants." And he looked up at her with those blue, blue eyes and said, "Did you seriously think you'd overtake a Ferrari in that heap of shit?"

She looked at him blankly.

"Babe, I'm really going to have to teach you about cars."

"Obviously I didn't think I'd *overtake* you, but I was counting on you stopping for gas or chocolate."

He grinned at that—a crazy Christian Kelly grin. "You know if you marry me you'll be strapping in for a wild ride, don't you?"

She got cocky then. "Is that your proposal?"

"No." His wicked gaze trailed up her body to her face. "The proposal comes *after* you say yes."

"Yes," Kezia whispered, and found herself pinned against the vehicle, hot metal on one side, hot man on the other.

"What if someone comes?" she protested, because even clothed, their bodies fitted sinfully close. Then she thought, to hell with it, and let his hot mouth burn her, as well.

"By the way." Christian came up for air and trailed a finger down the damp cotton of her dress to cup her bottom. Kezia tried to care that they were on a public highway, but couldn't. "The business I had with Bob last night. I bought your land back," he said casually. She gasped, then squeezed him so tight he started to wheeze. "I figure we'll build a house there for our annual six months in Waterview..." he managed to say before she shoved him into the back of the station wagon and climbed on top of him.

"That's another thing about your fancy car." She flicked open the snap on his pants. "No room."

Christian stopped her busy hands, intrigued. "What if someone comes?"

Kezia gave him a killer smile. "Count on it."

WITH A SELF-SATISFIED SMILE Kezia locked her station wagon. I am *such* a loose woman and I like it. On the strength of that, she sashayed over to where Christian waited by the Ferrari. "Does this look like a sashay to you?" she asked, concentrating, then caught him looking at her with an intensity that stopped her in her tracks. "What?" she asked, suddenly shy.

"Damned if I don't love you, Kezia Rose," he said, and she touched his mouth in an unconscious gesture of disbelief.

"What's more, I can prove it."

He bent to retrieve something through the open window of his car and handed her a loose bunch of purple flowers. Overcome with the heat, they drooped in her hand.

"They're lovely," Kezia enthused to protect his feelings, then tears came to her eyes as she recognized them. They were the pansies she'd planted at Deborah Kelly's grave.

"I love you, Kezia," Christian said again, and this time she believed him.

## CHAPTER TWENTY

IT WAS A bloody good country wedding marred by only five instances of shameful behavior, Bob Harvey declared to Joe when it was all but over.

Sipping whiskey, Bob ticked off a fat finger. "One. A telegram from a dead woman, which was a bloody stupid joke. More surprising that Don fell for it and read it out." Bob scratched his head and quoted verbatim. "'Once a gambler, always a gambler. All debts discharged. Be happy, my darlings. Muriel.'" He shook his head. "Bloody thing doesn't make sense."

Joe gave a noncommittal shrug and took a sip of his ginger ale.

"Two." Bob held up another digit. "The *junior* bridesmaid, Bernice May ignored calls from younger competitors for a rethrow of the bridal bouquet." He gestured to the dance floor in disgust. "Now she's making a spectacle of herself with the two grooms-men, one of whom needs a bloody good haircut."

Joe watched Bernice May in her floral housedress twirl the Viking, Jordan, and suggested innocently, "Go tell him."

Bob pretended not to hear. "Three—Marion letting John Jason wear his Batman costume *and* bring three rats to the church.

"Now, Bob," Joe said reasonably, "how could I know Roland would be found alive and well in Christian's Ferrari?" The two men looked at each other and began to roar. *Okay, Christian was a friend now but hell, the look on his face.* Weakly, Joe wiped tears from his eyes.

"Four." Sobering, Bob returned to his grievances. Kezia *laughing* in church when she saw Christian waiting behind a makeshift picket fence. Understandable reaction—some bloody crazy city trend that no self-respecting countrywoman would buy into. But still, in *church,* Joe."

But Joe wasn't listening; he was smiling at his wife who was dancing with their son.

Bob yanked on his sleeve to regain his attention. "But the worst thing…the very worst…and you might not have noticed this, sitting at the back with the rats—" Bob lowered his voice and gestured for Joe to draw nearer. "—Kelly *cried* at his wedding. Worse," he added darkly, "he didn't care!"

Joe hid a grin. For the sake of Bob's sensibilities, he hoped the old farmer wasn't around when the Kellys' baby was born in seven months' time.

Introducing...

# n o c t u r n e

### a spine-tingling new line
### from Silhouette Books.

**These paranormal romances will
seduce you with dark, passionate tales
that stretch the boundaries of conflict,
desire, and life and death, weaving
a tapestry of sensual thrills and chills!**

---

**Don't miss the first book...**

# UNFORGIVEN

by *USA TODAY* bestselling author

# LINDSAY McKENNA

*Launching October 2006,
wherever books are sold.*

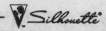

# SPECIAL EDITION™

**Experience the "magic" of falling in love at Halloween with a new *Holiday Hearts* story!**

# UNDER HIS SPELL

## *by KRISTIN HARDY*

### October 2006

Bad-boy ski racer J. J. Cooper can get any woman he wants—except Lainie Trask. Lainie's grown up with him and vows that nothing he says or does will change her mind. But J.J.'s got his eye on Lainie, and when he moves into her neighborhood and into her life, she finds herself falling under his spell....

## Those sexy Irishmen are back!

Bestselling author

# Kate Hoffmann

is joining the Harlequin Blaze line—and she's
brought her bestselling Temptation miniseries,
**THE MIGHTY QUINNS,** with her.
Because these guys are definitely Blaze-worthy....

All Quinn males, past and present, know the legend
of the first Mighty Quinn. And they've all been
warned about the family curse—that the only thing
capable of bringing down a Quinn is a woman.
Still, the last three Quinn brothers never guess
that lying low could be so sensually satisfying....

**The Mighty Quinns: Marcus, on sale October 2006**
**The Mighty Quinns: Ian, on sale November 2006**
**The Mighty Quinns: Declan, on sale December 2006**

### Don't miss it!

*Available wherever Harlequin books are sold.*

# SAVE UP TO $30! SIGN UP TODAY!

INSIDE *Romance*

The complete guide to your favorite
Harlequin®, Silhouette® and Love Inspired® books.

✓ Newsletter ABSOLUTELY FREE! No purchase necessary.

✓ Valuable coupons for future purchases of Harlequin,
   Silhouette and Love Inspired books in every issue!

✓ Special excerpts & previews in each issue. Learn about all
   the hottest titles before they arrive in stores.

✓ No hassle—mailed directly to your door!

✓ Comes complete with a handy shopping checklist
   so you won't miss out on any titles.

- - - - - - - - - - - - - - - - - - - - - - - - - - - - - - - - -

## SIGN ME UP TO RECEIVE INSIDE ROMANCE
## ABSOLUTELY FREE
*(Please print clearly)*

_____

Name

_____

Address

_____

City/Town                State/Province              Zip/Postal Code

(098 KKM EJL9)                        **Please mail this form to:**
                **In the U.S.A.:** Inside Romance, P.O. Box 9057, Buffalo, NY 14269-9057
                **In Canada:** Inside Romance, P.O. Box 622, Fort Erie, ON L2A 5X3
                            OR visit http://www.eHarlequin.com/insideromance

IRNBPA06R        ® and ™ are trademarks owned and used by the trademark owner and/or its licensee.

# THE PART-TIME WIFE

### by *USA TODAY* bestselling author

# Maureen Child

Abby Talbot was the belle of Eastwick society;
the perfect hostess and wife. If only her
husband were more attentiive. But when
she sets out to teach him a lesson and files
for divorce, Abby quickly learns her husband's
true identity...and exposes them to scandals
and drama galore!

On sale October 2006 from Silhouette Desire!

*Available wherever books are sold,
including most bookstores, supermarkets,
discount stores and drug stores.*

Silhouette®
Desire®

**Introducing an exciting appearance by legendary *New York Times* bestselling author**

# DIANA PALMER

## HEARTBREAKER

He's the ultimate bachelor...
but he may have just met
the one woman to change his ways!

Join the drama in the story of a confirmed
bachelor, an amnesiac beauty and their
unexpected passionate romance.

---

"Diana Palmer is a mesmerizing storyteller
who captures the essence of what
a romance should be."—*Affaire de Coeur*

---

**Heartbreaker *is available from Silhouette Desire
in September 2006.***